my
husband's
daughter

my husband's daughter

emma robinson

FOREVER

NEW YORK   BOSTON

Forever
Hachette Book Group
1290 Avenue of the Americas, New York, NY 10104
. read-forever.com
twitter.com/readforeverpub

First published in 2020 by Bookouture, an imprint of StoryFire Ltd.

First Grand Central Publishing Edition: March 2022

Forever is an imprint of Grand Central Publishing. The Forever name and logo are trademarks of Hachette Book Group, Inc.

The publisher is not responsible for websites (or their content) that are not owned by the publisher.

Library of Congress Control Number: 2021945936

ISBN: 9781538709535 (paperback)

Printed in the United States of America

LSC-C

Printing 1, 2022

For Alex and Helen
With love

my
husband's
daughter

PROLOGUE

Curled up on the sofa like a kitten, all pouted lips, soft breaths, and waves of hair spilling over the cushion. The most beautiful child ever to be born.

I touch your shoulder to stir you into a half-sleep, too grown now to be taken in my arms. Instead, you lean against me as I lead you to bed, mumbling how you are not tired *and* don't want to go. *Once I pull the sheet to your shoulders, in mere moments those eyelids flutter closed, traitorous lashes swept downward once more.*

Then I wait awhile at your bedside, hand at my chest.

How can you be mine? You were unplanned, a surprise, an unexpected gift. Somehow, you made your way into my life and burrowed into a space that wasn't there. Now I don't know where you end and I begin. You are my heart. My world. My daughter.

And I will do anything to give you the best life I can.

Anything.

CHAPTER ONE

Rebecca

Good food, interesting company: a Friday-night dinner with the partners and directors of Jack's advertising agency and their spouses had been surprisingly pleasant until Jack mentioned their wedding last year, which—inevitably it seemed these days—led to the topic of babies.

It was a gift from heaven for Linda McCray, the wife of the financial director, sitting across the table from Rebecca in the managing director's large dining room. Judging by her vacant gaze while her husband discussed profit margins with the man to his left, she'd been politely bored for most of the meal, but her ears pricked up at the mention of marriage and babies. "You've been married a year? It'll soon be time for the pitter-patter of baby feet then."

Rebecca forced a smile. This dinner was important to Jack. It was the first time he'd been invited to the house and he had been uncharacteristically nervous. Having started in the creative side of the business, then moving to management, further promotion would happen only if he "fit in" with the board. Rebecca had teased him but she hadn't felt at ease since they'd got here either. She was usually employed by people like this, not sitting at the table making small talk. Like a good little wife. "No, we're not having children."

Linda's eyes widened and her face turned a shade pinker. "I'm so sorry, I didn't realize…"

Rebecca should have just let it go, let her think that they weren't having children because they weren't able to. It would serve her right to squirm because she shouldn't have made assumptions. But something—possibly the third glass of Malbec—made Rebecca feel belligerent. "It's not that we *can't*. We just don't want children."

Linda's face changed immediately and she lowered her voice, leaning closer. "Is it Jack? Because men change their minds. My husband…"

Rebecca shook her head. "No. It's both of us. I don't want children. Never have."

Then there was the smile. The *I Know Better* smile. "Maybe you're just not ready yet. They are a lot of work, but it's the best thing you can ever do, believe me."

The best thing Rebecca could think of doing was traveling first-class round the world. Not pushing a small person out of herself. Still, they were at a dinner at Jack's boss's house; it wasn't the time for a full-on debate on a woman's right to make choices about her own body. She smiled tightly. "Maybe. I'll let you know if I change my mind."

But Linda wasn't for changing the subject. At the other end of the table, three men were discussing the new menu at the golf club, and Jack's head bobbed up and down as he tried to add to their analysis. His thick head of blond hair made him look like a young child trying to make a good impression on the gray-haired grown-ups. Rebecca was on her own. At least Linda was keeping her voice low. "We only have a finite time in order to have a baby, you know? If you keep putting it off, it might be too late. What happens if you regret it?"

Rebecca twisted the silver bangle on her wrist, wishing she was at the other end of the table discussing the golf club. It might be a good venue to add to her portfolio. Plus, it would save her from this irritating conversation. From experience, women like Linda seemed to find her lack of interest in having children personally offensive. She tried to keep her voice light. "What happens if I *do* have children and regret it, though? This way, if I do suddenly have an epiphany in my fifties, at least it's only me that I'm letting down, isn't it?"

She picked up her wineglass to signal the topic over, but before she could change the subject to something innocuous, Linda kicked it up a notch. "But what about Jack? What if he wants children? Don't you owe it to him?"

Was she serious? Had they woken up in a Jane Austen novel? Shouldn't she be taking Rebecca for a turn around the drawing room before she imparted her sage advice? Rebecca was about to tell her exactly what she thought of that opinion when, thankfully—for Linda's sake—Jack caught the end of their conversation. He reached for Rebecca's hand under the table and squeezed it. "Don't worry about me, Linda, I'm in complete agreement. Like kids; couldn't eat a whole one." He winked at Rebecca. "Anyway, George tells me you've got the planning permission for the renovations on your house. When does it all kick off?"

Rebecca returned the squeeze of Jack's hand. He was good at diverting trouble. She wasn't normally one to fly off the handle but she was so tired of people like Linda preaching on about the wonders of motherhood. It was like a cult. She had nothing against children. She'd even been one once. She adored her nephews. Wasn't averse to the children of friends. But she had no desire to have one of her own. Ever.

Back home, after repressing her rage through the dessert and coffee and the cheese course, Rebecca was finally ranting to Jack on the sofa in their living room. "Can you imagine if I'd reversed the conversation? Told her that she shouldn't have had children because of the overpopulation of the world? I'd have been lynched."

Jack kissed the top of her head. "There's no point reasoning with someone like that. They think their way is the only way. You shouldn't rise to it."

It was easy for him to say. Somehow, no one judged a man who wasn't bothered about having children. But when a woman said it, she was either an unnatural witch or a deluded soul headed for a life of lonely regret. "I just wish people would keep their opinions to themselves."

"Yep, me too. But you're not going to change the Linda McCrays of this world. Plus, have you seen their son? A sweaty, spotty, sullen teenager. She's probably jealous of your freedom. And that's before you point out that you don't need to sort out a babysitter to go on the weekend in Bruges that your ever-loving husband is planning."

It took a minute to realize what he'd said. Rebecca sat up. "Are you? Really?" She reached over and kissed him. This was a perfect example of what she had tried to explain to Linda. Why would anyone want to risk what she and Jack had by putting a baby into the mix? She leaned back and looked at him. "Did you check the calendar first?"

Jack laughed. "Of course. I barely go to the toilet without checking the calendar. I do value my life, you know. That's also why I'm telling you now rather than springing it on you. I learned from Parisgate."

She laughed and kissed him again. They'd been together for six months when he had booked a surprise trip to Paris on the same weekend that she had two big events going on in two different towns. In his defense, he hadn't realized that she actually attended the events that she planned. He might tease her about her über-organized schedule but it made life a lot less stressful if everyone knew where they were supposed to be and what they were supposed to be doing. Simple. No surprises.

Jack picked up his wineglass from the table. "It would be nice to be allowed to surprise you sometimes, you know. There might be a whole lot of fun you're missing out on by wanting to have everything planned out to the nth degree."

Missing out on what? Poorly organized parties or weekends in a hotel she wouldn't have chosen? "Nope. I am quite happy with the arrangement we have. Don't you start on me. I've had enough from Linda tonight. Next you'll be suggesting we do have a baby."

Jack pulled a face. "No way. I'm fully with you on that one. That would *not* be a good surprise."

Rebecca hadn't eaten much at dinner. Nerves at making a good impression on Jack's boss followed by suppressed anger at Linda's comments had made her throat so tight that she'd resorted to pushing the food around her plate rather than eating it. But now she was hungry. "I'm going to get some cheese and crackers. Do you want something?"

"No, I'm fine with just wine, thanks. But you go ahead."

Sleek white cabinets, Miele appliances, and granite worktops: the kitchen was still new enough that Rebecca got a thrill every time she entered it. Working from home, she had ended up the unofficial project manager for the whole thing, and it had been a major pain for two months because of the extension and the bifold doors and then the fitting of the kitchen itself. When she'd tried to speak to Linda about how stressful the whole thing had been—but how she was so happy with it now—Linda had attempted a clumsy analogy to the pain of childbirth: like a dog with a bone.

There were no crackers in the usual place in the pantry. She called back to the living room. "Jack, have you moved the crackers somewhere else? The water biscuit ones."

There was silence from the other room. There was no way she would have put them anywhere else, but she checked the cereal shelf. None there. "Jack? Can you hear me? Have you seen the crackers? They were definitely on the online shopping order." Still nothing from next door. Not with the canned goods. Or the cupboard with the herb and spice jars. Confused, she opened another cupboard door to get a tea plate and…there were the crackers. Jack was leaning in the doorway, laughing. She shook her head at him. "You jerk. Did you hide them in there?"

"Got to give you a few surprises in your life."

She pulled the plastic-wrapped crackers out and threw the empty box at him. He ducked behind the door, chuckling to himself.

When she returned to the living room, Jack was back on the couch. He patted the seat next to him. "Have you got any plans for the morning?"

One of the downsides to being an event planner was that those events often happened on a Saturday. "Not during the day. I've got the Andersons' dinner tomorrow night, but that should run like clockwork. As long as the PA I'm dealing with doesn't fret herself into pieces. Are you still out early for golf?"

Jack sipped his wine and nodded. "Unfortunately, yes. I would definitely rather be spending Saturday morning in bed with my beautiful wife, but it was their MD's suggestion and I couldn't say no. I need to be at the course at 8:00 a.m. so I'm there to meet everyone as they arrive. Fingers crossed everything goes well and they'll give us their business by the time we get to the last hole. If so, we'll take them out to lunch and then Rob and I will need to go back to the office and get the paperwork sorted and sent out. I might not be home until late afternoon."

It wasn't often that they got both weekend days together, whether it was her work or Jack's. "That's fine. If you're seeing Rob, can you take that last box of his stuff that's in the spare room?"

Rob was Jack's junior colleague who'd recently camped out in their spare room for two weeks after his girlfriend had kicked him out for being a philandering idiot. She loved Jack's caring nature, but his readiness to take in waifs and strays brought a chaos she wasn't so keen on. His brother had stayed with them for a month last year in between selling one house and buying another and—pleasant as he was—she'd almost moved out to a hotel to get away from his tendency toward forgotten half-empty coffee mugs and haphazard toiletries in the bathroom.

Jack stretched, unbuttoned the top of his shirt, then leaned forward and stole a cracker from her plate. "Will do. If you're at a loose end, maybe you could google some restaurants and bars in Bruges. The beer will be amazing. They have hundreds, apparently. And a different kind of glass for each one."

Rebecca held the plate out of his reach so he couldn't take another cracker. "Sounds great. And, as you say, it's just us, no kids to organize. We can go where we want, when we want. Footloose and—"

She was interrupted by the sound of the doorbell, followed by a knock at the front door.

CHAPTER TWO

Cara

Come on. Answer the door. The length of time between pulling the bell and waiting for the door to open was agony. It had taken a while to work out where the doorbell was; it was one of those old-fashioned pull contraptions that ring an actual bell. Of course. Jack always did like to show he was better than anyone else.

Should she try again? Maybe they hadn't heard? They were definitely in because they'd pulled up outside half an hour ago. Half an hour. That's how long she'd been waiting in the car, trying to pluck up the courage to go in as well as rousing a reluctant Sophie from the backseat, where she'd fallen asleep. On the upside, this late hour might work in her favor.

The last remnants of summer seemed to have disappeared in the last few days, and tonight's cold October air had blown the last of the sleep from Sophie. Now she jumped from one foot to the other, chattering with the excitement of being allowed up so late. "I like the door, Mummy. It's blue. My favorite color."

Cara smiled at the blue bobble hat pulled so far down over Sophie's ears that she could barely make out her nose between that and the scarf tucked up around her chin. "It is nice, isn't it? Hopefully it will open up soon."

As if she'd conjured it with her words, the latch on the door clicked and it opened to reveal an attractive woman of around thirty, holding a glass of red wine. Even though her hair was shorter—cut to chin length with full bangs—Cara recognized her from the picture she'd found on an old friend's Facebook page: Rebecca. Did she live here too?

"Hello?" Rebecca tilted her head, her shiny hair swinging back and forth.

Her vivid blue wrap dress, manicure, and expertly discreet makeup made Cara feel shabby and scruffy. It must be nice to have the money to look like that. "Hi, I'm looking for Jack Faulkner. Does he live here?"

Rebecca glanced down at Sophie and then back to her. "He does. I'm his wife, Rebecca. Is he expecting you?"

Wife? So, he'd turned out to be the settling-down type, after all. "Can you just tell him that Cara is here to see him? Cara Miller."

This was ridiculous: she sounded like a ten-year-old asking for her friend to come out and play. Jack was always a soft touch, but he didn't need his wife to play bodyguard, surely? Was she ever going to let them in? Rubbing Sophie's arm as if to warm her up had the desired effect: Rebecca held the door open. "Do you want to step into the hall?" She stood away from the entrance and leaned back to call out, "Jack! There's someone here to see you."

Inside, the warmth hit them like a slap after the crisp October evening. Though they rubbed their feet on the doormat, their boots made damp footprints on the black and white floor tiles. Cara took in the high ceilings, the Tiffany lightshade, Jack's sketches framed in black, lining the left-hand wall. She pulled the hat from the top of Sophie's head, her blond curls lifting with the static. The heat wasn't the only reason for taking it off; it was important that Sophie look her best.

Jack also had a glass of red wine in his hand when he appeared in the doorway to what was presumably their living room. Sitting in the car, she had wondered if he would recognize her straightaway, but the look on his face answered that question. "Cara? What are *you* doing here?"

Rebecca looked from one to the other. Did she know who Cara was? Had Jack ever mentioned her before? "I...er...I need to talk to you about something."

She couldn't blame Jack for being shocked. It had been a while. And Rebecca looked completely taken aback.

"Do you want to come through to the living room?" Rebecca held out a hand toward the door. "We've just finished a bottle of wine but I can make you tea and"—she looked at Sophie—"milk?"

Though a girlfriend had felt likely, Cara hadn't factored in a wife. It would be far better to speak to Jack alone. "Black coffee would be great, thanks."

Sophie pulled on her mother's hand. "I need to use the bathroom, Mummy."

Rebecca pointed to a doorway under the stairs. "There's a bathroom there you're very welcome to use. Just come through when you're ready."

CHAPTER THREE

Rebecca

As soon as she heard the bathroom door close, Rebecca turned to Jack. "Who is she?"

Jack flushed and fiddled with the glass in his hands. "An exgirlfriend. From years ago. Her name is Cara. I'm sure I've mentioned her to you before? I have absolutely no idea why she is here."

Of course. She knew the name was familiar. "*That* Cara? The one you were dating just before we met? I had no idea you'd stayed in touch with her. How did she know we'd moved here?"

Jack held out his hands. Opened his mouth as if to speak, but barely a sound came out. He dropped down onto the sofa and ran his hands through his hair. "I didn't... We haven't... I'm as confused as you are, Becca. Honestly."

Rebecca rubbed her eyebrows with her thumb and forefinger. She wasn't a jealous person. Of course Jack had had girlfriends before her. But why was Cara here? *People from your past don't just decide to make house calls out of the blue on a Friday night.*

The lock on the bathroom door clicked, and Cara and her daughter appeared at the door. Rebecca smiled at them and pointed to the large armchair, big enough for both of them. "Why don't you sit down."

Cara perched on the edge of the armchair and pulled Sophie toward her. "You have a lovely home."

Jack looked irritated. "Thanks. Look, I don't mean to be rude, but why are you here? We haven't spoken in years and now you just turn up at eleven o'clock at night."

Cara stuck out her chin. "Is there anywhere Sophie could play for a little while? I don't think she really wants to sit and listen to grown-ups talking, do you, baby? How about you go and do some drawing while Mummy chats with Jack." She opened her bag and rummaged around, then looked up at Rebecca. "I've left her paper and colors in the car. Do you have anything she could use to draw?"

That was convenient. Clearly, she wanted Rebecca out of the way. At least they'd find out what was going on. "I've got some paper in my office. Shall I show you where it is, Sophie?"

Cara nudged Sophie, who trotted obediently after Rebecca. She tried to give Jack a pointed look, but he was still staring at Cara as if she had two heads.

Rebecca's home office was a small room on the opposite side of the hallway to the sitting room, with a desk, chair, and very small white filing cabinet. Rebecca pulled some paper out of the printer underneath her desk and laid it out for Sophie to draw on. Above the neatly updated wall planner behind the desk were two shelves of brochures for venues, restaurants, and hotels. Next to them, a box of stationery that included a new packet of highlighter pens in pastel colors. She slipped them out of their pouch and laid them on the paper. "You can use whichever ones you want to."

Sophie's little face lit up. "Thank you."

She looked so tiny perched on the office chair, like a little bird dressed in denim dungarees and a blue polka-dot top. Rebecca was torn between staying to check she was okay and wanting to get back to the living room as quickly as possible. Her mind was chewing over Cara's sudden appearance. There must be a reason why an ex-girlfriend would turn up out of the blue after five years. She watched as Sophie picked up a highlighter pen and pulled it across the page as her left hand twisted the bottom of her curly blond hair.

It was the hair that gave it away.

Maybe her mind was already almost there before she walked back up the hallway. Before she overheard Cara and Jack's conversation. Before she saw him running his hands through his hair like he always did when he was confused. The thick blond hair he kept short to prevent it from curling.

Jack was leaning forward in his seat when she got to the doorway, shaking his head at Cara as if he couldn't shuffle his thoughts into the right order. "So, you've been thrown out of your home, you've got no one else to ask, and you've come here? When we haven't spoken in, what, five years?"

Why had they been thrown out of their home? Rebecca's heart was beating hard in her chest. She wanted so much to be wrong. She sat next to Jack, put a hand on his arm to stop him from waving it around. "Money? Have you come to ask Jack to lend you some money?"

Cara was the only one in the room who was composed. "Not exactly." She paused. "I was kind of hoping you might be able to let us stay for a few days. Me and Sophie."

"What?" Jack stood and started to pace. This was how he always processed something complex.

Rebecca's stomach was turning over. She knew what was coming and yet she still hoped she was wrong.

Jack stopped pacing and turned to Cara. "I'm sorry. I just don't understand. What are you thinking? We dated for a short while years ago, and then you turn up here and ask if you and your daughter can stay in my house with me and my wife? This is crazy, Cara. Even for you."

Cara flinched at his words but Jack didn't notice; he was pacing again. "The more I think about it, the worse this is, Cara. I can't believe you would just turn up here, dragging your poor daughter behind you and... and... what?"

The last question was directed to Rebecca, who was shaking her head to try to stop him. It was too painful to watch and she needed to know. Right now. She looked at Cara. "She's not just *your* daughter, though, is she?"

Cara took a deep breath and let it out slowly. "No," she said. "She's not just my daughter." She turned in her seat to face Jack. "Sophie is your daughter too."

CHAPTER FOUR

Rebecca

Rebecca's heart sank to her feet. Jack reeled as if he'd been shot. His face drained of color and he closed his eyes. When he opened them, his expression was more complex than shock, although Rebecca couldn't quite put her finger on it.

When he spoke, his voice had dropped to a whisper. "Are you sure?"

Cara nodded. "One hundred percent. I know it's a bombshell. If circumstances were different..."

Rebecca's initial shock was replaced by confusion. "What do you mean? If you hadn't needed somewhere to stay, you would never have told him? You would have just let him go on in his life ignorant that he had a child?"

Jack placed a restraining hand over Rebecca's. "Hold on. Let's just take a minute here."

Rebecca crossed her arms and pressed her lips together. Of the two of them, Jack was the one who always avoided confrontation, always saw the other side of an argument. *But even he must be angry right now?* Cara's chin was jutting toward them. She looked harder, tougher than she had in the hall. Then her eyes softened when they resettled on Jack. "I didn't find out that I was pregnant until after you... after we split up. I wasn't even sure that I was going to keep the baby and then I knew I did want to and..."

Jack covered his face with his palms and then pulled them down slowly, dragging the skin with them. He looked...guilty? "But five years, Cara? Five years and you've never said a word?"

Cara looked down to her lap, where she was picking at her fingernail. Her hands were red and her nails ragged. Rebecca had her nails manicured every two weeks. Nothing flashy. Blunt, neutral, tidy: part of her professional appearance. Although she had to grudgingly admit that Cara was pretty; her short choppy dark hair, angular face, and tight jeans made her look so different from Rebecca. Not Jack's type at all. How had they even met?

Cara looked up but continued to pick at her fingers. "I meant to. Before the baby was born, then again when she turned one. I even found you online but...I could never get the courage up to do it."

Jack sighed and dropped back in his chair. Couldn't he see that this woman was manipulating him with her big blue eyes and trembling lip? Jack was a sucker for anyone in tears, and Cara obviously knew that of old. Rebecca was trying so hard to bite her tongue, but Jack just sat there, shaking his head. If he wasn't going to say anything, Rebecca certainly was. "And what about Sophie? What does she know? Did she not ask about her dad? Have you told her Jack is her father?"

Cara's tone was unbearably condescending. "Where we live, there are lots of little girls who only have their mum. She hasn't questioned it up to now."

She was looking at Rebecca with something approaching contempt, as if she were a naive little girl with no knowledge of the real world. It was enough to drive the last remnants of patience from Rebecca's chest. "And what about now? Why does she think you are here? Who does she think we are?"

Cara narrowed her eyes. "She doesn't think anything about *you*." She turned to Jack. "But I've told her that you are an old friend of mine. That you might be able to help us. Might"—she paused and took a deep breath—"might give us somewhere to stay until we work out what we are going to do next."

Rebecca nearly choked. Stay? This complete stranger really did expect them to open their door and let her and the child *stay*? She looked at Jack and saw her surprise reflected back at her.

The door to the living room creaked and Sophie appeared in the doorway. "Mummy?"

Cara stood and walked the three steps to crouch beside her daughter. She was so slim and petite, if you didn't look at her face, you might mistake her for a child herself. Just the kind of woman to bring out Jack's natural protectiveness. "What is it, baby? Mummy just needs to speak to her friend for a few more minutes."

Rebecca noted the use of the singular "friend." Was this woman expecting her to offer to take her daughter back to her office and let them continue their conversation without her? No way that was happening now.

Sophie held out a picture of a roughly drawn triangle with four lines coming out of it and a floating circle. "I did a picture of you."

Cara took the picture. "That's fantastic. Can you draw some more for Mummy?"

Sophie shook her head. "The paper is all finished."

How had she gone through that pile of paper already? Still, at least this was a way to get Cara out of the room for a few moments so that she could speak to Jack alone. "There's more in the printer under the desk if you want to get her some?"

Cara pushed herself back up to standing. Without even glancing at Rebecca, she held out her hand to her daughter. "Come on, Soph. Show me where you've been drawing and I'll get some more paper for you. Maybe you can draw me a picture of you that I can keep in my bag."

As soon as they were out of the room, Rebecca stood and pushed the door closed. Now it was her turn to pace. "What the hell are we going to do?"

Jack looked exhausted. "I have no idea. No idea at all."

Rebecca had to keep moving. How could he just sit there? *Think. Think!* "She's expecting to stay here. What are we going to say to that? Do you know her well enough to allow her to stay in our house?" There was something unsettling about Cara's appearance. Her thinness, her hooded eyes, the tight set of her mouth. "Can she be trusted?"

Jack blinked several times. "I think so. I mean, I haven't seen her in such a long time. She was quite wild back then, but I guess she must have settled down if she has a kid."

Rebecca wanted to shake him; it was as if he was thinking in slow motion. Cara would be back any minute and, one thing was certain, they would have to present a united front on this. Much as she'd like to show Cara the door and relegate her to the gray box of Jack's past, there was a little girl to think about. She still didn't know why they'd been evicted from their home. But if she and Jack didn't let them stay here, where would the two of them go?

As if to underline her thoughts, the wind outside moaned and the beginnings of rain pattered on the front window. "So, are you going to invite them to stay in the spare room?"

Jack's face was almost pleading. He could never say no to anyone in need. "What do you think?"

The door opened slowly and Cara poked her head into the room. "Okay to come back in?"

Rebecca sat down next to Jack. He straightened up and motioned with his hand for Cara to regain her seat. "Of course. We were just talking. It's a lot to get my head around."

His head around? How did he think Rebecca felt? She waited for Cara to sit back down and then asked, "Do you not have anyone else you can stay with? Family? Your parents?"

Cara shuddered and a dark shadow came over her face. "No. My parents' house is the last place on this earth that I would take my daughter."

There was something in her expression that sent a chill through Rebecca. She wasn't going to press her further on that. She nudged Jack. It wasn't fair for him to let her be the bad guy.

Jack ran a hand through his hair. "Uh, what about friends? Don't you have other friends you can stay with?"

Now it was Jack's turn to be on the receiving end of her condescending look. "My only friends don't have room for two extra bodies in their place, even if the landlord would let them get away with it. Do you have no idea what it's like in the real world?"

Rebecca felt uncomfortable. She was well aware that they led a privileged life with their comfortable home and well-paid jobs. She'd worked for that, though. It hadn't been handed to her on a plate. "Do you work?"

"Yes. At the hospital."

For some reason, that surprised her. "Don't they have any accommodation there that you could—"

Cara stood. "Maybe this was a mistake. I didn't know that you were…that the two of you were married. I didn't even realize you were in a serious relationship."

Jack held up a hand. "Stop. Look. Where will you go?"

Cara shrugged like a recalcitrant teenager. "I really don't know."

Rebecca took a deep breath. There was so much to take in, so much to discuss. No way could they let this woman go out in the cold and rain with nowhere to go. Especially with a young child. A young child who was Jack's *daughter*.

Her head buzzed with the mess of it all. She couldn't think about that right now. It was too much. Get the practicalities sorted out first. "You can stay here. But just for tonight. I'll go and make up the spare room."

Cara looked relieved. "Thank you."

Jack stood up. "I'll come and help you."

It was only now that Rebecca realized what had been so strange about Jack's expression. He didn't look quite as shocked as she would have expected.

CHAPTER FIVE

Cara

Slipping out of bed the next morning, Cara picked up one of the towels that Rebecca had left for them the night before along with brand-new Molton Brown toiletries. What kind of person had miniature toiletries ready to go at a moment's notice?

Rebecca. Cara had seen a picture of her and Jack on an old friend's Facebook page when she'd finally tracked him down. He didn't have a Facebook page of his own but this photo had been taken at a barbecue or outside event. The way he'd had his arm around her made it obvious that she was his girlfriend. But wife? She hadn't expected that.

Insomnia had its uses. As she did every morning, she grabbed her oversized makeup bag to sort herself out before Sophie woke up. Thankfully, there was a bathroom that Rebecca had told them they would have to themselves, so she could make herself look presentable before facing Jack and Rebecca for round two.

It was nine o'clock by the time they made it downstairs. The living room door was open, but no one was sitting on that ridiculously huge sofa this morning. Cara, hands on Sophie's shoulders, gently directed her up the hallway toward another door, where they found Rebecca in a large modern kitchen. She was drinking coffee from an oversized floral teacup, reading through a pile of glossy magazines, looking like a TV ad for a kitchen company.

Getting up from the stool at the island in the middle of the room, Rebecca smiled at Sophie; the face she showed Cara was far more guarded. "Good morning. Would you like some breakfast?" She reached up into a cavernous cupboard above their heads and brought out four brightly colored mini boxes of cereal, which she set in front of Sophie. "I have these from when a friend stayed here with her son. Would you like one?"

Sophie's eyes widened and she nodded. "Yes, please."

Cara didn't want Rebecca fussing over Sophie. Where the hell was Jack? "You don't need to wait on us. I can do it for her if you tell me where everything is."

Rebecca's smile was tight. "It's no trouble." She reached into another vast cupboard containing a large set of perfectly matched and organized dishes. "Jack left already. I suggested that he stay home this morning but he has a *very* important round of golf with a potential client."

Both her tone of voice and the way she banged the cupboard door closed suggested that she hadn't been pleased by that decision. Maybe all was not perfect in paradise?

Cara's mobile buzzed in her pocket. She slid it out and looked at the screen. It was Lee. Their landlord.

Cara. Your rent is really late, mate. I don't want to get all heavy. What's the problem?

She slid it back in her pocket. She'd deal with him later.

Rebecca pulled out the silverware drawer for a spoon. While she was hidden from view by the door of the huge double fridge, Sophie pulled Cara down to her height and whispered, "Can we stay here all day, Mummy?"

"We'll see," Cara whispered back. If all went as planned, they'd be staying there a lot longer than that.

CHAPTER SIX

Rebecca

All relationships—professional or private—work best when people know their role. Rebecca was the one who organized their home life and Jack was happy to fall in with it. At work, he was a "blue sky thinker"; he would come up with the ideas, and the efficient team he'd built around him would work out the logistics and the processes. Their home life often followed a similar pattern. More than once, she'd accused him of being an ostrich about the practicalities of the new kitchen plan or a holiday destination or a social event he'd thought up. It was all very well him telling her that she should stop planning life to the nth degree. But it was her meticulous attention to detail that enabled their lives to work.

And when he'd informed her last night that he was still going to the golf course in the morning, she had seriously questioned his sanity. "Are you kidding me?"

He'd been lying on his side, looking at her, his eyes pleading. "I've been trying to land this client forever, Rebecca. You know I have. We've been courting their huge advertising budget since last summer, and they've finally agreed to meet with me. And we're meeting at eight in the morning. There's no way I can cancel now."

"And what am I supposed to do with Cara?" She'd practically spat the name at him. She was trying not to judge before she knew her properly but she hadn't liked what she'd seen so far.

"Just give her some breakfast and tell her that I'll call her later tomorrow. Obviously, we need time to sit down properly and talk about this."

Rebecca had stared at him. "This? This what? The little girl? Sophie? Your daughter?"

Jack had squirmed next to her. "Look. Let's not get ahead of ourselves. We don't even know for sure that she is mine."

Rebecca had laughed hollowly. "Seriously? You can't see it? She looks exactly like you. I mean, get a DNA test, of course, but I think we both know what it's going to say."

Jack had put his hands up to his face. For a very brief moment, she'd thought he was crying but then he'd looked up and sighed deeply. "Okay, okay. You don't need to keep saying that."

Again, she'd had the feeling that he hadn't seemed as shocked as he should have been. "Did you... know?"

Then *he'd* looked shocked. "What? No. Of course not. Did you think I'd been keeping a secret daughter all this time?"

She'd been surprised at the strength of his reaction, the fierceness of his whisper. Why had he spoken to her in that tone? This wasn't them. They never argued like this. Maybe this conversation would be better at another time, when they weren't so exhausted, so ready to bite chunks out of each other. There'd been no point dragging the conversation out all night, anyway. Especially as she'd wanted to get up early before Cara woke up. As much as she'd felt sorry for Sophie being dragged around town on a Friday night, she wasn't entirely comfortable having two complete strangers sleeping in the house. Although, she'd had to remind herself, Cara wasn't a stranger to Jack.

This morning, as soon as she'd heard the crunch of the gravel as his car pulled away, she got out of bed and into the shower.

Even on a weekend, it was important to her to be showered and dressed before breakfast, ready to begin her day.

Jack was ambitious. What her dad would have called a "go-getter." It was one of the things she'd most liked about him when they'd first met. There had been over two hundred people at the Christmas party she'd organized for his advertising agency, but he had stood out from everyone she'd spoken to. His clothes, his speech, the way he interacted with all the staff at the party showed how he was driven, focused: just like her. In the last two years he had been promoted three times, and each time his new boss would comment on his dedication and vision. His golf game with a major client was important, of course it was. But surely it could be rearranged considering the circumstances? Apparently not.

Before shutting off the shower, she let the water clean the suds from the shower gel and shampoo bottles. She'd already made a note on her phone to replenish the guest bottles she'd given to Cara last night. There was so much she wanted to ask Jack about Cara. The longer they'd spoken with her last night, the less she could understand how the two of them had been a couple. Jack had been brought up in a big house in Fincham village; Cara most definitely had not. All Rebecca had been able to get out of him was that they'd met at a club, that it had been during a "wild period" of his life that he wasn't particularly proud of. His eyes said that he didn't want to talk about it, and when Jack didn't want to talk about something, he would just shut down, become monosyllabic. She'd learned how to handle him. If she wanted to know more about Cara and him, she would have to catch him at the right moment. Theoretically, she had no right to be angry with him. They hadn't been together when he was with Cara, so it wasn't as if he'd cheated on her. But a child? This wasn't part of their plan. Ever.

*

After making Cara a black coffee, they left Sophie in the kitchen eating her cereal and watching cartoons. Sitting opposite Cara in the living room, Rebecca pushed the hair away from her face and took a deep breath. *Where to begin?* "So..."

Great start, Rebecca. For all her abilities to schmooze hoteliers and stately home owners into capitulating to her clients' more unreasonable demands, she was not good at dealing with personal stuff like this.

Cara wasn't helping her either. She just stared back at her. "So?"

Rebecca coughed. "What are your plans?"

Cara frowned. "For today?"

She really wasn't helping. "In general. About somewhere to stay."

"Are you kicking us out?" Cara leaned forward, her eyes wide.

Rebecca almost choked. Cara made her sound like a monster. "No, I'm not throwing you out. I just assumed you'd want to stay somewhere more...permanent."

Cara laughed and sat back in her chair. "I'm just joking. Yes, I'll start to call around this morning. It was just too late last night and it was a Friday night so..."

"Yes, yes, of course." She was making Rebecca feel terrible. In the light of morning, Cara looked exhausted. Maybe she'd lied about sleeping well; Rebecca never slept the first night in a different bed. Hotel rooms were the worst; her mind could never shut off from the fact that other people had been in the bed the night before. Jack had laughed at her when she'd begun to travel with her own pillow. She found her voice softening. "Look. You don't have to rush off. I mean, we're not using the room for a few days and—"

Cara practically bit her hand off. "Really? That's great. Thanks."

Dammit. Why had she said that? Surely Cara could see that she was just being polite. Anyone else would have realized. But how could she backtrack now and tell her that she wanted them gone today?

Cara sat back in her chair and sipped at her coffee, seemingly oblivious to Rebecca's anxiety. "Have you and Jack been together a long time?"

How had she changed the subject so easily? Rebecca nodded. "Four and a half years."

Cara paled a little at that. She was probably doing the same math Rebecca had done last night. If Sophie was four, Cara would have still been pregnant when Jack and Rebecca had met. Rebecca's stomach started to churn again. "Look, I don't want to sound rude, but… are you really sure? That Jack is Sophie's father?"

Cara looked her in the eye. "One hundred percent."

Rebecca's phone rang. Izzy. "Sorry, I need to take this. It's my business partner."

Cara waved a hand and got up. "I'll go and check on Sophie."

"Hi, Izzy. What can I do for you?"

"Oh, Rebecca, great. I was hoping you'd pick up. Just checking in because I know you've got the Anderson dinner in the schedule for tonight."

She frowned, realizing the events of last night had driven it from her mind. A three-course meal for the entire company and their spouses to thank them for a record-breaking year. Maybe she would have been less critical of Jack's golf game if she'd remembered she would have to go out this evening. "Everything is organized and ready to go. I'll be there an hour before to make sure the canapés and pre-event drinks are ready and waiting."

She could almost hear Izzy smile at the other end. "Of course it's organized. I know not to expect anything less. I, on the other hand, am anything but. Which is why I'm calling you in a panic. I'm out at Greenfield Manor with the Hunter-Woollards and I've forgotten those brochures you collated for me. Any chance there's an electronic version you can pop onto an email? I don't want to look a hot mess."

Rebecca bit her lip. She loved her colleague but Izzy's disorganization drove her nuts sometimes. *Why*, she mused furiously for a moment, *am I always the one who has to clean up other people's messes?* Messes that could be avoided with foresight and planning. Still, Izzy was her friend, and Rebecca had known what she was like when they'd started the company together. "Of course. Can you give me half an hour?"

There was a pause on the other end of the phone. Rebecca knew what was coming. "Sorry to be an absolute pain, but I really need them now. Please, pleeease could you send them straightaway? Or are you in the middle of something?"

Rebecca sighed. She could hardly tell Izzy that she was tied up talking to the mother of her husband's secret daughter. That one needed a face-to-face. "You are a complete pain, but I'll do it. It's a good thing I'm your friend."

Jack had warned her that starting a company with a friend wasn't necessarily a good idea. "You could run an events company with your eyes closed," he'd said to her. The problem was, successful event planning wasn't just down to organizational skills. Izzy had the vital element that Rebecca didn't: connections. She'd been born into the world of the Hunter-Woollards and the Jamiesons and all the other wealthy families that they managed events for. If Rebecca went out on her own, how would she pull in the customers she needed? Jack didn't understand because he was from that world too.

In any case, she and Izzy worked well as a team, playing to their individual strengths. Rebecca did the corporate events and Izzy looked after the private stuff, which was more touchy-feely and frequently involved the hand-holding of anxious husbands or fickle brides.

It would take only a few minutes to find the brochure PDFs and email them, anyway. The advantage of an effective digital filing system. Then she could finish her conversation with Cara. "I'll just be in the office," she called through to the kitchen.

But when she got to the upstairs landing, Cara startled her by walking out of the bathroom. When had she come up here? Cara stopped in her tracks when she saw her. "Oh. Er, hi. I didn't hear you come up, sorry. I was…"

She waved in the direction of the bathroom. Her eyes were watery and she was wiping at her nose with the back of her wrist. Why was she looking so guilty? What had she been doing in there that had made her so embarrassed?

CHAPTER SEVEN

Cara

The whole of Saturday had crawled by, and Cara had been perched on a stool in the kitchen for the last two hours, watching Sophie draw a house and willing Jack to walk back through the door.

She checked the time on her mobile. There were three more missed calls from Lee. She wanted to tell him to let her place go to someone else but just needed to wait a little longer. Once she'd spoken to Jack properly, she'd know whether to risk losing the apartment. Hopefully, she could get him alone. Without Rebecca there.

This whole situation would have been so much easier if Jack was alone. She hadn't been naive enough to think he'd be single, but married? What had he told her when he'd finished with her? *I'm not the settling-down type.* It had been so sudden, a punch to the gut. That's why, when she'd realized about the baby, she'd had a good idea what he'd tell her to do.

"This is the garden." Sophie held up her picture. In front of the house was a bright green lawn populated with clumps of red and orange, which Cara assumed were flowers.

"That's nice. What about a pond with some fish?"

Sophie screwed up her beautiful face. "A pond? In the front garden? You don't have a pond in a front garden."

It was almost six o'clock. Cara's stomach began to churn, and it wasn't from the smell of the casserole that Rebecca had put in the oven. Businesswoman, hostess, chef: Was this woman some kind of goddess? It was extremely unlikely that Sophie would eat casserole, but she didn't tell her that. For now, they needed to be the easiest houseguests in the world. Maybe she could bribe Sophie with the offer of sweets tomorrow if she ate some of it.

Rebecca had made conversation over lunch. Asking Cara how she and Jack had met. There was something about the way she'd asked that had made Cara feel as if she was being tested. When she'd said that they'd met in a club, Rebecca had seemed satisfied.

The night she'd met Jack had been one of the best nights of her life. Other than Soph being born, obviously. She'd been living on a friend's sofa—someone from school. Cara had taken her out for a drink to thank her for putting her up. Not that she could really afford the prices in the club, but with a figure like hers had been, there was usually someone who would buy her a drink.

Anyway, Jack had been out with some friends. They'd looked as if they'd just stepped out of a posh catalog, and Cara and her mate had got to chatting with them. They'd had a fair bit to drink and everyone had had a good time—they were nice guys. Jack was something extra, though. It wasn't just that he was great-looking and had a lovely voice. He was also kind and gentlemanly; didn't seem like he was just out for a good time like most of the men she'd met since leaving home. He'd taken her number and asked her out on a proper date. Her mate had teased her relentlessly the next morning. Kept calling her "Lady Cara." To be honest, she hadn't thought he'd call. Guys like that didn't tend to go out with girls like her. But he did.

Rebecca had been pretty busy in her office all afternoon. Cara could hear her on the phone quite a lot. Laughing and joking with whomever she was speaking to. Because the office door was closed, Cara had managed to bring the suitcase in without Rebecca seeing. She didn't want her thinking that she was moving all their stuff in. Not yet, anyway. Danielle, her neighbor and friend, had lent her the car for the whole weekend, so there was no rush.

Rebecca had said that Jack would be home around four. She must have been impatient for his arrival, too, because Cara heard her come out of her office a fraction of a second after the front door creaked open. As hard as Cara tried, it was impossible to make out the details of their murmured conversation. Moments later, a heavy footfall sounded as if someone was taking the stairs two at a time.

Rebecca appeared in the doorway. "I need to leave for my event now. Jack's just gone upstairs to take a shower. He won't be long."

At last. Some time alone. "Okay. Thanks."

Rebecca hovered for a few seconds then seemed to think better of whatever she was going to say. As soon as she'd gone, Cara opened the camera on her phone to check her appearance. The suitcase she'd brought in contained more of her clothes, and she'd changed into a fresh outfit an hour ago. It was important to give this her best shot.

CHAPTER EIGHT

Rebecca

Immaculate white tablecloths, silverware in perfect alignment, floorspace sparkling, clear, and empty: this was the best part of the evening. Rebecca checked her clipboard. Pre-drinks scheduled for 7:30 p.m. before a three-course dinner for two hundred at 8:00 p.m. A car was arranged to collect the keynote speaker from his hotel at 7:15 p.m., and he had assured her his speech lasted twenty minutes. Of course, he would think his words about the success of the company would be vitally important and inspiring, but there were a couple hundred guests coming who would just want to get to the free bar and the dance floor. Her job was to keep everyone happy.

"What time would you like us to bring out the canapés?"

Eric, the headwaiter, stood just to her left, and she glanced at him before checking the clipboard. "Let's stick to seven forty-five, but if a lot of people come early, I might ask you to bring them out earlier. We'll need something in their hands to avoid them downing too much of the Prosecco before dinner." See, she could be flexible when she needed to be.

Whitmore House was one of her favorite venues and she sent a lot of work their way. They were professional and organized and everything always went smoothly. Eric acknowledged her plan with a short nod. "Very good."

Another check of the clipboard even though she could have recited the order of events by heart. It was difficult to keep her mind on the job at hand. What were Jack and Cara doing at home? Reminiscing about old times? Sophie would probably be in bed soon; the two of them would be alone. Like two parents sitting down to a relaxed evening. Her stomach prickled at the thought.

Though she'd always been certain that she didn't want children, Rebecca found it tricky to know at which point in a relationship to tell a new boyfriend. If she said it too early on, she ran the risk of freaking him out if he thought she was assuming the relationship was serious. Too late and she'd be in too deep, at risk of getting badly hurt or hurting him. The best way was to let it happen naturally. Just slide it into the conversation when the subject of children came up.

With Jack, it was about three months in. He had given her the spare key to his flat the week before, so she'd known that things were moving fast and she would have to tell him soon. But it had been hard. She'd been falling for him. If he had imagined the usual "live together followed by marriage followed by babies" scenario, the whole thing was going to crumble.

They'd been out for dinner and the couple next to them had a baby. It was cute. But very noisy. The poor mother had been trying to calm the baby down and looking apologetically at the other diners. Rebecca had smiled at her—it wasn't her fault the baby was crying—but she still wished that they weren't there.

Eventually, the woman's husband had taken the baby from her and shuffled the noise outside.

"Poor guy." Jack had leaned forward, speaking quietly. "He practically inhaled that steak. Why do people take kids to restaurants like this?"

Rebecca had shrugged. "Maybe they can't get a babysitter. And they want a nice meal. They might not have a choice." She had been fully aware how much children took over your life. She'd seen it firsthand with friends of hers. *Now is as good a time as ever.* "One of the reasons I don't want children."

Jack had looked surprised. "Really? Are you definite on that?"

She hadn't been able to tell from his tone which way this was going to go. But there was no point in continuing if he wanted kids—it would just be more difficult the longer they were together. "Yes. It's not that I dislike children. I just don't want to be a mother."

Jack had raised an eyebrow. "Really? The guys at work keep winding me up that the next step after moving in together will be marriage and babies. A couple of days ago, one of the marketing execs was complaining that his wife had started dropping ten-ton hints since her sister announced her pregnancy. He just keeps saying the same thing to anyone who'll listen: 'I know how this works—if their sister or best friend has a baby, you're screwed.'" He had laughed.

Clearly, he hadn't been bothered by her announcement. Had he realized she was serious? "Yeah, I know that seems to be the norm. But I really don't want that. I'm selfish, I guess. I don't want the responsibility of another life."

Jack had shaken his head. "It's not selfish. It's good that you know what you want. To be honest, I haven't put much thought into it at all. I don't think I'd be particularly great father material either if it meant I'd have to stand outside in the cold rather than being in here with you and this glass of wine."

They'd both looked out the window where the dad was pacing up and down, rubbing the baby's back.

The waiter had come to take their plates. "Would you like to see a dessert menu?"

Jack had looked at Rebecca and she'd shaken her head. He'd dropped his napkin onto the table. "I think we're all done, thanks. Can you bring us the bill?" As the waiter left, he'd leaned in close and lowered his voice. "How about we go back to mine and have some fun *not* making babies?"

The subject had come up again several times before they'd got married—usually after attending a christening or going on holidays with other families—but Jack had never shown any signs that he was changing his mind, and she definitely wasn't.

The door to the large function room squeaked open and Angela Matthews poked her head around the door. Angela was the managing director's PA and had hired Rebecca and Izzy to organize tonight's dinner. For a moment, Rebecca didn't recognize her in full makeup and a low-cut, sparkly dress, scanning the room as she walked toward Rebecca with a growing smile on her face. "Wow. You were right about this place. It looks fantastic."

Angela had been to see Whitmore House only during the day. But it became something else in the evening when the electric candles on the centerpieces gave the room a romantic feel.

"I'm glad you like it. Everything is ready for the evening and I'll be on hand if you need anything." When they'd started their company, she and Izzy had agreed that personally attending every event would be their USP. Speaking from experience, that "anything" could include a range of disasters from a senior member of the board complaining about the wine to showcase his inflated view of his own knowledge, to one of the more junior members of staff mixing a dangerous cocktail of nerves and pinot grigio and throwing up in the toilet by 9:30 p.m.

Angela patted her hair with an anxious hand. "Actually, there is something. Have you heard that there is going to be a meteor shower visible this evening? Could we get everyone outside to watch it? Might be a memorable addition to the evening?"

She hadn't even finished when Rebecca started to shake her head. "No. I don't think that's a good idea. These things are always very unpredictable. You could get everyone outside and then find it's not visible. Disappointment will take the edge off of everything you're doing here."

Now Angela started to twist the ends of her hair. If she wasn't careful, she would ruin what looked like a salon curling job. "But the managing director is interested in that kind of thing. I'm sure he would appreciate the attention to detail."

So, she was trying to impress her boss. Completely understandable, but he wouldn't be half as impressed when it took twenty minutes to get everyone outside, the women in their strappy dresses and spiky heels shivering with cold and sinking into the mud, the men pretending they didn't feel it while the cold took the edge off their merriment. And then—when the cloud coverage was too thick or the timing was wrong and no one got to see anything anyway—it would put a damper on halfway through the event, which even "The Grease Megamix" would find difficult to wrench back. Still, this woman was the one who had hired their company, and she and Izzy were hoping for repeat business; it was important to be tactful. Or lie. "I read something earlier that suggested it was going to be difficult to see the shower because of the weather. Maybe we should keep quiet about it to avoid disappointment." Angela didn't look convinced but Rebecca was saved by the first arrivals. "Excuse me, I just need to check that the Prosecco is ready for your guests."

Since they had started to take on bigger clients, it had become more like this. The larger the spend, the more they wanted to be involved. It was irritating. Especially when she'd put so much time into ensuring that everything was planned to the last detail.

Izzy was different: She kept her scheduling a little more fluid. Tried to say yes to everything the client wanted, no matter how last-minute the request. "That's what they are paying us for," she said all the time. "You need to be more *reactive*."

Secretly, Rebecca thought this was actually a euphemism for Izzy's lackadaisical approach to the planning process. She was more about the look and feel than the precise details. It was what made them such a good team. But it was also what drove Rebecca crazy. What was wrong with making a plan and sticking to it?

Busy with getting everyone to their seat in time and ensuring the vegetarian and vegan options didn't go to the wrong people who had "forgotten" what they'd pre-ordered from the menu, she didn't cross paths with Angela Matthews until she bumped into her coming out of the toilet between the starter and the main course. "Oh, good. I was hoping to grab you. I've just been speaking to Stuart—the managing director I mentioned—and he thought it was a really good idea to go out for the meteor shower."

With everything going on at home, Rebecca was less than patient. "As I said, that's not going to work."

Judging by Angela's expression, her tone must have been less polite than she'd aimed for. "But there's plenty of time to—"

Rebecca waved her clipboard. "We have to get through two more courses and have the coffee served in time for the keynote speech. Honestly, just leave everything to me. You should be enjoying yourself. Really, leave it to me."

She left before Angela had a chance to reply. Why couldn't people just stick to the plan?

As she'd expected—and planned for—the evening went off without a hitch. A few people had ventured outside to watch the meteor shower, which was annoyingly spectacular according to the drink-addled enthusiasm on their return.

She caught a tight-lipped expression on Angela's face as she left. Her thanks were curt. The whole evening had gone off without a hitch, and she wanted to be sniffy about missing a few streaks in the sky? There was no pleasing some people.

As she walked back to her car, her phone rang. Izzy. "Hiya. Checking up on me?"

"No, just catching up on some emails now that the kids are in bed and thought I'd see how tonight went."

"Yep. All good. Just about to go home."

"Right, it's just, I got one from Angela Matthews. There's a ton of typos so I'm assuming she's had a few drinks. Something about a meteor shower?"

Rebecca sighed. "There was a meteor shower tonight and she wanted me to get everyone out onto the lawn to watch it. I just explained that it was a bad idea."

Izzy took a deep breath. "You need to be more flexible, Rebecca. Go with the flow. Just because something isn't on your clipboard doesn't mean it can't happen."

Rebecca wasn't in the mood for a lecture on how to run an event. Izzy had asked her to be her business partner because of her strengths—organization, planning, meticulous attention to detail. "Can we talk about this tomorrow? I need to get home and I'm really tired."

"Of course, sorry. I'm sure Jack is waiting up for you with a glass of wine. Enjoy your day off tomorrow. Think of me watching kids' TV at six o'clock when you are reading the morning papers in bed. We can talk about this when I see you on Monday."

When she saw her on Monday, Rebecca would have a whole lot more to talk to her about. Right now, she wanted to get home and find out how Jack's conversation with Cara had gone.

CHAPTER NINE

Cara

It had taken a while to get Sophie to bed. She'd been having a few nightmares recently and wanted Cara to lie with her until she was asleep, so it was almost 10:00 p.m. by the time she came back downstairs. Jack was on his laptop, tapping away.

When they'd been together, he'd been at the start of his career. He'd worked long hours then, too, but hadn't been against partying into the small hours and going to work on a handful of hours' sleep. These days he was clearly more responsible. What would her life have been like if she'd been the one he'd married?

He looked up as she came into the living room. "We need to talk."

You think? Cara resisted the urge for sarcasm. "Yes, we do."

"Obviously, we need to work out what to do about Sophie. And you need to find somewhere to live."

Barely looking at her, Jack's polite tone made them seem like strangers. Had he conveniently forgotten that they'd once been so obsessed with one another that they could happily spend a whole day in bed? "Rebecca said it was okay for us to stay."

"And it is. It is. For *now*." He'd emphasized the "now." How long was he willing to give her?

"I've tried to find somewhere for us but I haven't had much luck." It was fortunate she'd had so much experience lying her way into jobs and places to stay in the last few years. It was a breeze pulling the wool over Jack's eyes; she wasn't so sure that Rebecca wasn't figuring her out. "I'm sure you don't want me to take Sophie somewhere cramped. Or damp. Or unsafe."

Jack looked horrified; his world really was a million miles away from hers. "Of course not. I am well aware of my…responsibilities. Now that I know about Sophie, we can talk about what she needs. What you need to look after her."

What she needed was more time. *Two weeks should be enough.* By then, he wouldn't want to let Sophie walk out of his life. "I have been talking to a real estate agent about an apartment that will be available soon. It's on a nice street and it's clean. There's even decent heating. The current tenants are moving out in a couple of weeks. I know it's a big ask but can we just stay here until then?"

Jack looked as if she'd asked to stay for two years. But he was a good man, she knew that. In fact, she was banking on it. "Well, I'll have to speak to Rebecca, but obviously we are not going to throw you out on the street." He paused, shook his head from side to side. "I still can't believe all this, Cara. Why the hell didn't you tell me that you were pregnant? When we were still together?"

"I didn't know when we were still together."

"That's irrelevant. She's my daughter. You had no right to keep that from me. It's not fair to me. And it's definitely not fair to her."

Fair? He wanted to talk about fair as he sat on his luxury furniture in his huge house? "You'd made it pretty clear that you weren't interested in seeing me again. And then I heard that you'd met someone new. The bed must have still been warm."

He flinched. "How did you find that out?"

Cara shrugged. "Just because I didn't see you after that last night doesn't mean I didn't hear what was going on in your life. No one wants to be replaced that quickly and easily."

Jack sighed and leaned forward, his forearms on his knees. "I'm sorry if I hurt you, Cara, I really am. But this is some revenge, keeping Sophie a secret all this time and not telling me about her. Arriving on my doorstep with no warning."

Did he expect *her* to feel sorry for *him*? "Are you seriously telling me that you hadn't heard I was pregnant?"

"There might have been a comment or two. Someone who'd heard something. But, you know, we weren't together by then."

The familiar anger began to bubble in her stomach. Who was he trying to kid? Cara might not have gone to a university like him, but she damn well wasn't stupid. "You know it takes nine months to grow a baby, right? She was born nine months after we split. It's not difficult to do the math, Jack."

Jack reddened. "I just heard a rumor. I wasn't about to sit down and get the calculator out. Call me naive, but I would have assumed that you would tell me if I had a daughter."

There was a part of her that wanted to vent the rage she'd kept inside for the last five years. But she had to keep it together. Focus on the plan. When she spoke again, her voice was purposefully softer and empty of blame. Looking down at her hands and then up through her eyelashes, she bit her lip. "I suppose I foolishly hoped you would find out somehow. Would come and find us."

Jack came to sit beside her on the sofa. He'd never been able to bear it when she cried. He put a hand on her shoulder. "Hey, come on. Don't get upset."

She wiped at her eyes with the back of her wrist. Crying on demand was a very useful skill. "I'm fine. I just want to get past this. I want you to accept Sophie. Get to know her." She looked into his eyes. "She's your daughter."

Jack didn't look away this time. "If I'm honest, I had wondered before now if you'd gone through with the pregnancy. The guys teased me about it when we heard but then it just kind of got forgotten. I should have called you to check." He paused, seemed to be searching for the right words to say. "I knew the moment

I saw her that she was mine." As he finished speaking, he looked over her head and froze.

She followed his gaze to the living room door, where Rebecca stood looking at them, still in her coat.

He stood up and moved to help her take her coat off. "Hi, love. I wasn't expecting you home so soon."

Rebecca shrugged him away. "I can see that. And I wasn't expecting to find out you lied to me when you said you didn't know you had a daughter."

CHAPTER TEN

Rebecca

The silence in the room almost pulsed with tension. Vaguely aware of Cara—head down as she made a hasty retreat upstairs— Rebecca kept her eyes fixed on Jack. Her whole body trembled with an explosive cocktail of fear and anger. "You knew you had a child, Jack? You *knew?*"

Jack walked slowly toward her as if she were an unexploded bomb. "I didn't say that, Becca. You came in at the end of the conversation. If I'd known, I would obviously have done the right thing."

"Obviously?" she fired back. "There is absolutely nothing *obvious* about any of this."

He tried to reach out to take her arm but she took a step back. He held his hands aloft in submission. "I know, I know, I'm so very sorry that—"

"You're sorry? *Sorry?*" She was tired and shocked, and the reality of a child and an ex-girlfriend and a side to her husband that she'd never known was crashing around her ears. "I don't even know who you are right now. You are the man who won't let me kill spiders. The person who persuades me to let his friend's brother's son crash in our spare room for two weeks because he's spent the last of his student loan. Who told me"—her voice started to crack, her throat constricted, but still she waved him away when he reached out—"who told me I was so much better than I thought I was, that I could trust you, that you were…" A sob escaped from her throat. It was infuriating to cry when she was so angry, when she wanted to tell him exactly how scaldingly furious she was right now.

Jack still stood in front of her. "I don't know what else I can say except that I am so incredibly sorry, Becca."

She saw tears on Jack's face, too, and that just increased the anger in her gut. "You should be more than bloody sorry! It's not fair, Jack. I don't want children. I've never wanted children. I've had *years* of people telling me I'll change my mind. Giving me patronizing nods. Thinking I had some part of me missing somewhere. But I don't. I just don't want children. And you said you didn't want children either." She held up her hand to stop him from interrupting. "And then, last night, I find out that you have a child. You have a child that you knew nothing about. And do I shout and scream? No. I do not. I try to be a good person. I try to be calm. It's not his fault, I tell myself. He's as shocked as me."

Jack clasped his hands in front of him as if he were praying. "I *was* shocked. I didn't—"

She held up her hand again. "And tonight, I find that, no, you weren't as shocked as me because, hey, actually, you might have had an *inkling* but you decided not to look into it. It wasn't important to you that there might be a woman out there raising your child."

He opened his mouth but the flash of her eyes made him close it immediately.

"To be honest, I can't even get into that right now because my head won't let me take it in. Right now, I have to consider the fact that you have a child in your life, and—if I want to stay with you—I have to accept that there is a child in my life too. I'll be honest with you, if you had had a child when I met you, I would have stayed away because—for me—a child is complicated. It's messy. It's not what I want."

Her whole body was trembling. It was like delayed shock. Jack's face was ashen as he reached for her again but she flicked him away, her throat so tight she could barely speak. They'd never argued like this before. She hated confrontation and she hated losing control. There was too much in her head, her heart; she couldn't work out where she was going with this. What the hell was she going to do? "I can't...I just can't speak about this now. I'm going to bed. Seeing as the spare room is occupied, you can sleep down here."

The next morning, Rebecca stayed in bed uncharacteristically late, even for a Sunday, trying to wrap her mind around everything that had happened since Friday night. Before she spoke to Jack, she wanted to have a plan, a list of questions, an agenda. He'd brought her coffee in bed and mumbled that Cara had made an early start this morning and gone back to her old place to collect her things. After last night, she probably wanted to get there and back before they changed their minds about letting her stay. When he'd tentatively suggested a traditional Sunday roast lunch at the local bar, Rebecca had opted instead for the sushi restaurant on the other side of town. Jack hated sushi.

The sushi restaurant had the advantage of side-by-side seating: easier to avoid looking at him. His pitiful face would only provoke her further. For five minutes, they both sat and watched the colored bowls circulating past. Rebecca focused on tearing the paper from her chopsticks. "Remind me again how you and Cara got together."

Jack coughed and moved around on his stool. That was another thing he hated about this restaurant, the uncomfortable seating. Good. "Ah, like I said, we met in a nightclub. I was out with the boys; she was out with a mate. We got to talking. You know how it is."

She felt him wince as she snapped her chopsticks apart. "You owe me more than that, Jack. If Cara is going to be part of our lives, I need to know what kind of relationship you had. How serious it was." They'd done the relationship history chat but rarely ever referred to their exes. When she'd admitted that she'd split from her long-term boyfriend after discovering that he'd cheated on her—more than once—Jack had been horrified. Circling her with his arms, he'd promised that he would never hurt her, never lie or risk their relationship. And now? Was history repeating itself?

For a few moments, he didn't reply. Rebecca ignored the fact that he was looking at her and reached out to take a yellow bowl of avocado maki. She really wasn't hungry, but she pinched one between her chopsticks and put it in her mouth.

Jack followed her lead, maybe to buy a bit more time, and took a portion of fried rice, which he pushed around the bowl with a plastic fork. Eventually, he spoke. "Well, she caught my eye because she was, well, obviously attractive." He glanced up at Rebecca to gauge her reaction. "Are you sure you want to know all the details?"

Did he think she'd be jealous? It was a fact: Cara *was* very attractive. Possibly too thin but definitely attractive. She swallowed the maki almost whole. "Keep going."

Jack stared at the flower in her Jasmine tea, watching it unfurl. "I think it was also because she was…I don't know, there was something about her. She was different. The women I'd dated up to then had all been of a certain type. Private school. Very confident. Cara was confident, too, but there was an undercurrent to her confidence. She was kind of…fragile, I guess."

This was more like the Jack she knew. Protective and caring. On holiday in Greece that summer, she'd had to dissuade him from adopting a three-legged dog who'd followed them home from the beach. He had a big heart. And could be a complete sucker.

They were interrupted by one of the chefs wielding a fish knife. He nodded toward their lack of food. "You want something made to order?"

"No, we're fine with what's here, thanks." Rebecca took a bowl of chicken gyoza and held it aloft to prove her words. As soon as he'd gone, Rebecca prompted Jack. "So, she was different?"

Jack sighed. Had he hoped she was going to let him skip anything? "Yes. She was funny and independent and didn't care what she said about anything or anyone. She was a lot of fun, to be honest."

"Did you sleep with her that first night?" There was no reason why this should be remotely relevant but it was out of her mouth before she could stop it.

Jack gulped his Asahi beer. "Yes. We went back to the place she was staying. I stayed overnight."

"And where was she staying? Her own place? With a friend? Parents?"

Jack leaned forward so that he could see her face. "Rebecca, look at me. Why do you want to know all this?"

"I just want to know what kind of person she is. She's staying in my house, Jack. You seem to have complete trust that we can just come and go from the house, leaving her there alone, and not come back to find we've been robbed or she's invited another bunch of homeless mothers to spend the night, or the week, or the month!" The strength of her anger—albeit hissed under her breath so the young couple next to them couldn't overhear—surprised even her, so it was no wonder that Jack looked as if he'd been slapped.

He raised his hands in submission. "Okay. Okay. She was staying on a friend's sofa. I don't know if you picked it up from what she said, but she really does not have a good relationship with her parents. She never went into details but I have always assumed that her father wasn't a good man. Possibly even abusive in some way. And her mother, well, all she ever said about her mother was that she couldn't look out for herself, let alone anyone else."

Though she didn't want to, Rebecca felt a twinge of sympathy. "I see."

Jack dropped his gaze, went back to twirling his bottle of beer. "Which is why she ended up moving in with me."

Rebecca was nearly asphyxiated by her second bite of the gyoza. She turned around on the high stool so fast it squeaked. "What?"

He looked at her imploringly. "What could I do? She was sofa-surfing from friend to friend—I think she even stayed in an abandoned house at one point. And there I was in a large apartment subsidized by my parents."

Middle-class guilt. Was that part of the attraction of Cara? A charity case that he could look after and benefit with his wealthy largesse? She knew she wasn't being fair. Jack could no more control the type of family he'd been born into than she could. And he had never been boastful about his parents' wealth.

But she couldn't help the twinge of discomfort at the fact that he had moved Cara in so quickly. She and Jack had dated for almost a year before they'd decided to take their relationship to that next level. "Exactly how soon did she move in?"

Jack coughed, seemed to suddenly realize that his bottle was empty and signaled to one of the staff that he'd like another. "The next night."

They sat in silence for the minute that it took the second beer to arrive. Rebecca was starting to get a picture of Cara's behavior and it wasn't warming her toward her unwanted guest. "I see."

Jack must have realized how it sounded. "It wasn't really official. She stayed over and then she didn't have anywhere lined up to go and then she ended up staying a few more days and then it was easier to give her a key and—"

"How long?" Rebecca interrupted. "How long did you live together?"

Jack grabbed an orange bowl of yakisoba that had almost passed them and placed it in front of her. "That's your favorite, isn't it?"

She stared at the bowl of noodles, tangled with chicken and vegetables. "How long, Jack?"

"It must have been seven or eight months. I was still working in King's Cross when I met her, and I'd moved to Liverpool Street when it all came to an end."

Rebecca felt sick and it wasn't the sushi. "Which is when you met me."

Jack shook his head. "No. I had finished with her before then. You know that. You came back to my apartment that first night. You know I wasn't living with anyone."

Rebecca blushed at the memory. There was absolutely nothing wrong with sleeping with someone on a first date. But she had never done it before—and they hadn't exactly even been on a date. "Okay, so why did it end?"

Jack shrugged. "I don't know. I think we were just too different. All the things I liked about her—the unpredictability, the don't-give-a-shit attitude—just wore thin. I realized that I wasn't in love with her. And our lives—what we wanted from our lives— were just too different."

For all her dark good looks and great figure, Rebecca couldn't imagine Jack taking Cara for Sunday lunch at his managing director's house. "So, how did you break it off? And what happened to her?"

"I was as kind as I could be. We sat down and talked about it. I said that I just didn't feel the same way anymore. I even offered her money to help her out for a few days."

The answer to her next question suddenly seemed of paramount importance. "And did she take it?"

Jack shook his head. "No. She was quite upset. It wasn't... It didn't go well."

Rebecca would imagine not. Not only was she losing her boyfriend; it was her home too. "So, that was it? She left that night?"

Jack ran a finger around the inside of his collar; he looked uneasy. "Almost. About a week later, we ran into each other at the bar. We'd both had a lot to drink, she got upset, I comforted her, and..."

How damn predictable. "And she ended up coming home and spending the night in your bed."

Jack winced. She could see how painful this was for him to admit, but right now she didn't care.

He pushed his rice away. "I'm not proud of myself. And you don't just switch your feelings off. I had missed her."

The next part was obvious but she had to ask. "And this night together. This unexpected night where you couldn't stop yourselves from falling into bed. Did you use contraception?"

Jack's face told her all she needed to know, but she waited for him to say it. "No. No, we didn't."

"I see."

"I know what you're thinking. It's crossed my mind, too, but Cara wouldn't have got pregnant on purpose. She just isn't like that. If you knew her better, you'd know too."

If Jack wanted her to stay calm, to not lose her temper again, defending Cara was definitely not the way to go. "And you knew she'd got pregnant and did nothing?"

"No. I didn't *know*. I was telling the truth about that. It was just an offhand comment down at the bar that someone had seen her and she'd looked pregnant. And I'm fully aware that I should have contacted her to check. I spent most of last night asking myself why I didn't."

Rebecca was going to spend a lot longer than one night asking herself, and Jack, that question. For now, she'd asked everything she wanted to. Of Jack. "We need to go home. I don't know how long it will take to clear out her apartment, but Cara doesn't have a key to get back into ours."

A tentative smile hovered on his face. "Does that mean you're okay with them staying just a couple of weeks?"

She moved her hands from the table so that he couldn't take them. It was too soon for kiss and make up. But she'd spent some time thinking this through while she'd stayed in bed this morning. "It means that they can stay. Whether I'm okay about it is another matter. You need to speak to Cara while I am working at Izzy's tomorrow, and I do not care if you have a meeting scheduled with God himself, you are going to stay home and make a plan as to how this is going to work."

By the look of relief on Jack's face, she could have asked him to spend the next day rolling around on broken glass and he would have said yes. At least having Cara in the house would give Rebecca the opportunity to get to the bottom of this mess. Jack might be certain that Cara hadn't got pregnant on purpose, but Rebecca wasn't so sure.

CHAPTER ELEVEN

Cara

Sunday mornings were always quiet on the Bramley Estate and Cara's footsteps echoed up the concrete staircase as Sophie counted each one. She definitely hadn't missed the stale smell of the communal hallway: a nauseating mixture of domestic waste and urine. At the top of the stairs they turned left. The peeling red front door of 3b had scuff marks along the bottom, where she had perfected opening it by administering a low kick at the same time as turning the key.

They'd been in the apartment only ten minutes when there was a knock on the door. Lee was about her age, possibly even a couple of years younger. It was his dad who owned her place, along with several other apartments on the block. Reg was a builder who'd done well for himself and was now living in Majorca. Lee had been left in charge of the rentals business; his older brother ran the construction side of things.

Lee always looked as if he'd just stepped out of the shower and smelled as if he'd doused himself in expensive aftershave. His clothes were crisply pressed and covered in logos. The rentals business paid well. "Cara, babe. You're killing me. Where've you been?"

Not many landlords came out to meet you on a Sunday, but Lee had a soft spot for her. *Sometimes you have to work with what God gave you.* "I'm so sorry, Lee. It's just been a really tough week. I'll get the rent, I will. Can you just give us a few more days?"

The wobbly bottom lip—and a gesture in Sophie's direction—had its desired effect. Lee looked mortified that he'd made her cry. "Hey, hey. Don't get all upset. It's fine. Look, you've always been good for your rent in the past. I'll give you some time. What do you need? A week? Two weeks?"

It was so easy she almost felt bad for him. "That would be wonderful. I'll definitely have it by then. Thank you so much."

Lee actually blushed as he backed out of the room. "It's all right. I'll come back in a couple of weeks. You take care of yourself and the little'un. See you later."

As soon as he'd gone, she wiped the crocodile tears from her eyes with the back of her hand and started to stuff the last few items into one of the boxes she'd brought up with her. Another knock on the door made her jump. Had Lee changed his mind?

To her relief, it was Danielle from next door, box-bleached hair piled up on the top of her head in a messy bun, coat over her pajamas, shopping bags providing ballast either side. "Hello, stranger. I thought that was you I saw through the window. Are you back?"

Cara shook her head. "Nope. Just getting the rest of my stuff. Once I've dropped it off, I'll bring your car back. Thanks for lending it to me."

"No problem. I wasn't using it this weekend." Danielle's eyes took in the boxes. "So, you're really doing this?"

"Yep." Cara chucked a painted pebble into one of the boxes. "Are you missing me yet?"

Danielle shrugged. "Can't wait to see the back of you."

Cara laughed. "Who knows? I might be back here in a week. And even if I'm not, you'll still see me."

Danielle pulled a face. "The girls are starting school next September. Who's going to brave the school run with me? I can't be hanging around that playground on my own."

It was impossible to look her in the eye. "I'm not applying to Hopton Primary."

Danielle frowned. "Why not? It's only at the end of the road. All the kids from the estate go there. Where are you applying?"

Might as well get it over with. "St. Catherine's."

Danielle laughed. "St. Catherine's? Are you mad? You'll never get in there. It's got a tiny enrollment area and they don't accept..." A light dawned in her eyes. "Sophie's dad's house is in the area, isn't it? Is that why you're doing this?"

Cara put a finger to her lips and sideways nodded toward the bedroom, where Sophie lay on the bed with her coloring book.

Danielle turned so that her back was to the bedroom door and lowered her voice. "So, how did it go? Has he got a big house?"

"Yeah. Really big house. And a wife."

Danielle's eyes widened. "Wife? You never mentioned he was married."

"I didn't know until I got there on Friday night." Cara threw the last few things into the box. There was nothing else she wanted to take.

Danielle was staring at her, concern evident on her face. "Look, I'm going to say it one more time: Are you sure about this? I know we always moan about Lee and what a lazy lump he is, but I've stayed in much worse places. If you leave this place and need to get rehoused, they are going to put you in a one-room with shared facilities in a high-rise somewhere awful."

Cara had thought about that. "We're not going to need to be rehoused."

Danielle folded her arms. "How can you be sure? Especially if Sophie's dad is married. I can't see his wife putting up with the two of you in their house for very long."

Danielle was digging for gossip, but there was no way Cara was going to tell her why she was so confident. That she knew Jack better than he realized. And that she had a plan.

CHAPTER TWELVE

Rebecca

Although they both worked from home, Monday mornings were kept free for Rebecca and Izzy to meet up, sync schedules, and catch up on their plans for the week. Since Christmas this had always happened at Izzy's house because her stockbroker husband, Tim, had surprised her with a garden office: a wooden building with large glass windows, a desk to work at, and a round table for her and Rebecca to "conference" at, as he had mockingly put it.

They sat at the table now, with coffees from the state-of-the-art machine and a plate of Waitrose cookies. Rebecca was working up to her revelation: they might as well get their business meeting done first.

Starting up their business three years ago had been risky, but Izzy had an address book of great connections and they had plenty of experience working for a company called City Events in London. In fact, she had been working with Izzy the night she'd met Jack. They'd always been a good team, playing to each other's strengths.

Meeting at Izzy's allowed for casual clothes. Still, Izzy had that kind of wholesome appearance where she still looked beautiful with her hair in a ponytail and no makeup. "Right, don't shout at me. I need you to take over the Ross-Hamilton wedding."

Rebecca nearly spat out her coffee. "What? I don't do the weddings. I don't do any of the touchy-feely stuff. That was the agreement. I do corporate."

She had been really clear on that with Izzy from day one. It wasn't that she didn't like weddings or retirement parties or christening dos. It was that people organizing a party for a family occasion were unpredictable, emotional, needy. She much preferred working with professionals. However demanding they could be, they were at least clear and dispassionate about the whole thing. She could plan the event, present it to them, tweak anything that needed changing, and then move on. No histrionics because the flowers on the cake were the wrong shade of purple.

Izzy pushed the plate of cookies nearer to Rebecca. "I know, I know. And I wouldn't ask you but you know how long we've been waiting on an appointment for poor Jonty to have his rotten tonsils removed. I can't go through another winter of him needing weeks off school at a time. I just can't. And Tim's away for work that week, so someone will have to be here. Samantha 'soon-to-be-Hamilton' Ross will flip her lid if I'm not there and firing on all cylinders. It would be much better if you take it over from now and then you can be on hand."

Posh cookies weren't going to even come close to appeasing Rebecca. Why did people with children always get to play the family card? Of course, she understood that Izzy would want to be with her little boy, but she had some serious stuff of her own going on right now.

Plus, the Ross-Hamilton wedding? Izzy had been moaning for the last year about how crazy the bride-to-be was driving her. Nothing was quite right, and even when it was, her opinion on it might change within days. And now she wanted Rebecca to take over. "Can't you carry on for now and then I'll cover it the week of the wedding if I have to? I mean, you must be pretty much there, right?"

Izzy nodded. "Oh, I am. Everything is done as far as I know. But you know how these things work. Stuff happens at the last minute. Balloon artists come down with food poisoning, caterers drop cakes, there's an international shortage of avocados."

Rebecca groaned. She did know. And that was exactly why she didn't do weddings. But what could she say? "Okay. Give me the file."

Izzy clapped her hands and passed it over. Her glee at off-loading the wedding filled Rebecca with dread. "Thank you, thank you! I owe you one. Have a quick glance and then we can get Samantha Ross on the phone and book a meeting."

The file was twice the thickness of the ones Rebecca kept on her events. A quick look at the event summary page explained why: magicians, bouncy castles, doves, fireworks. This wasn't a wedding; it was a festival. She looked up at Izzy. "Are you serious?"

Izzy didn't react. "Have a look at all the helpful notes I've made in the margins. Do they make sense?" She picked up a cookie from the pile and broke it in half.

Rebecca picked up a page and squinted her eyes as she read the text. "Yes, I think I can decode your scribbles."

Izzy poked her tongue out at her. "Okay, Miss Perfect Pants. We can't all have a color-coded system for rotating the bath towels. Some of us lesser mortals get by with a sticky note and by the seat of our pants. I know that your wedding was a well-oiled machine."

Rebecca put the folder down on the table, took a deep breath. "Jack has a daughter."

Izzy must have aspirated the cookie in her shock. It took her a whole minute to stop coughing. "What?"

Rebecca nodded. "Yep. Friday night his ex-girlfriend turned up on our doorstep with Jack's four-year-old daughter."

"Oh my God, Rebecca. How has it taken you"—she counted out on her fingers—"*three* days to tell me this? What a bombshell. Are you sure the child is his?"

It was a relief being able to speak to someone about it all. "Oh, it gets better. Jack knew about the girl. Sophie."

Izzy's eyes nearly bulged out of her head. "What? For how long?"

She knew she was being unfair to Jack, but she needed someone on her side right now. "He had his suspicions at the time, apparently. He heard she was pregnant after they split, but that didn't prompt him to look her up and find out for sure."

"Wow." Izzy was looking at her openmouthed. "So, how are you feeling?"

That was a good question. "Angry. Upset. Shocked."

Izzy nodded. She picked up her mug and sipped at the coffee. "It would be a big shock for anyone."

How could Rebecca explain that this shock was double? Finding out that Jack had a daughter was bad enough, but discovering that he might have known about her and done nothing? That was even worse.

Izzy frowned. "I just want to check. Sophie is definitely Jack's daughter? You are getting proof?"

Rebecca nodded. "Yes, a DNA test. But you only need to look at her to know. Even he admitted he can see it."

"And how does Jack feel about having a daughter?"

They had always been in agreement on the children subject. They'd congratulated themselves on finding someone else so like-minded. But now he was a father. Would that change him?

"We haven't had a chance to talk about it really. He wants to get to know her, obviously. Be a part of her life."

Was this true? He hadn't even really spoken to Sophie that she knew of. Was that because he was worried about upsetting Rebecca? Because it wasn't as if she was going to stand in his way.

Izzy tilted her head. "Well, that's good, isn't it? That he's taking responsibility?"

It was good—of course it was. But where did that leave her? "The thing is, neither of us wanted children. But I can't help thinking, now that he has one, will it make him feel differently? Is he going to regret our decision?"

Until she'd said those words aloud, she hadn't realized how much that had been on her mind.

Izzy was nodding in understanding. "Have you asked him?"

She shook her head. Asked him? Even the thought of asking him was far too frightening. What if he said yes? She couldn't bear to think about it. It would tear their relationship apart at the seams. If only he hadn't slept with Cara again that one time after they'd split up. What a cruel twist of fate that it had happened when their relationship was already over. If it *was* fate, that was. "I mean, how easy is it to even get pregnant by *accident?*"

Izzy smiled. "Obviously, I'm not the best person to ask. Our pregnancies took a lot of planning and a lot of money."

"Of course. Sorry. I mean, how did you know you wanted a baby?" They were good enough friends that Rebecca could ask Izzy anything, yet she hadn't asked her this before. She was ashamed to realize that she hadn't been interested.

Izzy smiled. "I can't really explain it. It's not like I always wanted a baby or anything like that. But when I met Tim, I don't know, something went off in my head. And we talked about it and he felt the same. In fact, now that we've got two, he keeps saying he wants to keep going until we've got a whole tribe of them. That's because he's not the one who has to grow to the size of an elephant and give birth each time."

Rebecca joined in Izzy's laughter. But she couldn't help thinking of Cara. There had been no loving partner to laugh about prenatal classes and peer at scan photos with and to rub her feet as Rebecca knew that Tim had done for Izzy. Had Cara been in the delivery room alone? Or had there been someone to hold her hand? Where was that person now?

Izzy sat back in her chair. "I still can't believe this is happening to you. And they are at your house right now? How long are they going to be there?"

Again, the thought of Jack and Cara alone together made her stomach tighten. "Another couple of weeks. She's told Jack that she's got a place to move into after that."

Izzy frowned. "And you don't believe her?"

"It's not that exactly." It wasn't that Rebecca didn't want to tell Izzy her suspicions; it was that she didn't really understand them herself. Cara had been a model houseguest so far: tidy and polite. But there was something…something she couldn't put her finger on. She just didn't trust her.

Izzy twisted her ponytail around her forefinger, nodding to herself as she thought this through. "Hang on. How far away were they living before? Doesn't the little girl need to go to her school?"

That one, Rebecca did know the answer to. "No. She just turned four in September. Cara said she starts next year. Funnily enough, she happened to mention that she's going to apply to St. Catherine's, which is only a short walk from us."

Izzy raised an eyebrow. "Funnily enough, indeed. You know that St. Catherine's is hugely overenrolled? I have a friend who actually bought a second house near you to get her son in. You'd have no chance if you weren't in that small area."

It didn't take long for Rebecca to work out what the raised eyebrow meant. "Surely she isn't planning to use our address for the application?"

Izzy shrugged. "I don't know. But I do know that a mother will do anything it takes to get the best for her child."

Rebecca groaned. "What the hell am I going to do?"

Izzy reached over and squeezed her hand. "What can you do? If Sophie is Jack's daughter, he needs to step up. Which means that you're going to have to step up too."

Though Izzy was absolutely right, it didn't make it any easier. "You seem to be forgetting that I don't know the first thing about being a parent."

"Luckily for you, I've had some practice. Get your notepad out. Let's make a plan."

*

On the drive home, Rebecca ran over the rest of their conversation in her head. Sophie was Jack's daughter. That wasn't going to change. Rebecca loved Jack, so she would have to learn to love Sophie. The girl didn't need another mother; she had one of those already. Together, they would work out a system. She could do this. She *would* do this.

Hopefully Jack would have upheld his half of the bargain and made a plan with Cara for when they would look after Sophie. It was pointless getting herself all wound up about whether Cara had got pregnant on purpose, or whether Jack should have acted differently five years ago. This was their reality now and she was going to make a good job of it.

Nevertheless, for a reason she couldn't—or wouldn't—explain to herself, when she arrived home, she opened the front door really quietly and walked slowly toward the living room.

When she peered in, she saw Jack on the floor with Sophie, letting her crayon around his hands on a sheet of her drawing paper. Cara was sitting in Rebecca's favorite chair with a mug in her hand, smiling indulgently at the two of them.

They looked like a happy family of three.

CHAPTER THIRTEEN

Cara

On Tuesday morning, Rebecca ruined Cara's plans by offering to drive her into town.

Yesterday, when Rebecca had got back from her business meeting, the atmosphere had been very odd. Jack had attempted to talk about arrangements for Sophie a couple of times in the afternoon, but Cara had managed to divert the conversation to apartment-hunting or Sophie's progress in preschool. Rebecca had been a different prospect. There'd been more raised voices from their bedroom last night. Rebecca telling Jack he needed to stay home again tomorrow and "get this sorted out."

It was a relief to have a reason to leave the house today, but Rebecca's ears pricked up when she told them she was popping out. "Why don't you leave Sophie here with Jack? I can drive us both into town—I need a few things anyway."

How could she refuse? It meant changing her arrangement with Dave, though. *Damn.* "Great. Thanks."

As they pulled away from the house, she sent a text to cancel the meeting. Hopefully Dave wouldn't be too upset. As soon as she'd dropped her phone into her lap, Rebecca spoke. "Did Jack speak to you before I got home yesterday about making a plan?"

It was probably best to feign innocence until she knew the lay of the land. "A plan?"

"For Sophie. What days you want us to look after her and so on. Every other weekend? An evening each week? Whether we will take her for a week during the holidays?" Rebecca reeled off these options as if she were making an appointment with her hairdresser.

"No. No, he didn't."

Rebecca sighed dramatically. They approached a roundabout and she flipped the turn signal lever with her ring finger. Even this she did precisely. Everything about her was measured, planned, meticulous. After exiting the roundabout, she started again. "It might be best if you and I have that conversation. I usually deal with our calendar at home so I'm sure Jack will be happy with whatever suits the two of us."

God, she was irritating. "And Sophie."

Rebecca glanced at her. "Of course, Sophie. But children are very resilient. Or so I've heard."

Where had she got that from? The friend she met yesterday? The internet? "Children are all different. In my *experience*."

Rebecca pressed her lips together. Cara's tone hadn't been lost on her. She didn't speak for the next five minutes until they got to the parking lot. Cara jumped out, hoping against hope that Rebecca wasn't going to suggest they walk around together.

Thankfully not. Rebecca beeped her key fob to lock the car. "I need to go to the pharmacy and a couple of other places. Why don't we meet at the Costa on the main road in half an hour? We can have a chat before we go back to the house."

Cara wanted to refuse—it was obvious what that chat was going to be about. Rebecca had got Cara out by herself to push her own agenda. "Half an hour. Great."

Now that she was here, she might as well get Sophie some new leggings for preschool. She went through them like nobody's business. Paint stains, ripped seams, holes in the knees. Mind you, she'd had only cheap ones from the discount store and they weren't built to last. Now she had the money for M&S and Debenhams, which were a lot better.

It was outside M&S that she bumped into Dave. "All right, Cara? You're going the wrong way. I thought we were meeting at the café."

She almost jumped. It was weird seeing him here, out of context. He looked rough too—bags under his eyes, sallow skin, really bad. She scanned the area. *Please don't let Rebecca see me talking to him.* "Oh, hi. Did you not get my text? I can't..."

He frowned. "I don't understand. I've got the stuff you wanted."

For one horrible moment she thought he was putting his hand in his pocket to bring it out, but he was just getting his mobile to see her message.

Her heart was racing. "Yeah, I'm sorry but—"

"Oh, yeah. Got your message." Dave held up the phone with a grin. "Did you just change your mind or—"

Rebecca had appeared at Cara's elbow. "Hi. I finished in the pharmacy so I thought I'd join you. Hope I'm not interrupting?"

Had she been watching her? Keeping track where she went?

Dave smiled and held out his hand. "Not at all. I'm Dave."

Cara clenched her fists. Would Rebecca notice his fingernails? The marks on his arms?

To her credit, if she was disgusted, she didn't show it. She shook his hand. "Rebecca. Are you a friend of Cara's?"

He coughed a dry laugh and glanced at Cara. "Not exactly, we—"

Now she had to interrupt. "I'm really sorry, Dave, but our parking meter is about to run out and I really need to pick up some things for Sophie in here. I'll see you around, yeah?"

The confusion in Dave's eyes twisted her stomach, but she couldn't help that now. She turned into M&S, praying that Rebecca was following her. If Rebecca had finished whatever pretend errand she'd been on, Cara could grab a couple of pairs of leggings and get back to the car before they bumped into anyone else.

Cara had only had a credit card for the last six months. Before that, she'd been strict with her money, drawing out cash each week and not spending beyond her means. Maybe she had gone a bit crazy with it, but she still hadn't been expecting it to be declined. The assistant pulled it out of the machine. "Declined. Do you want me to try again?"

Could she have maybe put the wrong pin in? She felt hot. Rebecca was right behind her and there was no point trying her debit card. What else could she do? "Yes, please."

But the same thing happened. Declined. The shop assistant was kind. "Have you had it in your pocket next to your mobile phone? That happened to my boyfriend. It wipes the data or something."

Or maybe the assistant's boyfriend had maxed out his account like she had. What the hell was she going to do now?

Rebecca stepped forward, holding a card that looked like it was silver-plated. "Why don't I get it for now and we can sort it out later once you've talked to your bank?"

Cara wanted the ground to open up. First Dave, now this. Rebecca was going to have lots to report back to Jack tonight. She took the bag from the assistant. "Thank you for helping me out. I'm not sure why that didn't go through."

Rebecca smiled. "It's fine. We can figure it out later. Shall we go and get that coffee and we can talk about the arrangements for Sophie when you move out?"

If Cara could have lain down on the floor and closed her eyes, she would have. It was all too much. She needed...something. Dave flashed in front of her eyes. Did she look like him right now? "Actually, can we get back to your house and talk there? I want to check on Sophie. It's the first time Jack has looked after her and I want to make sure she's okay with it."

Rebecca shrugged. "All right. But I think he'll be okay. He's great with my nephews. And you're going to need to let us watch Sophie on our own eventually, you know."

She did know. "I'll pay you back for the clothes. I'll pick up some extra shifts."

They were almost back to the car and Rebecca reached into her handbag for the ticket to pay. She fed it into the machine. "Don't worry about it. It's only a couple of pairs of leggings. Jack will have to buy things like this for Sophie anyway, right?"

That was a good point. He would have to start paying for some of Sophie's clothes. And a lot more besides.

CHAPTER FOURTEEN

Rebecca

"I'm telling you, there is something suspicious going on."

Rebecca had been bursting to speak to Jack since she'd got back from the shopping trip with Cara, but she had to wait until Cara took Sophie to bed. In retrospect, she had sounded slightly unhinged when she rattled off her suspicions to Jack in the kitchen.

The kettle rumbled in the background as Jack opened the cupboard for three mugs. How quickly he had got in the habit of that. He must know he was still on thin ice, as he was taking a while to choose his words carefully. "This whole situation is weird, I'll grant you. I know that Cara can come across a bit prickly. But drugs? I can't see it."

Could he not see it because he looked at everyone through spectacles of optimism, or did he not *want* to see it because of his past feelings for Cara? "Just think about it for a minute, Jack. She's been kicked out of her flat and her credit card got declined. She's obviously in financial difficulty." It felt unnecessarily hurtful to actually *say* that Cara was contacting Jack only because she was in trouble, but the evidence was all there.

Jack rubbed at his cheek. "So, she's got some money issues. That hardly makes her a criminal. She's a decent person, Bec. I know you have to take my word for that, but she really is."

Rebecca stiffened. Decent people didn't hide a child's existence from their father for years. Why was he siding with Cara all of a sudden? "You didn't see her *friend* today: really shifty and twitchy. I would bet money he is an addict. And she was *definitely* not happy for me to catch the two of them together."

The kettle clicked off and Jack filled two of the mugs, his back to her. "*Catch* the two of them? You make it sound like you were trying to trap her."

This conversation was not going the way she'd expected. There had been something about Cara from the beginning that didn't ring true. Why was Jack so blind to it? "I just think we need to keep a close eye on her. For Sophie's sake."

Jack turned and raised an eyebrow. "For Sophie's sake?" He stepped around the kitchen island to where she was perched on one of the stools. Standing behind her, he circled her with his arms and rested his chin on the top of her head. "I know this has been tough, Becca. It's thrown everything up in the air and we have no idea how it's going to settle. You're hurt and confused. I am too. It's understandable that you don't trust Cara yet."

She blinked back angry tears. Is that what he thought this was? "It's not about me, Jack. You need to stop thinking of Cara as this fragile little thing that you feel guilty about abandoning. She's the one who is guilty of lying to you all these years. Has she even given you a proper reason for that?"

Jack's breath was warm on the top of her head as he sighed. "Not really."

Rebecca clenched her fist and brought it down on the worktop like a gavel. "Exactly. And if she can lie about something as big as that, what else is she lying about? Her job, for instance. It's now Tuesday and she hasn't even mentioned going into work."

"Tomorrow."

They both twisted in unison at Cara's voice in the doorway.

"I have a shift tomorrow. I was going to ask if one of you would be available to pick Sophie up from preschool."

Rebecca's face burned as if they'd been caught doing something wrong. Jack let go of her and stepped toward Cara. "Of course. Just let us know where it is and what time, and we'll be there."

Cara managed a thin smile. "Good. Thanks. I'm off to bed."

As soon as she left, Rebecca let out the breath she hadn't realized she'd been holding. "Picking her up from preschool? Does that mean you're taking a third day off work?"

Jack shook his head. "I can't. I have the Wednesday team meeting first thing. I'll be able to leave early in the afternoon if I have to, though."

Wednesday morning, Cara and Sophie left the house at eight thirty, so at least Rebecca wouldn't have to leave them in the house alone when she went to meet with Samantha Ross.

At 10:00 a.m., Cara called, her voice strained and anxious. "I don't want to have to ask this. Sophie's preschool has a gas leak. All children have to be picked up as soon as possible. I've tried Jack's phone three times and he's not picking up. I can't leave work. Is there any way you could go?"

Jack always turned his mobile off when he had a meeting. Good for him that he had the luxury of focusing on the job at hand—now she was going to have to be the one juggling *his* child around *her* job. How was that fair? But she could see no other way. "Okay. Give me the address and I'll go and get her."

After writing the address on a sticky note, she broke the habit of her professional lifetime and tried to reschedule her meeting, but Samantha Ross was borderline hysterical when she suggested it. "The wedding is in less than three weeks. Izzy promised you were dependable. You cannot do this to me." Rebecca would have to take Sophie with her.

When she picked up Sophie, her blond curly hair bounced around as she talked excitedly about the gas leak. "Sue made us wait outside and we all had to hold hands and Daniel wouldn't hold hands with Sam because Sam had a runny nose and Sue got cross and said it was really 'portant that we stay together and then the man came and he had a huge box and he told us to stay outside and…"

It was a constant stream of information, though fortunately Sophie didn't seem to need any input or even a response from Rebecca, so it became background noise as she tried to get her thoughts together for her meeting with Samantha.

Izzy had told Rebecca that Samantha was the only child of a successful trucking company owner, and that although she could be perfectly pleasant and polite, she had no comprehension whatsoever that the world couldn't be moved in order to have exactly what she wanted. When she opened the door to them, wearing a gray jersey jumpsuit tucked into chunky suede boots, her fake tan and suspiciously plump lips explained the word "Bling!" scribbled several times in the margin in Izzy's wedding file.

Partly due to the damn car seat, which had taken Rebecca a while to wrestle into place, they were ten minutes behind schedule. She hated being unpunctual. "I'm so sorry I'm late. As I explained on the telephone, I had to bring Sophie with me because there was a gas leak at her preschool."

Samantha waved away the apology, her meltdown from earlier forgotten. "No problem. I *love* kids. Would you like some cake, Sophie?"

Sophie's eyes rounded like globes at the array of tiny cakes being offered to her; she looked at Rebecca for permission. What would Cara have said? It was just a cake. That must be okay. "You can take one, but try and keep the crumbs on your plate." She turned to Samantha. "Can she maybe sit somewhere and draw while we go through the plans?"

Samantha nodded. "Of course. Why don't you sit at the big table? You can spread yourself out then."

Rebecca nodded to Sophie, who took herself over to the table. She felt guilty for resenting her presence. None of this was her fault. She sat on the sofa and opened her file. "Okay, then. Everything seems in place for the big day. Are you getting excited?"

"Really excited. My mum will be here in about fifteen minutes. I wanted to look at the seating plan again before she gets here. Otherwise, we'll have a world of pain getting her to agree to it." Samantha rolled her eyes in mock exasperation at her difficult mother. Apples not falling far from trees sprang to mind.

Seating plan? Rebecca opened the file to the agenda she had put together for their meeting. The seating plan wasn't even on it. "Sorry, I thought you'd agreed on that weeks ago? Izzy has an email in the file saying it has gone to the chalkboard company to be painted." She didn't add that Izzy had described the whole process as being akin to getting a root canal with no anesthetic.

Samantha smiled sweetly, displaying a set of perfectly white teeth. "I know. But we bumped into a couple we met on holiday and I kind of invited them. We can have another blackboard painted, can't we? How long can it take?"

Rebecca took a deep breath and tried to focus on the huge fee they were being paid for this wedding. She slipped the paper copy of the plan across the table. "Okay, where would you like them?"

As Samantha leaned toward the coffee table to read who was sitting where, they heard the front door open and a strong female voice call out, "It's only me. Shall I come in?"

As if it might explode, Samantha thrust the seating plan back at Rebecca. "That's my mum. I'll text you their names. Stick them anywhere. She can't see the plan because I've put my stepmum at the head table and she'll go mad."

The rest of the meeting was relatively painless, apart from a standoff between the two women when Samantha wanted to change the salmon option because her friend had said it would make the room "smell all fishy." Inexplicably, she recruited Sophie to her cause, who pronounced salmon to be "disgusting" and said they should have "cheesy pasta" instead.

Samantha clapped her hands. "Macaroni and cheese. Perfect choice."

Her mother sighed. "Sam, your father is spending a small fortune on this. He's not going to want people eating macaroni and cheese."

"It'll be fine, Mum. Very gastropub. I'm sure the chef can serve it on slate or something and make it look cool. In fact, maybe we should rethink the beef?"

Rebecca needed to steer the conversation elsewhere before Sophie recommended chicken nuggets. "Okay, macaroni and cheese it is."

When they got back to the car, Rebecca called Izzy with an update.

"How did it go?"

"We survived. I thought it was just going to be a courtesy visit but she actually wanted to change things. And I had to take Sophie with me at the last minute. You are not going to believe this but Samantha was asking Sophie for ideas."

"Actually, I do believe it. Samantha can be bonkers. How come you had to take Sophie?"

"Her preschool called Cara because there was a gas leak. Cara couldn't leave work and neither of us could reach Jack, so it had to be me. I really need to make sure that we get this child-care thing sorted out. I can't suddenly drop everything at the last minute like that."

Izzy actually laughed. "Welcome to the world of parenting. You have everything organized and then an upset stomach or a bad night's sleep or any number of small issues can destroy all your plans."

Rebecca understood that, she really did. And people who chose to have a child had to factor that in. But Rebecca *hadn't* chosen this. She hadn't chosen any of it. Sophie wasn't her daughter. She was Jack's. So why was she the one who'd had to pick up the pieces? And how had Cara coped with this kind of emergency before now?

After ending her call to Izzy, she turned in her seat to look at Sophie. "I've got an idea, Sophie. Why don't we drop in on Mummy at work to say hello?"

CHAPTER FIFTEEN

Cara

Gray desks, gray carpet, gray people: if someone wasn't already depressed, the bleak design of the courthouse offices would bring it out in them. Cara's ticket was number seventy-four and it had already taken an age to click round to number seventy-one when Sophie's preschool had called about the gas leak. It was a useful lesson for Rebecca in the reality of child-care emergencies, anyway.

Normally she was here with a fight on her hands. Benefits that had been screwed up or to negotiate payments that had to be made when she needed more time.

"Yes, can I help you?" Damn, it was the one with the hard face on reception this morning. The younger one was nicer, kinder.

"I need some advice on birth certificates."

Almost camouflaged against the desk in her gray suit and blouse, the receptionist looked over the top of her computer monitor and down her nose. "What kind of advice?"

None of your damn business. Was she expecting her to talk about her private life out here in front of everybody? If she had looked like Rebecca in one of her designer wraparound dresses, she would have received far different service, no doubt. "I need to make a change to a birth certificate."

Now she had the woman's full attention. "Change? Do you mean you want to change the baby's name?"

For goodness' sake. "No. I need to add a name. The father's name."

To be honest, if they'd let her at the time, she would have put Jack's name on the birth certificate when she'd registered Sophie's birth. But when you're not married, you need to have the father there with you to put his name down.

When they'd first split up, she'd been distraught. Jack had called her at work and told her not to be late because he was cooking dinner for them that night. Stupidly, she had thought for a moment that he might have something special to tell her. She hadn't been thinking an engagement ring or anything— they'd been together for only eight months—but maybe a trip away.

That's why she had been so blindsided by his announcement during the strawberry cheesecake that it was all over. He'd explained that he wanted to focus on his career, that he didn't want to be in a relationship. It didn't matter how he tried to dress it up: he didn't want her anymore.

She was embarrassed now about how she'd behaved. Anger, then tears, then begging him to give her another chance, to give their relationship another chance. He had held her hand, stayed calm. But it was a no. He'd wanted out.

He'd tried to give her money too. Said he'd help with the deposit on an apartment. But her pride had finally kicked in; she wasn't about to be paid off. Wasn't about to help him feel better.

The stern receptionist took off her glasses and leaned closer. "Is the father with you?"

Did she mean literally or metaphorically, as in were they a couple? Cara opted for the former. "No. He's at work. I just wanted to know what the process is. What evidence you need."

She had almost called him when Sophie was born. Too many years watching stupid romantic comedies where the partner comes rushing into the delivery room—the woman on the bed making groaning noises in full makeup with a perfect film of perspiration across her top lip. She had got as far as looking him up online. And that's when she'd seen the picture of him and Rebecca.

The receptionist was scrutinizing her, maybe trying to work out what her story was. "We don't need evidence of paternity. He just needs to come with you, and you both need two forms of ID. She walked her fingers down a series of shallow shelves and plucked out a form. "Here you go. Accepted forms of ID are listed on the back."

Cara took the form and replied with a smile and sarcastic tone at the miserable woman. "Thank you so much."

Revising the birth certificate sounded a lot easier than Cara had thought it would be. Jack's name on the document was the first big hurdle. Once that was done, she could move to the next stage of her plan.

CHAPTER SIXTEEN

Rebecca

King George Hospital was a maze of a building—every corridor the same. The clinical atmosphere, the smell, the hushed tones. Lots of people didn't like hospitals, but Rebecca did. They were so organized and clean. Calm.

This was the first time she had been to this one and it took a while to work out which door led to the main reception area. She'd hoped that Sophie might recognize her mum's workplace, but she said she'd never been here either. Rebecca had a vague idea that Cara had mentioned outpatients.

"Can I help you?" The receptionist looked tired and overworked. She clearly had better things to do on a busy Wednesday than locate a staff member for a random stranger. Rebecca would need to use the charm she usually reserved for the most stubborn clients.

"Hi, yes. We're looking for Cara Miller. She works here."

The receptionist frowned. "This is the patient reception area. People on their way to medical appointments."

"Yes, I know that. It's just that her mobile phone is dead and I can't get ahold of her." She held up Sophie's hand. "This is her daughter. Could you call her to let her know we're here? Or point us in the direction of her department? She works in the outpatient department, I believe."

A phone started ringing insistently on the desk and the receptionist placed her hand on the receiver, ready to pick it up. "The outpatient area is round the other side. You'd be better off going back out; turn left and walk around the building. Past maternity."

Rebecca opened her mouth to thank her but she had already picked up the call, so she nodded and mouthed the words instead before turning to exit in the direction the receptionist had indicated with a wave of her hand. "Come on, Sophie, let's go and surprise Mummy."

Of course, she'd lied about trying Cara's mobile. It was too easy for someone to ignore your calls, but if you turned up in person, they had to speak to you. It was a method she'd used to good effect when clients wanted a venue that was highly sought after or even unbookable. When she met with the owners in person, she could usually find a way to get what she wanted.

There had been a strange atmosphere at home last night, like something had shifted. Jack hadn't seemed to want to ask Cara any of the hard questions Rebecca needed answers to—"When are you leaving?" for example. That was another good reason to drop in on her here: maybe they could have a conversation away from home and Rebecca could get to the bottom of what was going on.

Her phone buzzed in her bag. She stopped and propped her bag on a low wall so that she could get to it. She didn't recognize the number. "Hello?"

"Hi, is this Rebecca Faulkner?"

"Speaking."

"Hi, this is Burberry House. We're calling about the Ross-Hamilton wedding. We've had a call from Samantha Ross. She wants to know if we allow entertainers who juggle fire. Just checking with you whether this is definitely happening because there will be insurance implications."

Good heavens. This bride was going to be the death of her. No wonder Izzy had practically skipped out of their meeting after

Rebecca had agreed to take it over. She couldn't look like she didn't know what was going on, though. "Oh, yes. Sorry, can you give me twenty minutes or so? I just need to double-check that with her and I'll get back to you."

Burberry House staff were obviously used to the shenanigans of the rich and spoiled. "Marvelous. Any time today would be great."

As soon as she'd ended the call, she dialed Samantha. Predictably, the phone rang and rang before being answered. "Hello? Rebecca? You must be psychic! I was just about to call you!"

Of course she was. It had been at least forty minutes since they'd last spoken, after all. Rebecca let out her breath slowly and smiled in the hope she could sound more upbeat than she felt. "Hi, Samantha. I've just had a call from Burberry House, asking about a fire juggler?"

In the background, clinking silverware and clattering dishes suggested that Samantha and her mother were already out to lunch. "That's what I wanted to talk to you about. Mum and I just bumped into a friend of hers and we were talking about the wedding, and Janice—that's my mum's friend—told us about this amazing act she's seen. Apparently, they just wander around your guests juggling crazy objects. I thought it would be great to have them at the wedding. We called them up and they're available. So lucky."

"Lucky" wasn't the word Rebecca would have used. "It might have been better if you'd told me about this first and let me deal with the venue about it."

She was outside the maternity department now, judging by the pregnant women on their way in and out of the large glass doors. Some of them had bumps so big they could barely walk. Leaning back, almost rocking side to side in order to move their feet forward. Like ducks.

Samantha sounded as if she was having a conversation with her mum at the same time. There was a muffled laugh and then she spoke to Rebecca. "Sorry! To be honest, I've thought better of it now. Just tell the venue to forget I asked."

She had to remember once again that Samantha was a client who was paying them a hefty fee. "Okay, fine. But if there's anything else, please call me first?"

Samantha laughed again. "Okay. I promise."

Beyond a huge "Outpatients" sign, sliding doors took her to another reception desk. This time there was a waiting line. Maybe this hadn't been such a good idea. She leaned down to Sophie. "Maybe Mummy is busy. Let's see if we can find one of her friends."

Moving away from the waiting area, she stood in the corridor for only a couple of minutes before she found what she was looking for: a member of the nursing staff. In her experience, receptionists were a lot more officious than the people behind the magic doors. "Hi," she called to the nurse. "Do you know where Cara is working today?"

The nurse slowed and frowned. "Cara?"

"Cara Miller. She's a…." She had absolutely no idea what Cara's job was. She'd just talked vaguely about working in the outpatient department. "I think she's a nurse here. I'm her friend and I need a quick word with her."

The nurse shook her head and picked up speed again. "There's no Cara I know of, sorry."

"Thanks."

The nurse didn't seem to be lying, but maybe they all worked different shifts. Rebecca hadn't actually checked that the nurse worked in the outpatient area and wasn't just walking through. She'd wait for the next one.

It was five more minutes before another nurse appeared. This one had her coat on; she looked as if she was going home. Rebecca waited for her to wave good-bye to the receptionist and followed her outside. "Excuse me!"

The nurse turned and smiled at her. "Yes?"

"Sorry, I know you've probably had a long shift but I really need to speak to my friend who works here. Cara Miller? This is her daughter, Sophie. She needs to see her mum." She winked at Sophie as if this was all a bit of fun.

"She must work in a different department. There aren't any Caras here."

This was frustrating; surely someone must know who she was. "Are you sure? She's about my height, slim"—she might as well admit it—"and very pretty."

The nurse shook her head. "I'm sure. I've been here for five years and I work on both shifts, and there's definitely no Cara who works here."

She smiled and gave them a mini-wave as she walked in the direction of the parking lot they'd just come from.

Confused, Rebecca crouched down so that her face was the same level as Sophie's. "Does Mummy definitely work at this hospital, Sophie? Has she talked to you about it?"

Sophie's forehead wrinkled above her nose as she thought about that. "I think so. I think she does."

Clearly, Sophie had no more idea about this than Rebecca did because it sounded very much as if Cara did not work in the outpatient department. Why had she lied about that? And if she wasn't working here, where was she working? Or was she not working at all? Was that why she didn't have any money?

And where the hell was she right now?

CHAPTER SEVENTEEN

Cara

Sophie had been a relentless babble of excitement about weddings and dinners and had gone to bed very happy. Which was more than could be said for Rebecca, judging by her face when Cara came back downstairs.

Picking up cushions from where Sophie had sat on the floor, Rebecca didn't make eye contact when she spoke. "I went to your hospital today."

Damn. What was she doing checking up on her? Cara knew Rebecca didn't trust her. So much for the friendly face. *Take it slowly.* "Oh, yes? Did you have an appointment? Everything okay?"

Rebecca smiled with the tight lips of someone trying to keep their temper. She must have known that Cara was playing it out. "I wasn't there for me. Sophie and I were on the way home and thought we'd pop in and say hello."

Now Cara wanted to smile. Who turned up at a busy hospital and expected to be able to speak to someone who was working? "I see."

Rebecca was tidying the new markers she'd bought for Sophie earlier. Proper branded Crayola ones. She placed them back in the box one by one, darkest to lightest colors. Who had time in their life to be that particular? She seemed to be struggling with what she was going to say. Cara waited. No need to offer any information before she was asked for it.

Eventually Rebecca located the words. "No one seemed to know where you were. In fact, they didn't recognize your name at all."

Now they were getting to the crux of it. She *had* been checking up on her. "It's a big hospital. Staff change all the time."

Rebecca folded the lid of the marker box closed. So slowly, carefully; Cara wanted to snatch it from her. "Yes, but I asked one of the nurses. She said she'd worked there a long time. And she didn't know you."

What was she, a private detective? "Yeah, well. She probably didn't want to give out any information about me. We have to be careful. We get all sorts turning up there and asking to see people. There are a lot of *weirdos* out there."

She kept her eyes firmly on Rebecca as she spoke, not wanting her sarcasm to miss its target. Clearly, it hadn't; Rebecca reddened and dropped the box into the yellow shiny tray she had bought for Sophie's art materials. Cara wondered if she had one of those to tidy Jack into if he sat still too long. Rebecca lowered herself onto one of the two armchairs and smoothed her dress over her knees. "Remind me again what exactly it is you do at the hospital. Are you an actual nurse?"

Was it the word "actual" or the tone of voice that was the most maddening part of Rebecca's question? Obviously, she didn't think Cara capable of such an important job. She almost wanted to say yes to surprise her, but that would be a lie too far. She crossed her fingers and gave her a half-truth instead. "Not a nurse, no. I'm a CNA—a certified nursing assistant. I take temperatures, blood pressure, that kind of thing. A lot of the same things that a nurse does but I can't give medication."

"I see." Rebecca didn't look as if she believed her. This could all end badly.

It was sort of true. Cara used to be a CNA. Maybe if she kept going, gave a few details, she could stop Rebecca from being so suspicious. "I work PRN shifts, which means I pick up available hours and I can work it around Sophie. It's difficult to work the normal shift patterns if I'm full-time. Child care is very expensive."

Rebecca hadn't looked interested in the details of Cara's work, but she pricked up her ears at the mention of child care. "Is that why you contacted Jack now? Because you need help with child care?"

Cara needed to stay calm. "I want her to know her father."

Rebecca's eyes flashed. Something was eating at her, disturbing her usual calm demeanor. What did she know? Or suspect? "But why now? I mean, why didn't you let him know before now? Five years is a long time to wait, Cara. Surely you've needed help before now?"

One thing she'd learned in the last few years was that the best line of defense was attack. "Do you not want Sophie in your life, Rebecca? Is that it?"

Rebecca reddened again. She would never make a poker player. "I didn't say that. Sophie is Jack's daughter. Of course he should get to know her. It's the right thing to do."

And heaven forbid this perfect woman should do the wrong thing. Cara had her on the ropes now, at least. She could push her advantage. "But you don't *want* to do it, do you?"

It worked. Rebecca started backpedaling before her eyes. "I didn't say that. Sophie is a lovely girl." She smiled, the mask back on. "You've done an excellent job with her."

Cara definitely didn't want or need Rebecca's approval. "I didn't do anything. This is how she came out. She's a good kid, always has been."

Rebecca rallied, as if she wanted to ask everything on her mind while it was just the two of them. "It must be quite a shock for her, though. Meeting Jack out of the blue. Didn't you prepare her in any way? There was probably a better way to do this than just to spring it on her and Jack with no warning."

Here we go. The childless woman who was an expert on raising kids. It never ceased to make Cara laugh when people who didn't have children talked about all the things they would do if they had a child: rigid bedtimes, healthy food, no digital devices. A couple of months as a parent to an under-five and they'd soon change their tune.

Still, at least this had taken them off the work conversation. Rebecca was trying to look nonchalant but these questions had been brewing for days. How little could Cara get away with saying? "A shock for you, too, I would imagine?"

Again, Rebecca looked caught off guard. She was just too easy. Clearly, she had never had to negotiate her way out of a tricky situation before. Some people's lives were just smooth and free of wrinkles. Cara couldn't decide if she envied her or hated her. Or both.

"Well, of course, it was a shock for me, but"—she held her head higher, clearly ready to take Cara on—"I can accommodate Sophie in our lives. We just need to agree to a plan that works for all of us. What about alternate weekends and one evening in the week?"

Rebecca thought she could just slip Sophie into their schedule like a regular appointment with a client? God, she had a lot to learn. "Maybe we should keep it flexible to start with. See how it all works out. Sophie has enough change to her routine coming up. Starting school next September and everything. I'm not sure how that is going to work out."

Rebecca's smile tightened. "Of course. But children need routines. Surely she will feel more secure if she knows where she is."

Cara bit her tongue. It would be too easy to take her down. Ask her what the hell she knew about raising children. Tell her that there was more to being a mother than buying fancy art supplies. It would be satisfying for five minutes and then Rebecca would probably go back to Jack and make life difficult for her and, more importantly, for Sophie. No, it was too soon for that. "Well, we'll cross that bridge when we come to it, all right?"

But Rebecca wasn't letting go this time. She'd clearly tired of waiting for Jack to work out a schedule and was taking matters into her own hands. "But we are at that bridge, aren't we? I mean, you'll be moving out soon and we need to have a plan in place by then."

Damn, she had her there. She needed to buy more time. "I really think Jack should be here for this conversation. His schedule seems rather busy. I'm amazed the two of you manage to actually see each other at all."

Rebecca bristled. "We make it work. We coordinate our schedules for time together."

Cara had to laugh at that. "Wow. That's romantic. What happened to spontaneity?"

Rebecca stood up, holding the rest of Sophie's drawings in her hands, ready to tidy them away somewhere. "Spontaneity can get messy. Unpredictable." Now it was her turn to look Cara dead in the eye. "It can lead to unplanned consequences. Our dinner will be at eight. I need to catch up on some emails now."

As soon as Rebecca left the room, Cara let out a breath and sank back into the chair. She'd managed to deflect this conversation for now but she was going to have to make sure that she wasn't left alone with Rebecca again. She wouldn't be asking her these questions if Jack was there, Cara was sure. And there was only so long she could avoid her interrogations. Rebecca was on to her.

CHAPTER EIGHTEEN

Rebecca

If Sophie asked when her mum was going to get home one more time, Rebecca's head might actually explode.

The last two days had been tense. Rebecca had tried to make it sound casual when she'd told Jack about her visit to the hospital, but he had also accused her of checking up on Cara. Why was he defending her all of a sudden? Then Cara had announced she had an interview with another agency on Friday to get some work in a chain of care homes where the hours would work better around Sophie. It was as if a truce had been called: neither of them mentioned anything further about their conversation on Wednesday.

Friday wasn't one of Sophie's days at preschool, though, so Rebecca was—again—the one to look after her while Cara was gone. But that was six hours ago. Surely she was done by now?

"When is Mummy coming home?"

Sophie's whine was beginning to sound like fingernails down a blackboard; it was impossible for Rebecca to concentrate on the budget spreadsheet for the Brooklands House dinner next month. There was a missing £250 somewhere among all these numbers and she needed to focus. Not be dragged away every ten minutes to answer a question or find a green crayon. Sophie was usually so self-sufficient. Why was she suddenly so needy? "I don't know. Any minute, I would think. I'll send her another message."

This was the third message she'd sent Cara, along with two voice mails. Dinner preparations needed to start soon if it was going to be ready when Jack got home from work. Why had she agreed to babysit?

Sophie's bottom lip trembled. "Is my mummy coming back?"

Why would she say that? This really was unlike the Sophie she'd seen so far. "Has your mummy ever left you before?"

Sophie shook her head but looked uncertain. "I don't think so."

A chill went through Rebecca. But there was no need to panic, surely? Cara clearly loved Sophie. No way would she abandon her.

As much for herself as for the little girl, she stood up and offered, "Why don't you come and help me make dinner? That way it will all be ready when Mummy comes home."

That brightened her up. Rebecca had a 1950s-style apron that Jack had thought was a humorous gift when she'd gone through a brief baking phase, and Sophie was delighted when Rebecca tied it on her, folding the bottom half back on itself at the waist so that it didn't drag on the floor.

"Right. We're having chicken wrapped in prosciutto with roasted new potatoes." She opened the fridge and brought out all the produce they needed. She liked this part of cooking. When she did bake a cake—rarely these days now that the novelty had worn off—she would measure all the ingredients into little bowls as if she were on a cooking show.

Sophie wrinkled her forehead. This was a common expression at mealtimes. One of the things Rebecca planned to do when Sophie stayed with them was work on her food choices. "What's persootow?"

"It's like ham. Like your sandwiches. Come and wash your hands before we start." Ham had been another issue. Apparently, the thick-sliced honey-roasted Yorkshire ham she'd bought was "disgusting." Cara had bought Sophie a shrink-wrapped pack of square ham you could see through and it grated on Rebecca every time she saw it in the fridge. The meat looked more plastic than its packaging.

Sophie eyed the ingredients suspiciously but slid down off of the kitchen stool and joined Rebecca at the sink. She loved the soap dispenser: Rebecca had to watch to ensure she didn't dispense enough soap to clean the entire kitchen. "That's enough."

Now that she had the soap on her hands, she rubbed them together. "Jack makes bubbles. Can you make bubbles?"

Rebecca had absolutely no idea that Jack could make bubbles with hand soap. When had he done that? "We haven't got time for bubbles—we need to get that dinner started!" She tried to come off as upbeat but she knew what a bore she must sound.

Rinsing her hands also involved Sophie getting water all over the surround of the sink and onto the floor. Rebecca tore off some paper towels and quickly wiped it up. Once she'd herded Sophie back to the island, she unwrapped the chicken breasts, then peeled back the film from the prosciutto and laid it next to a plate. "Okay, Sophie, all you need to do is wrap the pros—the *ham* around the chicken. Take one at a time."

Sophie picked up a chicken breast. The nose wrinkle was back. "It's slimy."

Best to ignore it. "Put it on the plate and then peel off a slice of ham."

Rebecca had assumed that peeling off a piece of prosciutto and then wrapping it around the chicken would be the easiest job she could give her. How wrong she was. By the time she looked up from the silverware drawer, roughly twelve seconds later, Sophie had peeled off three separate slivers of the thinly sliced meat and stuck them randomly along the chicken breast.

"No. Not like that." Rebecca reached out to take the meat from her hands, but Sophie pulled it away.

"I'm doing it."

"But you're doing it wrong. Look." Rebecca tried to peel the next slice of prosciutto but it was tricky now that Sophie had pulled off the corners. She tried to pick it away from the plastic but Sophie pulled it away from her. "It's *my* job."

Rebecca was trying to be patient, she really was. But it took every ounce of self-control not to rip the packet of ham—*prosciutto*—from Sophie's chubby four-year-old hands. It was excruciating. Pick, pick, pick. Tear off a tiny piece. Stick it on. Start again. She just wanted to get dinner on.

The agony didn't end there. Sophie insisted on peeling carrots, which ended up looking like they'd been mauled by a large rodent. Rebecca also spent the whole time hovering over her, convinced she was going to cut herself somehow on the vegetable peeler. It wasn't Sophie's fault, but Rebecca's shoulders were getting so tight that they almost grazed her ears. Cooking was normally an activity that reduced her stress levels, not increased them. She wasn't cut out for parenting; she really wasn't. That's why she hadn't planned on doing it.

Somehow, finally, they got dinner in the oven. While Sophie washed her hands again—another gallon of soap—Rebecca sent Cara another text. This time, she was more to the point.

Where the hell are you???

Half an hour later, Sophie was drawing place mats for everyone for dinner when the front door opened. Rebecca practically flew into the hallway. "Where have you been?"

Cara looked absolutely awful. If Jack saw her now, he wouldn't be so dismissive of the possibility she was taking drugs. She was also not remotely apologetic. "I've been walking."

All the stress of the last two hours surged up in Rebecca's chest. "Walking? What do you mean, *walking*?"

Cara hung up her coat. "You know. One foot in front of the other. Moving forward."

Rebecca was not in the mood for sarcasm. She also didn't believe her. "Well, while you were walking, I was babysitting your daughter, and she has been asking for you nonstop for the last four hours. I've been texting and calling and—"

Cara held up her hand to stop Rebecca from talking. "Please. Can I just have a minute before you launch into me?" She leaned her head back to call out, "Soph? Where are you?"

"Mummy!" Sophie's squeal was followed by the pounding of her feet as she ran into the hallway. She flew into Cara's open arms.

Cara rested her face on the top of her daughter's head. "Hey, baby." Her voice sounded thick, as if she'd been drinking.

Rebecca couldn't let it go this time. "Sophie, why don't you make us some nice place cards for names to go with your place mats? You can get the blue paper from the back room upstairs if you like."

Colored paper was a guaranteed winner. Sophie ran upstairs straightaway. Cara watched her go and then turned to walk into the sitting room.

Rebecca was a calm person. Whatever happened at work—last-minute booking problems, seating plan sagas, menu disasters—she could handle it with smooth professionalism and without once getting into a flap. But she could feel the roar in her belly about to erupt as she followed Cara into the sitting room. "What the hell is going on? You asked me to look after Sophie while you had a job interview. A couple of hours, you said. And you've been gone for eight. I've got a job, too, you know. People are relying on me."

Cara just sat there. On Rebecca's sofa. Looking at her like she couldn't care less about what she was saying. She was arrogant, thoughtless, and totally bloody selfish. She also had a very strange look in her eye. "Are you drunk? Or high?"

This time Cara laughed. "If only. No. I had some bad news."

"About the job?" Rebecca wasn't surprised Cara didn't get it. She wouldn't employ someone as bedraggled as her and with the attitude she had. "That doesn't give you an excuse to just go off and leave Sophie with me and—"

Again, Cara raised her hand. "I've been at the hospital today, but not to work. I'm ill, Rebecca. Really, really ill."

CHAPTER NINETEEN

Cara

When the symptoms had first started—stomachache, feeling bloated, constant tiredness—Cara had put it down to the fact that she was dashing about so much. What single mother didn't feel absolutely exhausted all the time? But it had gone on so long and she just couldn't shake it—plus, Danielle wasn't letting up on nagging her—so she booked an appointment with the GP.

To begin with, he'd been no help whatsoever. Barely making eye contact, he had taken her blood pressure and asked some basic questions about her diet. Did she eat regularly? Was she getting enough vitamins? What about fiber? Iron? In the end he had sent her away to get a blood test for anemia and suggested she get herself some multivitamins.

It was pointless going for the blood test; she'd known she wasn't anemic. But she did order an assortment of vitamins on eBay. The ones in the pharmacy were ridiculously expensive and Sophie had needed new shoes that week. The same site had cheap antacids, too, so she ordered a large pack of those.

They made no difference. In the next couple of months, the pain in her stomach had got steadily worse, moving to her pelvis. Sometimes a dull ache, other times a vicious cramp that took her breath away. Then her stomach had been swollen all the time; she'd felt bloated, like she was constantly full, even though her dwindling appetite meant she was actually eating less and less. Her jeans wouldn't snap and, a few times, she caught strangers glancing at her stomach as if they thought she was pregnant.

Eventually she'd gone back to the doctor and while she was in the waiting room, just by chance, she'd seen a leaflet about ovarian cancer. All the symptoms described were the same as hers.

She'd taken it with her when she was called in to see the doctor, but he wasn't convinced. He'd peered at the leaflet and then pushed it to one side. "Ovarian cancer is very rare in someone of your age. It's much more likely after menopause. Unless you have a family history of this type of cancer?"

Apparently, ovarian cancer could be genetic. When he'd asked her about her family history, she'd almost laughed at him. How would she know? Her family weren't big on openness and honesty. At sixteen, when she'd finally got out of there, her mother had been healthy. Physically, at least. And she'd had no interest in what had happened to her since.

This time, she hadn't been about to be put off with a diagnosis of anemia. There was something wrong and she'd wanted an answer. At last he'd examined her, pressing into her stomach as she'd winced in pain. Frowning, and making lots of reluctant noises, he'd finally sent her for a scan.

The letter with her appointment had arrived two days later. On the one hand, this was good. But on the other, did this mean that cancer was a real possibility? Danielle had come with her while both their kids were at school and preschool. Sitting next to her in the waiting room, she'd grasped Cara's hand. "Whatever this is, I'm here for you, right? Whatever you need." Her face was the picture of reassurance as Cara's name was called by the sonographer.

But Cara had been all alone when she was told that they'd seen a mass behind her uterus. She would need a biopsy but they would do another blood test that day. A very specific blood test this time—CA 125—and that's when it was confirmed.

Ovarian cancer.

After the diagnosis, everything had moved faster, almost in a blur. The biopsy showed the cancer had spread from the ovary into the womb. This time she hadn't even needed to wait for a letter: she was given an appointment with a consultant the very next day.

Dr. Green's office was small and almost filled by a desk, computer, and three chairs: her own fancy-looking leather one and two other hospital-issue. Cara had only ever needed one of them. Thick gray hair and piercing blue eyes made it difficult to guess her age. From the beginning she had been kind and gentle in her tone, while remaining painfully honest. "The tumor is quite large and we don't have the benefit of an early diagnosis, so we need to get started on treatment right away. First, we will operate to remove it. Then you will have six doses of chemo."

It had been like they were talking about someone else. She'd felt numb but strangely logical. "And then I'll be cured?"

Dr. Green had taken her time answering. "We won't know the full extent until we open you up, I'm afraid. Let's take it one step at a time."

Cara had Sophie to think about. She didn't have the luxury of *wait and see*. She needed to know exactly what she was dealing with. "But you are giving me chemotherapy? Which means you think that I will beat this?"

Again, the pause. The clock in Dr. Green's consultancy room had a very loud tick. "Our drug options are less for this than they are for other cancers. But the good news is that you are young and we are going to blast this with everything we have."

Still, she hadn't answered the question. "So, you are saying that it's still possible that I might die?"

Dr. Green had reached out and put a hand over hers, which Cara hadn't realized was clenched in a fist. "Let's take this one step at a time. We will operate as soon as possible. Because of the extent of the tumors, we will need to perform a hysterectomy. Would you like to talk to someone about freezing your eggs before that happens? Obviously, you wouldn't be able to carry a child yourself once we remove your womb but—"

"No." In what alternate universe was she ever likely to meet someone and have more children? She was done with men. Sophie was all the children she would ever need. "I have a daughter. I don't plan on any more children. I want this out of me as soon as possible."

Dr. Green had nodded once. "I'd like you to go home and think about that before you decide for sure. I'm going to give you a number for the ovarian cancer nurses. They can talk this through with you some more if you'd like?"

Had Dr. Green assumed she had a loving partner at home who she needed to discuss this with? The only person at home who was on her mind was Sophie. Who would look after her while she was in the hospital? How long would she have to stay in after a hysterectomy? Would Cara be fine to look after her while she was having the chemo? How would she work? Pay bills?

All of her thoughts had been about the daily routine of life while she was having treatment. It wasn't until she'd gone home and googled the statistics that she'd realized what Dr. Green had been trying to tell her. Of the seventy-five hundred women diagnosed with ovarian cancer in the UK every year, fewer than half survived five years.

And she was already at stage 3C.

Practicalities had carried her through the next few days: arranging for Sophie to stay with Danielle next door while she was in the hospital, speaking to the welfare people about how she was going to cover her rent and bills if she couldn't work, informing the agency who supplied her work at the hospital that she wouldn't be available for a while. The logistics were endless, but they did keep her occupied and unable to dwell too long on the consequences of what they might find when they opened her up.

At night, though, she would lie awake and watch Sophie sleeping. Fear would creep under the covers and almost suffocate her. Her mind a carousel of faces. If she wasn't here, what would happen to Sophie? Who was going to look after her baby girl?

Cara had forced herself to be upbeat and matter-of-fact when she told Sophie about her operation, explaining that she had something in her tummy that the doctor had to take out. Sophie had initially been inquisitive. Had she swallowed it? Was it a seed from an apple that had grown? What did it look like? It was only when she'd realized that she couldn't stay in the hospital with her that she'd got upset and clung to her with all her might. It had reminded Cara of the first time she'd taken her to preschool and Sophie had had to be peeled from her so that she could leave to go to work.

Sucking down the wave of emotion that that memory generated, it had taken every ounce of Cara's remaining strength to make it sound fun that Sophie would be sleeping over at Danielle's for a few nights. That's when she had taken out the credit card. To buy Sophie a My Little Pony sleeping bag and a Pinkie Pie plush toy to cuddle while she was staying there. She'd also bought treats and sweets for Sophie to take with her and share with Danielle's children. She'd wanted to buy something for Danielle, too, but Danielle had told her to behave herself. "You can take me out for dinner when you're all better."

The hysterectomy had left her sore and immobile for a while but it was nothing compared to the chemotherapy. Once a month for the last six months she had visited the cancer center to be hooked up to a brutal concoction of drugs that had made her feel far worse than the cancer had. Looking back, after the first dose she had been naively optimistic that the aftereffects weren't so bad. But every time had got progressively worse until the last appointments, which had left her feeling like she'd been beaten up for days afterward. That was when she'd made the decision to find Jack.

It was also where she'd met Dave. He'd been in for treatment for testicular cancer. She'd learned much more about *that* than she'd wanted to, to be honest. Dave was a talker and had delighted in telling her about all the alternative therapies he'd researched, including some high-strength CBD oil that a friend of his could "get hold of" that was "much better than that rubbish you can buy in the shops now." That's why she'd arranged to meet him for a coffee on Tuesday; he'd got her some to try. That's what she hadn't wanted Rebecca to see. Or the telltale needle marks in his arms, peeling skin on his hands, or his sickly pale face that might give away his treatment.

Right now, Rebecca looked paler than either of them. She opened her mouth and closed it again. Then opened it. "*Cancer?* I'm so sorry, Cara. I had no idea."

Cara had had her full quota of the words "I'm sorry" in the last few months. "Of course you didn't. There is no need to apologize. Really."

She could practically see Rebecca's brain frantically searching for the right words for what she wanted to ask. "And are you, will you...?"

"They didn't get it all." After the first operation, everything had been hopeful; Dr. Green had removed all the cancer she could see, and had even had a big smile on her face when she'd said they were going to blast her with chemo to make sure that "the bugger doesn't come back." Danielle had even bought a bottle of nonalcoholic wine so they could celebrate.

Today, Dr. Green had looked devastated. The scan from a few days ago showed that Cara's original tumors had metastasized, spreading to the surface of her liver and diaphragm. She'd promised that they would continue to fight it—making some changes to the chemo drugs was a start—but it wasn't good news.

Rebecca nodded slowly, looked down at her hands and up again. "I'm so sorry. I really, really am. And I understand...I mean, it all makes more sense now. Why you are here. I'm assuming that's why? Why you decided to get in touch with Jack?"

There was no point lying anymore. Even if she'd had the energy to do so, there was no point keeping it secret. "Yes. Yes, it was."

Rebecca was silent for the next few moments. It was obviously a lot to take in. When she spoke again, she did her best to be tactful. "Does that mean, uh, that you have introduced Jack to Sophie so that he can look after her when...if...?"

Cara was way too tired to skirt around this nicely. "So that if this treatment doesn't work, he can raise her. Yes. That's exactly why."

Before the diagnosis, the prognosis, there was no need for Cara to ever contact Jack. He had made it clear when they'd split up that it was over, so why would she put herself, and Sophie, through begging him to be in their lives? She had friends who were single parents and, as far as their experiences went, having an ex-partner in their lives was often much more stressful than the day-to-day and financial difficulties of doing it alone.

Of course, she had considered whether Sophie had a right to know her father. Whether it was worth taking the risk of reaching out to him. Maybe he would have stepped up. Been one of the good ones. But she'd witnessed firsthand what it was like for those kids whose dads let them down. Who had weekend plans canceled at the last minute. Christmases where they had to spend half the day in a car being shuffled between two addresses. She didn't want that for Sophie.

Sophie was hers. All hers. Her perfect, beautiful, clever, kind daughter. She would do anything to make her life easier than her own had been. Anything.

Rebecca's hand was over her mouth, her eyes wide, voice barely above a whisper. "You want Jack to raise Sophie?"

For a clever woman, it was taking her a while to understand. "No, I don't *want* Jack to raise Sophie. I want to raise Sophie myself. But if I die, there is no one else, Rebecca. No one. And I am not going to let her be taken into foster care or a children's home."

It was so bloody unfair. But there was no way that Sophie was going to be looked after by strangers. She'd heard too many horror stories, too many tales of how difficult it was for older children to be adopted.

"Why didn't you tell us this immediately?"

She'd been expecting that question. "I hadn't decided. I didn't know what Jack was like now. What he would be like as a dad. And when I realized that you were also going to be part of the setup, I needed to see what you would be like. As a mother. A stepmother."

Rebecca almost physically blanched at that. "I . . . I see."

"Why don't you want children?" Cara had been wanting to ask her this question for the last week but it had felt too invasive. Now that Rebecca knew about the cancer, nothing was off-limits. Jack had been vague when she'd asked him—maybe Rebecca would give her a straight answer.

But Rebecca just shrugged. "I don't know how to answer that question. I just don't. Maybe I'm not the maternal type."

Cara had hoped that being with Sophie might change their minds, that she'd have time to ease them into this gently, but the appointment today had confirmed that they might not have that luxury. "I see. But what about now? What about Sophie? What about Jack's daughter?"

If it was possible, Rebecca looked even paler. "I don't think it's appropriate for us to talk about this without Jack here. You need to speak to him tonight. To tell him everything. And then . . . then I guess we will come up with a plan."

Cara almost laughed. "A plan? This is not one of your events. You can't make a spreadsheet about this. We're talking about a little girl. Sophie needs to be looked after by someone who loves her. How can Jack fail to love her? He is her dad."

A small voice interrupted them. Sophie stood in the doorway, her hands full of inexpertly folded place cards. "Is Jack my dad?"

CHAPTER TWENTY

Rebecca

Rebecca was sitting in the living room, hands in her lap, waiting for Jack to get home. She had already sent him a message to check that he wouldn't be late, using the dinner as a pretext. Then she had tidied her desk, refolded everything in the linen cupboard, and checked all the spice jars to see if any were nearly out of date. Now she just sat and tapped her foot.

She heard the familiar ritual of Jack slipping off his shoes at the door and hanging up his suit jacket on the hanger he left on the coatrack for that purpose. When he appeared, leaning down to kiss her as he always did when he got home, he scanned the room. "Where are Cara and Sophie? Have we got an empty house?" He raised an eyebrow suggestively, but he'd soon have that playful expression wiped from his face.

"Cara went upstairs for a nap."

"A nap? It's six o'clock." Jack frowned and straightened up. "Did you two have a disagreement?"

That was the understatement of the year. "Yes and no. You might want to sit down."

Jack loosened his tie, pulled it off altogether, unbuttoned the collar of his shirt. She always enjoyed the way he did that. It was a mini-transformation from work-Jack to home-Jack. He perched on the edge of the armchair—the same armchair that Cara had vacated thirty minutes earlier. "Okay. Hit me."

If only he knew how apt that turn of phrase was. She felt as if she *had* been punched. Where to begin? "Well, first of all, Sophie knows that you are her father."

His eyes widened. "Really? How did that happen? I thought we'd agreed to wait a little while."

"Yes, well, she overheard Cara and me talking. We didn't realize she was there."

Jack sat back in his chair, let out a long breath. "So, this is really happening. Once Sophie knows, it makes it all the more real."

It had been less than an hour since Cara had dropped her bombshell, and Rebecca was still in shock. She needed to tell Jack as quickly as possible; maybe they could make sense of it all together. "There's more."

Jack sat up in his seat and leaned forward. "Did she not take it well?"

Rebecca had no idea how Sophie had taken it. Cara had scooted her straight upstairs to talk about it, and the two of them hadn't been down since. Looking at Jack now, his eyes searching her face, she could barely breathe. The next few moments were going to change things forever. "It's not that. It's something else."

She knew that dragging it out like this was pointless; she was going to have to tell him. She just didn't know how to. Didn't know how he was going to react. Would he be upset? Angry? She'd known for thirty minutes and still wasn't sure how to feel. Maybe it would help to build up to it a little. "It's Cara. She hasn't been entirely honest with us."

Jack folded his arms. "Is it this apartment she told us she's waiting for? Has it fallen through?"

If only it were that simple. Right now, she would have paid Cara's rent in a heartbeat if it would change things. "I have no idea. It's not that, though." She took a deep breath. *Just say it.* "Cara is ill. Very ill. Ovarian cancer."

Jack's face turned gray in front of her eyes. His voice dropped to almost a whisper. "Cancer?"

Her face must have looked like that half an hour ago. It all made sense now that she thought about it. The tiredness. The lack of money. That she was no longer working.

And other things too. The way she looked at Sophie sometimes, like she was drinking her in. Rebecca had misread it as possessiveness, but it was much more likely that Cara didn't know how long she would be able to look at her daughter. For the first time, her eyes filled and she chewed on her lip for a moment before she continued to explain. "Apparently, she was diagnosed less than a year ago. She's still having treatment, but the cancer is...aggressive."

She watched him, waiting for him to reach the same conclusions that she had. It didn't take long. Jack swallowed. "That's why she's here."

She nodded, still watching him, saying nothing.

"Is it..."

The look in his eyes nearly broke her. "Terminal? I don't know. We got interrupted."

Jack let his head fall back onto the chair and he stared silently at the ceiling. She would have given anything to know how he was feeling right now. Best to just wait, give him space to think.

He didn't move his head to look at her when he finally spoke again. "So, if she...dies, we get Sophie? Full-time. Living with us permanently. The full deal?"

Rebecca's chest was so tight. She took a deep breath then let it out slowly. "It seems that way, yes."

"Bloody hell." He closed his eyes.

"Bloody hell, indeed."

They sat in silence for a few moments and then Jack lifted his head. "I can't believe she has been living here for a week and not told us. And why—and please don't take offense to this—why tell you and not me?"

"No offense taken. I don't think she planned to tell me. She had an appointment today. It wasn't good news. So, it just kind of came out."

She wasn't about to tell him that she'd been almost shouting at Cara. She burned with shame at the memory. Not her finest hour.

Jack shook his head as if to free it from a fog. Initial shock over, he was obviously trying to get his head around the facts. "And did she say why she kept something like this a secret?"

That was something else Rebecca had had a chance to reflect on while she waited for Jack. Much as she wished Cara had been honest from the start, she could understand her reasons. "I think she wanted to check us out. Work out whether we were appropriate guardians."

Jack's eyes flashed. "And if we weren't, what? She would just waltz straight out of our lives again? Hi, Jack, here's your daughter; oh no, we're off again." His anger flashed hot and then cooled quickly. "Sorry. God, that was selfish. It's just…I can't believe it. Poor Cara. Poor Sophie."

Rebecca thought of the little girl wrapping the chicken this afternoon, her tongue poking out the side of her mouth as she concentrated. Why hadn't she been more patient with her? "Yes. It's awful."

The room had darkened but neither of them stood to turn on the light. Silence filled the space between them, Jack staring into the middle distance. It was too big to talk about. The implications for all of them were huge. Eventually, he rubbed his face with his hands and then looked at her. "Sorry, I'm just thinking about myself. What about you? How are you feeling?"

His concern for her made her heart hurt. Jealousy had made her horrible to him the last few days. She got up from her chair and sat beside him on the armchair. "I don't know. We obviously need to talk to Cara. Ask her to be totally honest with us."

He looked into her eyes, reflecting her own bewilderment back at her. "And if that *is* what she wants, for us to look after Sophie permanently, how do *you* feel about that?"

How honest could she be without sounding like a total heartless bitch? "I'd be lying if I said I was happy about it. I mean—a child? It was never part of our plan."

Jack nodded, though the shadow across his face made it hard to read. "I know. I know. But if Cara genuinely doesn't have anyone else and if she... If the treatment doesn't work, what choice do we have?" He leaned over and took her hand, squeezed it. "I wonder how Sophie is taking it that I am her father."

That was a slightly different subject, and the eagerness in Jack's tone made her feel uncomfortable. "What are you hoping for?"

He shrugged. "I hope that she's pleased. If I'm going to do this, step up and be her dad, then I hope she doesn't hate me." He attempted a laugh but it hung on the air between them.

Jack was Sophie's father. There was no way that Rebecca would ever stand in the way of him getting to know her. It was important. It was the right thing to do. She was pleased that he was the kind of man who accepted his responsibilities. And financially they would make a provision for her.

But living with them full-time? That was something very different. Was this really happening? "We need to talk to Cara about this. It doesn't sound promising, but they are finding new treatments all the time."

"Yes, of course. And maybe it's not as bleak for her as she thinks. But if it is, I have to offer Sophie a home. We both agree on that, right?"

Rebecca nodded. Of course she understood it. He would have to offer his daughter a home. But where did that leave her? Was she going to have to become a mother to Jack's child?

She knew nothing about being a mother. Had never wanted to be a mother. Had known that Jack was the man for her because he hadn't asked her to be a mother. Today she'd had to look after Sophie for just over eight hours and she'd barely coped.

And now he was looking at her and expecting her to "step up" with him into a role she would never have chosen.

What would happen if she wasn't up to the job?

CHAPTER TWENTY-ONE

Cara

Before making the final decision about whether to look Jack up, Cara had considered what kind of father he might make.

Ironically, their relationship hadn't been serious enough to actually discuss whether either of them wanted children—*who thinks about that when you're still in your twenties?*—but she had always assumed he was the kind of man who would have kids someday. For a start, he was the most caring person she'd ever met. When they'd lived together, he would cook for her and meet her from work and just generally look out for her. It had been nice. Really nice.

Which was why she'd been surprised and concerned by Jack's lack of interest in getting to know Sophie. Caught up at work, or playing golf, he'd been more than happy to let Rebecca pick up the slack in looking after his daughter. It was worrying. Had she played it wrong? Misjudged the man she thought she knew?

Today he was different. Since yesterday, when he'd found out about the bloody cancer, it was as if a wall of awkwardness had come down and she could see the Jack she'd known back then. Even better, with Rebecca out on a Saturday afternoon shopping trip, he was finally taking the time to get to know his daughter. For the last thirty minutes, he'd been lying on the floor with her, putting together a huge Lego kit that he'd ordered online—it must have cost a small fortune.

He wasn't the only one feeling more relaxed. Not having to hide the cancer—or endure Rebecca's pitying glances since she'd found out—meant Cara felt better than she had since they'd arrived. Plus, without Rebecca there watching their every move, it was easier to talk openly and honestly. "I'm really surprised that you and Rebecca aren't planning to have children."

Jack pressed the edge of a yellow brick onto what looked like a tiny window. "Really? Why is that?"

Although Sophie had had building blocks when she was younger, Lego had always been too expensive. The bricks Jack had bought were larger than normal, and Cara had been surprised how into them Sophie was. Even more surprised how into them Jack was. She couldn't remember her own father ever playing with her like this. "It's just, seeing you there, you look like a natural."

"Hmm?" Jack was concentrating on the instructions. The kit he'd bought was a huge castle and there were about a gazillion pieces. At the beginning he had boasted to Sophie that they would be able to work it out just by looking at the picture on the box. He'd made her giggle by throwing the instruction booklet over his head. Then Cara had laughed when he'd begrudgingly given in and had to crawl over and retrieve it from behind the sofa. And then had to disconnect and reconstruct a whole section that he'd got wrong. "It's not that I don't like kids. I just hadn't really thought about having one." He watched Sophie focus on pressing two bricks together and then stage-whispered at Cara, "I think she's better at this than me."

He grinned at her. The same grin that had won her over five years before. She knew he liked his freedom—that's what he had told her was the reason that they couldn't be together. *I've got a lot going on in my career. I just need to be free from commitment at this point in my life.* Funnily enough, it hadn't seemed so important to be free when he'd met Rebecca a matter of weeks later.

Anyone with an ounce of tact would have left the conversation there. But Cara didn't have that luxury. She needed to make sure that Jack was going to be the kind of father that Sophie needed. "And now? Now that you have the opportunity?"

Jack glanced at Sophie. He was probably right; they shouldn't be having this kind of conversation in front of her, but when else were they going to have it? She couldn't speak freely in front of Rebecca. And it wasn't as if she could ask him to talk privately without making it look like she was trying to "get him alone." He put down the Lego and spoke to Sophie. "I think I need a break from this. Can I leave you to it while I make some coffee for me and your mum?"

Sophie reached over and took the booklet from beside him. "I'll use the 'structions."

Jack grinned at her holding them upside down and pretending to read. "Good girl." He made a movement with his head to signify that Cara should follow him out to the kitchen. She waited for him to go ahead before she got up. No man was telling her what to do.

When she joined him, he waved a mug at her. "Coffee or tea?"

"Coffee, please. Black."

Of course, this was Jack so it wasn't going to be a spoonful of instant coffee. He filled up a top-of-the-line coffee machine with fresh beans and twiddled the knobs and dials like a barista. He avoided her eye as he spoke. "Sophie seems okay about me being her dad?"

She wasn't sure if this was a statement or a question. It wasn't like him to seek reassurance. At least it hadn't been when she'd known him well. "Yeah. She's a pretty resilient kid. And she seems to like you." She paused and smiled. "There's no accounting for taste."

It had always surprised her that Sophie had never really pestered her to know about her daddy. She had asked Cara once if she had one, and Cara had said that she did and had then made up some kind of mumbled explanation about him living a long way away. She hadn't seemed that bothered about it.

"What did you tell her? I mean, before. Why did you say that I wasn't around?"

"It didn't really come up."

Jack nodded slowly. The machine hissed steam and he wiped it with a cloth. "I suppose she is still pretty young." He seemed to be thinking about something. "Do you think she'll remember not knowing me? I mean, do you think she'll hold it against me later on?"

This was positive. "To be fair, she's more likely to hold it against me. It was my choice, after all."

Now Jack did turn and look at her. "I wish you'd told me."

Cara's throat tightened. In that moment, she wished she had too. Could things have been different between them? "Yeah, well. I'm here now. You get to make a decision for yourself."

Jack frowned. "A decision?"

"Yes. About how involved you want to be in her life, I mean."

Jack leaned on the kitchen island; she was sitting on the other side on a stool. "You think I'm going to turn my back on her? That I don't care for her? Is that what you're trying to suggest?"

She wasn't explaining herself very well. "No. That's not what I meant at all. But having kids, it takes over your life. You've already said that you weren't planning on having any. And you're not even starting out with a tiny baby. You're kind of in at the deep end."

She still remembered how overwhelmed she'd felt when she'd first brought Sophie home from the hospital. How she had plonked her car seat down in the center of her tiny living room and just looked at her. *It's you and me, kid.* She had thought about calling Jack then. The first of several times when she had thought about it over the last four years.

The steam nozzle hissed behind him. "Deep end or not, she's my daughter. And she's a nice girl. Funny. And smart. I like her."

It was ridiculous how quickly Cara's heart skipped at that. Of course, he would have been a monster to think anything else: Sophie *was* a really brilliant kid. "I'm glad you think so."

Jack turned back to the coffee machine and filled the first of the mugs. "And, anyway, you're talking as if the worst has happened, Cara. Let's be positive. You and Sophie will move into your own place soon, and then I'll have her over for weekends, maybe a day in the week? Even a selfish old fool like me can cope with that."

She knew that he was trying to make her smile, but Cara's stomach lurched. Just because this was the right thing to do, it didn't make it any easier. "We'll have to see how it goes, I suppose."

Jack slid her mug toward her. Everything matched in this kitchen—even the mugs were the exact same shade of gray as the tiles behind the worktops. "Of course. We need to take it slow. I'm sure it's a lot to take in for Sophie." He put his own cup under the coffee spout. "So, you really think she likes me?"

Cara laughed. *When did he get so needy?* "You've bought her gifts and you're willing to lie on the floor and play for hours. That puts you pretty high up in Sophie's world."

Now it was his turn to look happy. "Good, I'm pleased. To be honest, I'm surprised how much fun it is to just hang out with her. I haven't spent much time with children. I'm an only child so there's no nephews or nieces on my side, and I've pretty much avoided friends' kids as far as I can."

She already knew that he was an only child. It was odd how he behaved as if they barely knew each other. "What about Rebecca? Didn't she say that she has nephews?"

He shrugged. "Yes, but we don't really see them. We send them gifts at Christmas and on their birthdays, but we probably only see them a couple of times a year. She visits her mum once a month, but she's not that close to her sister."

Had it really been Jack's decision not to have children, or was that Rebecca's choice? Jack definitely seemed more relaxed around

Sophie without his wife there. And then there were the rows she'd overheard the first couple of nights. "What does Rebecca think about you having Sophie in your life?"

He shrugged again. "She knows I have to do it. To be honest, it was Rebecca who was adamant I should step up. I mean, I would have, obviously, but she was very clear about it. Don't worry, there are no issues there. It's not as if she's got to be Sophie's mother, anyway. Sophie already has one of those." He paused. "And now she has a father too."

Cara was glad to hear him say that and, yes, of course Sophie had a mum already. At least she did right now. What would happen if they couldn't shrink these tumors? If she wasn't here anymore? Jack might be ready to step up and be a parent. But what about Rebecca?

CHAPTER TWENTY-TWO

Rebecca

Being an event coordinator meant that Rebecca needed to look the part when she met prospective clients. Therefore, she didn't view a new handbag as an indulgence but more as a work tool. Plus, shopping for a new bag felt like therapy right now.

Izzy brushed the sequins of a clutch bag with something like reverence. "How are things going with Cara and Sophie?"

"Fine, yeah. I bought those books you recommended and Jack ordered some toys and, oh yes, Cara has cancer and might need us to take on Sophie full-time."

Izzy nearly dropped the purse she had picked up. "What the hell? Are you being serious?"

Like she would joke about something like that. "Yep. Apparently, she's been ill for a while. I mean, she looked sick when she first arrived. Still ridiculously attractive but sort of tired-looking. I assumed it was the upheaval of losing her apartment and everything." This was Izzy she was talking to; she might as well be honest. "Actually, I even accused her of taking drugs, which makes *me* the biggest bitch of the year."

Izzy winced. "Ouch. Still, in your defense, you couldn't have known. Why didn't she tell you from the beginning?"

"Apparently, she wanted to check us out. Make sure we would be good parents. Well, I say we, but it was Jack she wanted to get to know." The more Rebecca thought about it, the more she could see this from Cara's point of view. It had been five years since she'd seen Jack; he could have been the last person she wanted to look after her daughter. And she knew nothing about Rebecca at all.

Izzy looked like she understood. "Well, that makes sense, I suppose. And if you hadn't been up to it, what were her other options?"

Rebecca shrugged. It had been difficult broaching the subject with Cara without sounding as if they didn't want to take responsibility for Sophie. And Jack had been next to useless in speaking about it. He was more focused on getting to know Sophie better. "She doesn't seem to have any. She doesn't speak to her parents, and none of her friends appear to be in the financial position to take on another child. Plus, Jack is, of course, Sophie's father."

"Does Sophie know that? Have you told her?"

"She does now. She overheard me talking to Cara."

They were still wandering around the shop, Izzy picking up bags and putting them down again without really looking at them. She'd wanted to treat herself to something new but this bombshell must have put her off. "And how has she reacted to that?"

Weirdly, Sophie seemed to have taken it in stride. Rebecca had steeled herself for a seismic reaction. Surely finding out that the man she had just met was her father would have rocked her world? But Sophie had just accepted it, carried on playing with Jack this morning like he had been a part of her life forever. "She seems fine. Although, I am assuming she'll have questions when she gets older and realizes that he was missing from the first four years of her life."

Izzy nodded slowly. "Yeah. Although kids are remarkable. Life events happen that would tear an adult apart and they seem to be able to roll with it and move on."

That made sense if a child was getting over a broken game or even a lost pet, but this? And poor Sophie might have a lot worse to come. Rebecca picked up a mustard-yellow satchel, exactly the type of thing Izzy loved. "This is perfect for you."

Izzy stroked it lovingly. "That is very pretty but I need something bigger. I'll never fit the kids' snacks, toys, and a packet of wet wipes in there."

Rebecca could practically feel the satchel recoiling in horror. "It's a far cry from when I first met you. Do you remember when you'd go out with little more than a toothbrush and a spare pair of underwear?"

Izzy laughed. "I miss those times. Since having the children, I appear to be on my way to a mini-break every time I leave the house."

"I guess I'm going to have to get used to that too?"

Izzy took the satchel from her and hooked it back on its peg. "It could be worse. It's not like you have to do the whole baby stage. Sophie is four. You've skipped all the messy food and diaper changes."

Izzy knew her well. Rebecca wouldn't have dealt well with either of those things. "I know, and when I thought she'd be coming for weekends I was actually beginning to think I might be able to cope with it. I mean, she's a nice kid and I am used to arranging things to do, right? It might have even been fun to take her out places and spend time with her."

"It can definitely be fun."

Rebecca shook her head. "I saw myself in more of an 'entertaining aunt' role. You know, luxuries and treats and someone she might come and chat with when she was a teenager and her own mother was driving her crazy."

Izzy stopped and stared at her. "Wow. You really had been thinking about this. Although, I shouldn't be surprised. You are, after all, the girl who has a two-week rotating meal plan that changes every season and links to her online shopping app."

Rebecca remembered Izzy's laughter when she'd first told her that. "Well, that's just common sense. Who has time to think up a different meal every night?" Rebecca tried on a trilby and held out her hands for an opinion; Izzy just took it off and handed her a knitted beret. "Try this. So, you won't be the entertaining aunt. You'll be the…what, the…not-wicked stepmother?"

Rebecca pulled the hat down over her eyes. "Oh God, that sounds awful." In her head, pictures of Snow White and Cinderella spun on a loop. "Surely there's a modern word for it?"

Izzy picked out a scarf and tried it on in front of the mirror. "Maybe you could invent one? Patent it and make a fortune. What do you fancy? Extra Mum? Daddy Mum? Fun Mum?"

Rebecca pretended to stick her fingers down her throat. "They're all terrible." She put her hands up to her face and groaned. "I can't believe this is happening."

Izzy stopped and looked at her, reached out for her hand. "Let's go get some coffee. I need caffeine for this."

Costa was full but they managed to find a wobbly table in the corner that everyone else had wisely avoided. Rebecca folded two napkins four times to prop under the leg and stabilize it before Izzy slid a tray onto it. Five minutes standing in line had clearly given her time to process everything—she'd barely sat down before she started speaking. "First of all. Is this definitely happening? Without being completely tactless, is Cara saying that this will definitely be the case? And does she know how long she has?"

It felt so wrong to be talking about this. It was Cara's life they were talking about. Her actual life. But Rebecca needed to talk to someone, and Izzy was her closest friend. She shook her head. "No. At the moment, she's still having treatment. But if it doesn't work, her consultant hasn't been particularly positive about any other options."

"Wow." Izzy sat back in her chair and her eyes filled. "The poor woman."

Rebecca picked up her cup and blew on her coffee, her throat too tight to actually drink it. "I know. Hard to imagine how that must feel."

Izzy let out a breath. "And looking at her little girl, thinking that she won't see..." She looked into Rebecca's eyes. "It's a huge thing, you know. That she's trusting her daughter to you. Her greatest treasure and she's trusting you and Jack to look after her."

Rebecca put down her cup and stared into it, waited for the blur in her vision to right itself. "I know. I know that. But I don't know if I can do it, Izzy. I'm not sure either of us has any clue about what we'd be taking on. What do we know about kids?"

Izzy opened a small packet of cookies and tipped them onto a plate. "What does anyone know until they have them? Honestly, I'd read every baby manual written in the English language and it still hit me sideways."

This is what she was scared of. "That's what I mean. Everyone says how hard it is—when they're not trying to tell me it's the most wondrous thing a woman could ever do and what kind of freak I am for not wanting it, of course. Jack and I, we're pretty selfish people. We like our lives the way they are. He's busy with his job, I'm busy with mine, we schedule our time together and we make it work. But how is a child going to fit into that? This is a little girl's life. A little girl who will have lost her mother. What if we get it wrong? What if we let her down?"

This morning, she had increased her efforts to get to know Sophie and find out what made her happy. All the while she couldn't avoid seeing her as so small, so vulnerable. It all felt too much. She hadn't realized that her hands were trembling until Izzy covered them with her own to stop them. "Hey, you're going to get it wrong. That's part of being a parent."

"You don't get it wrong, though. Every time I see you with your family, the pictures you share online, it's all idyllic. Your life looks so brilliant, you seem so happy with what you've got."

Izzy laughed. "Believe me, when it comes to parenting, things are not always how they seem. I *am* happy. But that doesn't mean I don't find it hard. That I don't think longingly of child-free nights out when no one needs anything from me except the odd witty comment. But you can still have nights out. You just need to plan them in advance." She patted the hand that she was still holding. "You're good at planning."

Rebecca tried to smile. How could she explain to Izzy how she was feeling? If people judged her for not wanting to have a child of her own, how much worse did she sound that she didn't want to take on the child of a woman who might be dying? A child fathered by her own husband? But every time she thought about becoming a full-time mother to Sophie, it felt as if she were drowning. She couldn't breathe. "I can't plan a child's life on a spreadsheet, though, can I?" She tried to smile, but the corners of her mouth wouldn't obey and her chin started to wobble.

"Hey, Bec, it's going to be okay. I know this all feels like you have no control—and I know how you hate that—but you just need to take it a step at a time." Izzy reached down into her bag and brought out her ever-present sticky notes and a pen. "There's a lot of things you can plan for. Whether Sophie is coming for weekends or full-time, she'll need a bedroom. How about we start with that? Order some furniture, look at paint. If you start doing something, it might make it all feel more possible."

Rebecca blew her nose and took a cookie. Izzy was right. This lack of control, the feeling that this was all happening *to* her, was overwhelming. It would help to stop thinking and start doing. "Okay, where do I go to buy bedroom furniture for a little girl?"

CHAPTER TWENTY-THREE

Cara

Dark-wooden reception desk, original modern artwork, and a granite floor: the entrance to Jack's office building was very smart and Cara felt more than a little out of place on Wednesday morning. He'd referred to the name of his advertising agency a couple of times at home, and how he was enjoying their new premises in East London, so it hadn't been difficult to look it up and see that it was in Stratford, only a few stops away from where he and Rebecca lived in Essex.

She approached the receptionist tentatively, holding tightly to Sophie's hand. "Hi, I need to speak to Jack Faulkner."

The young receptionist raised a perfectly styled eyebrow at her. She probably didn't look much like a client with her sweater, jeans, and boots. Oh, and the child in tow. "Is he expecting you?"

"Er, no. I was just popping by on the off-chance that—"

As luck would have it, Jack appeared from a side door holding a pile of papers, which he dropped into a tray on the receptionist's desk. As he turned back to go, she called to him. "Hi, Jack."

Jack turned. Took a moment to realize it was her. "Cara? What are you doing here?"

She couldn't gauge whether that was a pleasantly surprised or uncomfortably shocked tone. The receptionist was also watching in interest. "Sophie and I were out and about. I realized that we were near your office so we thought we'd come by to see if you'd had lunch yet."

She stroked the top of Sophie's head to draw attention to her. Jack looked down at her with a smile. Who could say no to that face? "Hi, Sophie. Er, no, I haven't had a chance to stop for lunch yet. I usually grab a sandwich and eat at my desk, to be honest."

The receptionist picked up a call, so he moved away from the desk toward a group of low leather chairs around an oval glass table. Cara followed him. "Really? I would have thought Rebecca would have made you something super-healthy to bring in."

He laughed. "No. I think that would be above and beyond." He looked as if he was about to start backing toward the doors he'd come through.

She pressed on. "Well, why don't you come out with us, then? Sophie can show you the new drawing things she bought today."

Jack looked hesitant. Was he wondering what Rebecca would say about them going for lunch together? It wasn't as if it was a romantic date—Sophie was there. Cara looked at Sophie, who helped by holding up the shopping bag she'd insisted on carrying. "I've got lots of new colors."

That did the trick. He winked at Sophie and his face seemed to soften. That was promising. "Okay, just give me a minute to grab my jacket. There's a café around the corner that does excellent sandwiches. And cake." He frowned. "Oh, but I forgot. You don't like cake, do you, Sophie?"

Sophie jumped up and down and giggled. "I do! I do! I love cake!"

Cara's chest warmed with pleasure at listening to him teasing his daughter as if he'd done this for years.

The café smelled of good coffee and cake. A glance at the chalk-board price list almost made Cara turn around but they found a seat in the corner and Jack passed her a menu. "I can recommend the club sandwich."

Maybe it was the churning in her stomach that had taken her appetite. With her last chemo session looming, she wanted to get the birth certificate conversation out of the way. It had seemed like a good idea to get Jack alone to give him the form she'd picked up, but how was he going to react? "Actually, can I just get a black coffee for now? Sophie will have a grilled cheese if they have one."

Jack was watching Sophie; he'd been doing that a lot lately. As if he was trying to make up for lost time. Now he looked back at Cara and frowned. "Are you sure you don't want anything? I thought you said you wanted some lunch?"

That had been her excuse to come, and it wouldn't do for him to think she was sneaking behind Rebecca's back. She would have to order something and do her best to eat it. "You're right, maybe I should eat. I'll have a grilled cheese too. Do we pay now or after?"

"Don't worry, I'll get this." Jack took the menu with him to the counter to order.

Normally, she would have argued, hating owing anything to anybody, but she didn't have the energy. Her heart was fluttering in her chest and her breath was short. It was just nerves about how to broach the conversation. *Take it one step at a time.*

While he was gone, Sophie pointed to a child-sized table in the corner that had been set up with crayons and paper. Another little girl who appeared to be about the same age as Sophie was fully focused on what looked like a rainbow. "Can I sit over there, Mummy?"

With Sophie out of earshot, it would be easier to talk to Jack. "You can go over there as long as you promise to come straight back when your sandwich arrives." She kissed her on the top of the head and watched her skip over to the table, sit down, and start chatting with the other little girl, who pushed the container of crayons farther toward Sophie so that they could share. It was so easy to make friends when you were four. Before life had taught you to protect yourself.

There wasn't a line at the counter, which meant Jack was back at the table pretty quickly. "All done. They're going to bring it over."

It was best to get it out there as soon as possible, before their food arrived and Sophie came back to the table. She took a deep breath. "Thanks. Actually, there was another reason I wanted to see you. I picked up the forms from the courthouse last week. So that we can change Sophie's birth certificate."

She took the form from her bag and slid it across the table. Jack looked startled. Was she rushing him? "Oh, good. That's good." He pulled the form from its envelope but only glanced at it. "You could have given this to me tonight, though. There's no rush, is there?"

Cara didn't respond to the rush comment. "It just feels a bit tactless. Giving the form to you in front of Rebecca."

Now he looked confused. "Tactless? Why? It's not as if Rebecca doesn't know what's going on."

It was impossible to put it into words without coming across as difficult. When Sophie had been born, Cara had wondered if she should give him the chance to meet his daughter—for Sophie's sake if not for his. When she'd looked at that tiny baby in her arms, she'd known she would do anything for her. Anything.

Still, she had registered Sophie's birth as "Father Unknown" even though she knew who he was. She wasn't able to do anything else if the father wasn't there with her, anyway. She'd told herself that she would work it out another time. And then a year had gone by before she'd realized it. Then another. And another.

Jack was scrutinizing the form. "This all seems pretty easy and straightforward. Makes it all seem very real." He turned his face to where Sophie had two crayons in her hand at once, drawing two-color patterns with immense concentration. Did he see how amazing she was for only four years old?

Over the years, Cara couldn't fail to notice how much she could see Jack in her daughter. The color of her hair, the crease of concentration at the top of her nose. The feelings were a complex tangle. She had loved Jack. Still loved Jack. But every time she'd seen him in Sophie, it had reminded her that he wasn't there. And that she hadn't given him the chance to be part of Sophie's life. She'd carried the guilt of that too.

"I'm sure this feels fast, becoming a dad to a four-year-old overnight. But it's difficult for me, too, you know."

Jack slipped the form back into the envelope and looked at her. "Difficult?"

From the moment she'd picked up the birth certificate form, this thought had been creeping up from the back of her brain. She had been so focused on getting to this stage—meeting Jack, telling him about Sophie, ensuring he wanted to be involved in her life—that she was only now reflecting on what that meant. For all of them. "Once you sign that form and we get it certified, Sophie will belong to you as much as she does to me. I won't be able to make decisions about where we live or where she goes to school without consulting you. That's going to feel pretty strange."

The waitress appeared at the table with their drinks and Sophie ran over for a slurp of the pink strawberry milk shake that Jack had bought for her, then she ran back to the table and her new friend.

Jack tipped sugar from the chrome-topped dispenser onto a spoon. She hadn't noticed him having sugar at home. Maybe Rebecca didn't approve. "I hadn't thought about it being difficult for you in that way. I can see how it will take a bit of getting used to. You don't need to worry, though. You seem to be doing a pretty great job with her right now. I can't imagine I'm going to ask you to change anything. It's not as if I know the first thing about bringing up a little girl."

Cara kept her eyes on Sophie as she spoke, her chest tight. It wasn't really Jack she had been thinking about. Jack, she knew how to handle. "But what about Rebecca?"

"Rebecca?" Jack stopped stirring his coffee. His guarded tone almost made her lose her nerve.

But she needed to talk about the way she was feeling, needed to be sure before his signature on the form launched them into a new reality. "What if Rebecca has opinions about the way I bring up Sophie? What if she tells you that I'm doing something wrong? Or that she could do it better? What then?"

Jack put down the form and looked at her intently. "I don't know what you want me to say, Cara. Rebecca isn't like that. She's not going to have big opinions on child-rearing. She's not even into kids."

Cara didn't know what would be worse: if Rebecca tried to take over or if she had no interest at all. It felt as if everything was slipping through her fingers; she was losing control. "I'm just saying that you're her father. You should be the one who makes the decisions. After me, of course."

Jack sat up straight. Cara could imagine this face in business mode, holding a meeting with his team. "Obviously, we are going to need to sit down and talk about the logistics. You know that Rebecca is on board. She's the one who spent half of Sunday ordering furniture to get the back bedroom ready for Sophie; the one who has been pushing me into getting a regular routine agreed for her. I think she has taken all this really well, to be honest."

He was defending her. Cara needed to tread carefully if she was to get this right. "I know. She has. It's just, I'm not sure she is that keen on me, and that makes me worry how she is going to be with Sophie."

Jack sighed, ran a hand over his face. Surely he could understand her concerns. "That's not true. Rebecca—"

"Rebecca doesn't want children. She was very honest about that. I'm Sophie's mother. And you are her father. We are the ones who need to make any decisions. Together."

Jack twisted in his seat. "I understand what you are saying, Cara, I do. But Rebecca isn't about to start—"

"Promise me, Jack. Promise me that you will be a father to Sophie and not sit back and let Rebecca take over. She is *your* daughter."

Jack glanced over at Sophie then back at Cara. "I promise."

CHAPTER TWENTY-FOUR

Rebecca

Answering a call from a valuable client—whatever she was in the middle of—was event planning 101. But when that client called her sixteen times in twenty-four hours, there had to be a limit to professionalism. Rebecca pressed the end call button and returned her mobile to the windowsill. Samantha would have to wait.

Now that the clothes rails and boxes had been moved elsewhere, the back room seemed bigger. Definitely large enough for a small four-year-old girl. Although he usually enjoyed getting involved with the paint charts and fabric swatches—if not the finer details involved in getting the work done—it hadn't taken much to persuade Jack to give her free rein with the decor in here. If anything, he'd seemed relieved.

Rebecca stood in the middle of the room and took in the overall effect. Sunshine-yellow paint to match the polka dots on the new duvet cover had been a good choice: bright, welcoming, and positive. After Cara had admitted that she'd invented the idea of an available apartment, they'd all agreed she and Sophie should stay put until her final chemo treatment was over and she felt strong enough to move. Then they would help her find a place for the two of them and this room would still be Sophie's when she came to stay here. Any circumstances under which that didn't happen were too awful to contemplate.

Rebecca touched the wall lightly to check whether the paint had dried. Like Izzy had said, Sophie would have to have her own room either way. The walls were going to need a second coat tomorrow, but it was bright enough for Sophie to get the effect when she saw it later. Painting had also been good therapy for working out the frustration of the incessant calls from Samantha and every "just a little thought" that had entered her head in the last day.

It wasn't just Samantha who had irritated Rebecca; she was also annoyed with Jack. First, because he'd met Cara for lunch yesterday. It wasn't so much that they'd met up without her—although that was uncomfortable—but that he'd mentioned it as an afterthought when they'd got into bed last night. Apparently, Cara had "been in the area."

On top of that, after saying she could go ahead and order whatever she wanted for the bedroom, Jack had backtracked and warned her that she was moving too fast. "You need to give us all time to adjust before changing things." He was too late anyway; the furniture was being delivered today. Why was he not getting it that she needed to have something constructive to do? That this was something nice she could do for Sophie?

The bedroom window opened onto their back garden and she pushed it as wide as it would go to let the smell of the paint escape. Their garden wasn't huge but it was pretty. One of the weddings Izzy had coordinated last year was for a garden planner by the name of Tony who had been so happy with the wedding that he had offered his landscaping services to them at a reduced rate. Tony had done a fantastic job on theirs: a small patio for barbecues that they used as an overflow for parties and then a long lawn surrounded by bright bedding plants at various heights. Would they have to spoil the whole effect now by getting a swing on the grass? Maybe some kind of jungle gym?

She was done arguing with Jack about the Sophie situation. Co-parenting a child neither of them had planned was going to be a big test of their relationship, of course it was. But loving someone meant sticking by them. The anger that had bitten her for the first few days after Cara and Sophie had arrived had gone. Now that she knew about Cara's illness, she just wanted to get everything straight in her head.

Late last night, she'd washed, dried, and ironed the new bedding so that it would be ready to go on the bed today. Sophie wouldn't be able to sleep in here until the paint dried, but it had given Rebecca something to do other than watch Cara and Jack together. Jealousy wasn't an attractive trait and she didn't like to think of herself as showing it. The duvet cover was already inside out so she pushed her hands inside it to the bottom edge, gripped the corners of the duvet and started to shake the cover down it. Possibly a little more vigorously than was completely necessary.

She'd seen enough of her friends and relatives with children to understand the level of commitment that parenting entailed. For people with children, life took a certain shape. The baby years, transportation to and from school, saving for college. Even holidays were largely organized around their children.

But not having kids had meant they could shape their lives the way they wanted them to be. Their year wasn't structured according to school holidays. They didn't have to check hotel bookings to ensure they allowed children or the menus at restaurants to make sure there was something that a small person might want to eat. These things sounded trivial if said aloud, but it was a complete culture change.

She laid the duvet on the floor. This room had effectively been used as an overflow wardrobe because they already had the guest room, which Cara and Sophie were in now. When they'd bought this big house, it had attracted the obvious jokes from Jack's colleagues and friends who didn't know them well about filling it with children. Maybe the overenthusiastic real estate agent had known something that they didn't.

Still, as Jack kept trying to reassure her, it wasn't as if their lives were going to change completely. Cara would have her last chemo appointment on Monday. As soon as she was well enough, they could help her move into her own place—somewhere nice and hopefully not too far away—and that's where Sophie would live for the bulk of the week. They would still be free to do as they wanted most of the time. It just required them to factor in the weeks they wouldn't necessarily be able to go out to a nice restaurant or book a weekend away. To be organized.

And that was why, as she'd tried to explain to Jack, she had been pushing to know what the schedule was likely to be. Until they had a concrete idea of when they would have Sophie, she couldn't even begin to make sure that everything else worked.

The doorbell rang. She checked her watch: they were right on time.

On the front step, a delivery driver smiled broadly. "Morning, ma'am. Furniture delivery?"

"Fantastic, thanks. I'm all ready for you."

He returned to the back of his van, where his coworker was waiting to lift down a wardrobe. They struggled to the door with it and then through to the hallway. "Where do you want it?"

"Upstairs in the bedroom if you don't mind?" She didn't want Sophie to come home and see it in the hall. It would spoil the surprise.

The men put it down in the hall, and one of them let out a long sigh. "No problem, but you'll have to give us a minute. This thing is heavy."

Rebecca smiled. "Would you like me to make you a cup of tea while you do it?"

The deliveryman winked. "That would be marvelous. Two sugars for me and three for Pete, please."

She met them back in the hallway with two cups of tea to find they had already taken up the bed, the storage unit, and the matching wardrobe. "That was quick."

They both held out their hands for the tea. This time it was Pete who spoke while the other guy caught his breath. "That's a nice bit of furniture you've bought there. Solid. We didn't push it against any walls because of the wet paint. I bet your little one is going to love that bedroom. Very pretty."

Rebecca opened her mouth to say that Sophie wasn't her "little one" and then closed it again. Sophie was Jack's child. She *was* the little one in their family. People would look at the three of them together and probably assume that she was Sophie's mother. What was Sophie going to call her? At home, she would just call her Rebecca, of course. But how would she refer to her when she spoke to other people? "My dad's wife" made her sound like an afterthought. But stepmother?

The men finished their tea in about five gulps and handed back the mugs. "Thank you. We'd better get on."

The furniture looked perfect in the room as she had known it would. There were six fabric storage cubes that needed to be unpacked: red, yellow, dark blue, light blue, dark green, and light green to match the polka dots on the duvet cover. She assembled them and slotted them into the low unit. *Perfect.* Hopefully, Sophie would think so too.

She could do this. The stepmother didn't need to be the mother. Cara had that one covered.

CHAPTER TWENTY-FIVE

Cara

The chemo room at the King George Cancer Unit had been made as comfortable as the National Health Service could stretch to, but it was impossible not to feel the usual level of dread on Monday morning at the sight of the high-backed chairs around the walls.

"Hi, Cara. Good to see you, sweetness. How are you feeling today?" Angie smiled at her—all the cancer nurses were so kind. Even so, hopefully this would be the last time she saw them.

"Not too bad at the moment. Although that's about to change this week, obviously."

The first week after chemo was the worst. Nausea, headaches, throwing up: like the worst hangover she'd ever had in her life times a hundred. That's why she'd timed the knock on Jack's door when she had: it gave her the maximum amount of time while she was feeling well enough to be able to hide what was really going on.

"We'll get you hooked up and then I'll go and make you a cup of tea. Marjorie brought us in a huge tin of cookies this morning so I'll bring you some of those too." Angie nodded in the direction of an older lady with short white hair, who waved. Her husband was sitting next to her, reading the *Guardian*. A lot of people had someone come with them at least the first few times. Six hours was a long time to sit in the same place alone.

However nice everyone was, sitting here was probably the most on her own Cara had felt since giving birth to Sophie. She had been alone on the labor ward then too. Thankfully, Sophie's birth had been relatively short and uncomplicated. How she would have managed with a C-section recovery, she didn't know. That was typical Sophie, though. She was the easiest kid in the world.

"Okay, love, let's see your hand." The corners of Angie's eyes crinkled when she smiled, her light blue eyeshadow the same shade as her uniform.

Cara held out an arm and Angie took hold of her hand for the cannula, rubbing above her knuckles with her capable thumbs. The crinkle around her eyes changed to a crease across her forehead. Each time, it got more difficult to find a vein that worked. "Hmmm. This one doesn't look promising. Can I have a look at the other one?"

Cara offered up her right hand. It was amazing how quickly she'd got used to this. Blood tests. Chemo. More blood tests. It wasn't surprising her poor veins were recoiling inside of her or giving up altogether.

Angie was tapping the side of Cara's right thumb. "I think this might be a good one, although it'll be a bit awkward. Can you eat cookies with your other hand?" She smiled and Cara nodded.

Marjorie's husband had folded his newspaper and was holding it in front of them both. *They must be doing a crossword together.* They looked like any old-aged couple if you squinted one eye so that you couldn't see the tube connected to her hand. Marjorie looked remarkably well, and unless that was a very good wig, she also still had her own hair. Cara guessed it was only her first or second time.

"Ouch." The word escaped before Cara had a chance to suppress it. She didn't like to make a fuss—the nurses had a difficult enough job as it was. "Sorry."

Angie gave her a motherly rub on the arm. "No, I'm sorry, sweet. It's all done now. I'll go and get your tea."

This room was the one public place where Cara would be seen without her wig. Even Sophie had never seen her without it. Setting an alarm every day for the last few months, she had always managed to put it on before Sophie woke up. It was a relief to slip it off.

Now that the chemo had started, she let her head fall back and closed her eyes. At least now that Rebecca and Jack knew what was going on, she wouldn't have to hide it from them anymore.

She leaned down to take her mobile from her bag. It was awkward trying to use it with her left hand, but she managed to scroll through her pictures. She'd made an album of the pictures of Sophie, starting when she was a scrawny newborn, through chubby toddlerhood, to the bright, sparky four-year-old she'd become. Sophie loved it when she whizzed through them quickly, making it look as if she were growing up before their very eyes. Cara had made the album as something to focus on when the treatment made her feel bad. Now her eyes blurred as she got to the final picture: Sophie with a straw in a strawberry milk shake as big as her head. The picture blurred and she pulled a tissue from the box beside her to wipe her eyes.

Rebecca had offered to come with her today. That had been surprising; maybe it was her way of trying to make up for being so suspicious. Cara couldn't blame her for that. It wasn't as if she'd known what was going on. Long sleeves to hide the tracks on her arms, makeup to cover her sallow complexion, a short dark wig, time spent upstairs with Sophie where she'd actually just lain on the bed to recover some strength: she had been a master at disguising this damn disease.

And Rebecca had made a real effort in the last couple of days. She'd even made the back bedroom into a proper little girl's room: bright colors, coordinating boxes for toys, a bookshelf. Sophie had been so excited to see the desk that Rebecca had laid out with drawing paper and markers and colors in a little cup. *Money can't buy happiness, but it sometimes has a damn good try.*

When it had just been the two of them, Cara hadn't been able to give Sophie her own room. Their apartment hadn't been that bad, really. A small living room with enough space for a sofa, a TV, and a low cabinet. A tiny kitchen beyond with appliances that were old but clean and functional. She should have moved out when Sophie was old enough to need her own room but it had been impossible to find something with two bedrooms that was as decent as the one they had. Instead, Sophie had a small single bed along the wall of Cara's bedroom that she had painted pink for her: a princess bed.

When she'd called Lee to confirm that she was giving up the apartment, he'd been really understanding, even sounding a little choked up when she explained why. Her original deposit would cover any outstanding rent so there was no problem there, but saying good-bye to the flat had been harder than she'd anticipated; it had been their home since Sophie was six months old. She'd pulled herself up on their secondhand brown leather sofa and taken her first wobbly steps across the living room floor, bottle in hand, laughing like a happy drunk on a Friday night. Cara had knelt near the wall, arms outstretched, ready to catch her if she fell. Would Sophie even remember that they had lived there? Even if she did, how could it compete with the bright new room of her own that Rebecca had given her? It wasn't fair.

God, this was boring. Rebecca had given her a couple of books to read and she had taken them so as not to look ungrateful, but she knew she wouldn't read them; her mind wouldn't stay still long enough to follow the plot. Time went backward in here, and she hadn't found anything that could distract her thoughts. Maybe that was why other patients brought people with them; being forced to speak to someone else might be the only solution.

It was difficult not to picture how they'd looked in the sitting room yesterday: the three of them. To anyone looking in, they would have seemed the perfect family on a Sunday afternoon.

Handsome father, attractive mother, beautiful daughter. Jack looked as if he'd been drinking from Sophie's toy teacup set for years and Rebecca had spent more time getting to know Sophie over the weekend too. Asking her so many questions about preschool and friends and favorite foods that it had sounded like a job interview. Sophie hadn't minded; she liked nothing better than a captive audience for the outpourings of her four-year-old brain. On Saturday, they'd cooked together again too. Cupcakes. Cara hadn't had Rebecca pegged for a home baker but it turned out there really wasn't anything that woman couldn't do.

Sophie had been so proud of her tray full of cakes. The most amusing part had been Rebecca hovering over her as she iced them, trying to ensure some kind of symmetry. She had a lot to learn if she thought Sophie cared a jot about things looking even. She was definitely from the ad hoc school of creative output.

Cara should have been happy, of course she should have. Rebecca didn't even want children, yet here she was making every effort to do things with Sophie and even change her home around for her. However ungrateful it might seem, though, Cara couldn't stop feeling that it was too much, too soon. Despite Jack's promise to take the lead, Rebecca was taking over, and Cara didn't like it. Hopefully, now that Rebecca had shown that she was on board by creating the perfect bedroom, she would back off a bit. Otherwise, once Cara was back on her feet again, they would need to have a conversation about boundaries. She was Sophie's mother, not Rebecca.

CHAPTER TWENTY-SIX

Rebecca

Rebecca was so grateful to Izzy for seeing things more clearly than she could; her advice had been absolutely spot-on. Getting the bedroom set up last Thursday had been a great start. Although it was now Wednesday, and Sophie hadn't actually slept in the bed yet, she clearly loved the room and wanted to play in there whenever she could.

Cara had looked less impressed, which was a little disappointing. Although, to be fair, she'd looked too hollowed out to be enthusiastic about anything. Rebecca had never been this close to someone going through cancer treatment before, had no idea how poorly it could make you feel. The sickness was pretty common knowledge, but it was more than that. Cara looked different. As if the spark in her eyes had gone.

This morning, she must have been bone-tired because Sophie was up first. She came down to the kitchen on her own.

Rebecca glanced behind her, surprised not to see Cara following. "Good morning, Sophie. Where's Mummy?"

Sophie was chewing on the sleeve of her pajamas. "She's sleeping. I can't wake her up."

Rebecca's heart was in her mouth as she took the stairs two at a time, but when she knocked gently on Cara's door then pushed it open, Cara stirred on her pillow and tried to push herself out of bed, her voice thick with sleep. "Where's Sophie? I'm sorry, I was up half the night and..."

It was a shock to see her without her wig. In some ways, her face was more beautiful, her eyes bigger and bluer, her cheekbones more defined. But there was also a vulnerability that Rebecca hadn't seen in her before. Was this what Jack had seen in her? Still saw? "Don't worry about Sophie. I'll get her some breakfast and take her to preschool. You go back to sleep."

For a second, Cara looked like she was going to argue, but her body had other ideas. She sank back into the pillows. "Thank you. I'll pick her up later and..." She was asleep again before finishing the sentence.

Sophie was very quiet on the drive to her preschool, but she seemed happy enough once there, and she waved good-bye to Rebecca from the door. This time, there were quite a few dads and grandmas dropping the children off; lots of family members offering support.

On the way back, she drove past St. Catherine's and remembered that was where Cara wanted Sophie to enroll. She pulled over down the street and walked back.

St. Catherine's was housed in a large Victorian building hidden behind a tall black wrought-iron fence. The intercom system was far more modern than that, as was the electric gate that buzzed open when she told the receptionist who answered that she wanted to pick up an application form and brochure. Walking across the playground, she noticed hopscotch and chutes and ladders chalked onto the tarmac. Childhood games didn't seem to have changed since she was Sophie's age.

The reception area was just large enough for a table and two chairs upholstered in the same shade of green as the school sign. A man of about Rebecca's age stood at the reception window, speaking to the receptionist who had buzzed her in.

"Sorry. It's usually Albie's mum who drops him off. He stayed over with me last night because she's away. I just wanted to double-check that you know to call me if he needs anything today. He was a little bit unsettled this morning."

The receptionist knew how to deal with anxious parents. "I'm sure he'll be fine, Mr. Robson. His mum is on her honeymoon, isn't she? She explained that he'd be with his dad for the week."

Mr. Robson looked even more unsettled than before. "Yes. He stays with me all the time, anyway. Just not usually on weeknights when he has school. I wanted to make sure that you'd call me today if he needs me."

The receptionist picked up a pen and glanced down at her work before giving Mr. Robson a polite smile. "Of course. We have your number on file. I've already put a note on there to make you the primary contact for this week."

Rebecca recognized the obvious cues for him to leave and, after a moment's hesitation, it seemed Mr. Robson did too. "Great. Thank you."

The receptionist already had the school's information ready to hand over to Rebecca, and the phone on her desk rang to demand her attention, so Rebecca didn't hang around.

Mr. Robson was finishing up a call and getting into the car next to hers. He nodded at the materials in Rebecca's hand. "It's a very good school. My son, Albie, loves it here. Have you got a son or a daughter?"

"Oh, no, I haven't…" She realized how odd that sounded when she had just been inside the school to get enrollment information. "It's for my husband's daughter. His…ex-girlfriend is thinking of applying here."

Mr. Robson nodded. "Families come in all shapes and sizes, right?" He smiled and waved as he opened his car door and got in. "Good luck."

If only he knew how much she might need that.

*

Back at home, Rebecca checked on Cara, who was still asleep, and then made herself a cup of coffee to take into her office. Before starting work, she flicked through the brochure. It was pretty impressive. According to the accompanying letter, applications for entry to St. Catherine's needed to be in by the beginning of January. The open day for new applicants had been on October 3: they'd missed it by three weeks. Although maybe Cara had gone? She'd have to ask her. It had looked like a really nice school from the outside, and it would be easier if Sophie went to a school close to their house.

The next hour was spent returning phone calls from prospective new clients and making appointments. In between, though, she looked up the St. Catherine's website and their assessment report. The more she read, the more she could see what an excellent school it was. And hadn't Izzy said that people actually moved into the area to get their kids into it? She picked up the phone.

"Jack Faulkner."

"Hi, it's me."

As it always did, Jack's voice slid from clipped business tone to warm. "Hey, what's up? Nothing to do? Have you run out of coffee?"

"Very funny. Actually, I was calling to ask whether you'd spoken to Cara about school applications. I picked up a brochure for St. Catherine's today and it looks perfect for Sophie."

Jack didn't reply right away. "Where did you get a brochure from?"

That was a weird question. "From the school, of course. I dropped Sophie off at preschool because Cara was tired. The school was on my way back."

"I see."

Why was he being so strange about this? "It's just a brochure, Jack. Although, if we are going to apply there, it has to be by the beginning of January. Izzy said that it's really hard to get in, so—"

"Izzy said? Was she there too?"

Rebecca took the phone away from her ear and looked at it in exasperation before putting it back to her mouth. "No, Jack. Of course she wasn't there. What's got into you?"

Jack sighed on the other end of the phone. "I just think you need to slow down a bit, Bec. We can't be telling Cara where to send Sophie to school."

Heat rose to Rebecca's cheeks. That was unfair. "I'm just trying to be supportive, Jack."

"I know that, Becca. But we have to tread carefully, you know. We don't want Cara to think we're taking over."

Taking over? For goodness' sake, Cara was the one who had first mentioned the damn school. "Do you want me to be interested in your daughter or not, Jack?"

Now his tone was more conciliatory. Which was even more irritating. "Of course, of course, just... just take it slowly."

She couldn't win. "Look, I've got to go, Jack. I need to email some venues out to a client."

"Don't be like that, Bec. I just don't want to step on Cara's toes. The bedroom and now the school. It feels too... pushy, I suppose. I'm just saying that we've got to take it slowly. Both of us."

"I'll see you later."

Once she'd ended the call, she threw her mobile down on the desk in frustration. Jack hadn't been taking it slowly the other day when he'd spent a small fortune on toys that he and Sophie could play with. So why was her decorating a bedroom and picking up a brochure so "pushy"?

He needed to understand that it wasn't in her nature to be the kind of person who rolled around on the floor with Sophie, or blew bubbles with the hand soap. But this was something she *could* do. Researching schools, suggesting living arrangements, maybe even throwing birthday parties down the line—these were ways she could contribute.

Cara had thanked her for doing the preschool drop-off this morning, and Sophie's face when she had shown her the bedroom had been a picture. Jack needed to stop worrying about what they could and couldn't do and let her be a part of Sophie's life in the best way she could. Like Izzy had said, she should play to her strengths.

Speaking of Izzy, she needed to wrap and send her gift. She had been back to the shop yesterday and bought her that yellow satchel as a thank-you. Even if it was impractical, she wanted her to have it. While she was there, she'd seen a whole range of hair accessories for little girls and picked up some really cute red hairbands with bows on them. Surely even Jack wouldn't think that giving these to Sophie would be "too pushy"?

CHAPTER TWENTY-SEVEN

Cara

If there was one thing guaranteed to make Cara feel a failure as a mother, it was hair. Sophie's friends at preschool often had intricate braided creations far beyond her capabilities. In a pinch, she could manage a ponytail, pigtails, or a basic braid. Now and again, Sophie would ask her for more, but—try as she might—Cara just couldn't do it. Even step-by-step tutorials on YouTube didn't help: her fingers just wouldn't work in that way. It had been the same when an ex-boyfriend had tried to teach her to play the guitar. At least he had given up eventually; poor Sophie seemed to live in eternal hope that one day her mother might learn to give her the hairstyle of her dreams.

All of this explained Sophie's unbridled delight when Rebecca offered to French braid her hair on Thursday afternoon. The ensuing excitement was on a par with Christmas plus Easter multiplied by a birthday. "Really? You can do it?"

Rebecca laughed. "It's been a while, but I'm sure I'll remember when I get going. You need four sections of hair—that's right, isn't it?"

She had directed her question to Cara, who shrugged. "Don't ask me. I've never managed one in my life."

This time round, the side effects of the chemo were worse than ever before. Even the extra antinausea medication wasn't stopping her from vomiting, and the exhaustion was debilitating. Maybe it was because she wasn't the only one to look after Sophie now? She was psychologically allowing herself to feel ill whereas before she'd had to be the one to prepare meals or take her to preschool. When she was pregnant, an old woman on the bus had told her that morning sickness was the sign of a healthy baby. If only that old wives' tale signified a healthy result with the chemo. Sick of staying in bed, she'd decamped to the sofa, alternately dozing and watching Sophie play on the floor.

Rebecca dragged a stool from the kitchen to the living room to raise Sophie to the right height, then stood behind her like a stylist. She put on a posh accent. "And what would madam like this afternoon?"

Sophie giggled. "A French braid, please!"

Normally, Sophie would cry out as if Cara were murdering her, but as Rebecca brushed through her hair to detangle it, Sophie pursed her lips together, seemingly determined not to make any kind of noise that might make her stop. Each tug against a tangle caught in Cara's chest. There was something so maternal in the movements; a stranger coming into the room now would assume that Rebecca was Sophie's mother. It hit Cara like a bolt to her stomach: if Dr. Green had bad news, Rebecca soon might be.

"You have beautiful hair, Soph. Your curls look much better on you than they do on Jack." Rebecca smiled at Cara, who tried to smile in return. Rebecca was making an effort with both of them, that was obvious, and Cara should have reciprocated, however difficult it was to look cheerful when what she wanted to do was break down and cry from the unfairness of it all. And when had Rebecca started calling her *Soph*? Cara was the only one who called her that.

Sophie beamed at the compliment. Then ratted Cara out. "Mummy wants me to cut it all off."

"I didn't say that." Cara could hear that her voice sounded strangled, so she coughed to clear her throat. *Get it together.* "I just said it would be easier to manage if it was shorter. And I only say that when you accuse me of trying to pull it out. Maybe if you were as quiet with me as you're being with Rebecca, I wouldn't say it."

Sophie stared forward, didn't even look at her. "Rebecca doesn't hurt me."

It wasn't Sophie's fault that those words were slicing into Cara. Rebecca held up her strange-looking brush. "It's called a Tangle Teezer. My friend recommended it. It's brilliant at getting any knots out."

Cara nodded, not trusting herself to speak. Just one more thing to add to the list of things that Rebecca did better than her. She should have been pleased that Sophie was happy, pleased that Rebecca wanted to spend time with her daughter, giving her what she wanted. What kind of mother did it make her that she wasn't happy? That she was totally and utterly and horribly jealous?

Rebecca finished the flawless braid and looked around for a hairband. "Shoot—I've left the new hairbands in my handbag in the kitchen." She held the end of the braid up to Cara. "Are you able to hold this for a second?"

"Of course." Cara eased herself off the couch, legs as heavy as lead. Holding the ends of Sophie's hair to stop it from unraveling exposed her beautiful neck, a soft fuzz running like a seam from the bottom of her hairline. It had always been her most ticklish place. When Sophie was a small baby, Cara would only have to blow gently on it to make Sophie collapse into giggles. She bent forward now and put her lips on the warm dent where Sophie's neck met her shoulder.

Sophie wriggled her shoulder. "Stop it, Mummy, you will mess up my hair."

Before Cara could respond, Rebecca walked back in with a packet of hairbands with small red bows held aloft. When had she bought those? "Found them!"

Cara swallowed the lump in her throat. "You won't get her to wear that one. She hates red, don't you, Soph*ie*?" She emphasized the last syllable of Sophie's name.

Sophie's eyes moved but her face still pointed forward. "Actually, red is my new favorite color."

Since when did she start sentences with words like "actually"? And Cara could pretty much guess what Rebecca's favorite color was before she even asked. She collapsed back onto the couch. Watched as Rebecca fixed the bow to the bottom of the braid and then helped Sophie off the kitchen stool so that she could run to the bathroom and admire herself.

Rebecca watched her go and then turned to Cara with a smile. "It's amazing how it all comes back to you. I can remember spending hours doing my hair and my sister's hair."

"Well, I think you've got yourself a job for life there. Sophie will be wanting all kinds of styles now that she knows you're a whizz with a brush." She hadn't meant to sound bitter but it was hard not to let the acid in her gut come out of her mouth.

Rebecca looked startled. "You don't mind, do you?"

Cara shrugged. "Of course not. Does me a favor. She won't be bugging me to do it now that she has her own in-house hairdresser."

Rebecca nodded, looked down at the brush in her hand.

Sophie came running in. "It looks amazing. Can you take a picture, Mummy? Can you? Take a picture on your phone."

Cara forced a smile. She was being petty, and it wasn't fair to spoil Sophie's excitement. "Of course. It's in my bag in the bedroom. Why don't you go and get it for me?"

Sophie ran off again with her braid flapping behind her.

As soon as she was out of earshot, Rebecca turned to Cara. "I'm sorry if I overstepped. I just..."

This was where Cara should have apologized for her tone. Where she should have said that she was glad that Rebecca could do that for Sophie. Pleased that she was spending time with her, getting to know her. But she just felt angry, really angry, and it was hard to control right now. "It's nothing. I'm not feeling great and there's a lot on my mind."

Cara used the back of her hand to wipe away the tears in her eyes, bit her lip to stop any more from coming.

Rebecca seemed unsure what to say so she plumped for the old platitudes. "Is your appointment playing on your mind? Try not to think the worst. There are new treatments all the time. If you keep fighting, you can beat it."

Of course she would keep fighting. She'd fight as hard as she could to spend as long as she could with Sophie. But she needed to be realistic too. To make plans for Sophie's future, plans that didn't include her. However painful that was. Because wasn't that what every mother had to do? Put their child before themselves? She could hear Sophie running back down the stairs so she didn't react. Just gritted her teeth and nodded.

Sophie ran into the room holding Rebecca's phone in front of her, her mission to retrieve Cara's seemingly forgotten. "Your phone was on the stairs. It keeps ringing and ringing."

Rebecca took it from her. "Thank you. I must have left it there earlier. Well done for hearing it." She glanced at the display and grimaced. "I need to get this."

She walked into the kitchen and left the two of them alone. Sophie was jiggling about in excitement but keeping her head straight so the braid didn't fall out somehow.

Cara winked at her. "Give me another twirl, then."

Sophie turned slowly so that Cara could get the full effect. She looked so grown-up with her hair off her face. It was as if Cara were getting a glimpse of the young woman she would become.

Rebecca wasn't long on the phone and she had a strange expression on her face when she came back into the room. "That was the bride for the wedding I'm coordinating this Saturday. Samantha. Sophie met her two weeks ago. One of her flower girls has chicken pox and can't make it to the wedding." She looked at Cara meaningfully and side-nodded toward Sophie, obviously not wanting to spell it out too clearly and get her hopes up before Cara said it was okay.

As if Cara would stop her. "She wants Sophie to do it?"

The sharp intake of breath from Sophie was a clear indication that she hadn't guessed that was what Rebecca meant and also that she would be absolutely ecstatic to step in. She looked at Rebecca, who nodded. "Yes. She thinks Sophie is the same size."

"I'm not sure Sophie would want to do that, would you, Sophie?"

Cara made her face as serious as she could to tease her daughter, who jumped up and down and squealed. "Yes! Yes! Please! Can I? Can I?"

Cara looked at Rebecca. "I think that's a yes."

"Great. I'll call Samantha back and put her out of her misery. Heaven forbid she should have an uneven number of flower girls. Looks like you're going to get your hair styled by a proper professional on Saturday, Sophie. Not just a pretend one like me."

Sophie was looking at Rebecca as if she were a fairy godmother. Cara could almost feel her heart twisting in her chest.

CHAPTER TWENTY-EIGHT

Rebecca

Saturday morning at 10:00 a.m., the outside of Samantha's mother's house was lit up like a Christmas tree. Everywhere she looked there were fairy lights. Sophie's face was almost as bright when they got out of the car; it must have seemed like a palace to her.

When she saw the dress that she was going to wear, she looked as if it actually were Christmas. "It's so pretty."

As Samantha had predicted, the dress was a perfect fit. Pale blue silk, little cap sleeves, a calf-length skirt: Sophie looked beautiful. She twirled around so many times she made herself dizzy.

The whole top floor of the house had been taken over as a staging area. Makeup artists in one bedroom, hairstylists in another, dresses hanging in a third. The large rectangular landing was as busy as the concourse of Liverpool Street Station: with more bling.

Rebecca hadn't been able to get close to Samantha yet as she was surrounded by a brush-wielding woman and a force field of hair spray, but now she was waving her over. Sophie held tightly to Rebecca's hand.

Samantha looked like a movie star. Her blond hair was sculpted into large waves and her makeup was a work of art. Wrapped in a white robe, she sipped pink champagne from a glass flute with a glittery stem, and her arms were as wide as her smile as she held them out to welcome them.

"Sophie, baby, you look absolutely gorgeous in that dress. Thank you so much for being my emergency flower girl; I've got a little present for you later. Do you want to have some makeup done?"

Sophie looked up at Rebecca with eyes as big as tea plates, a puppy begging for a treat. "Am I allowed? Please?"

Oh, damn. She hadn't thought to ask Cara about that, and after Cara's reaction to the hair braiding on Thursday, she didn't want to step out of line again. Still, she didn't want to call her now in case she was sleeping. The aftereffects of the chemo had had her throwing up in the early hours of this morning. Rebecca glanced in the direction of one of the other flower girls, who was in seventh heaven as the makeup artist stroked shadow onto her eyelids. "Er, have you even had makeup on before?"

Samantha rolled her eyes. "They are professionals, Rebecca. They won't cake her in it. Just a little bit won't hurt."

That was easy for her to say. She wasn't the one who was responsible for someone else's child. She looked back at Sophie, who was biting her lip in nervous excitement. "Okay. Maybe just a little bit."

She turned to walk Sophie over to where the beautician had set up, but Samantha caught her arm. "Can I talk to you quickly for a minute?"

She seemed nervous about something. Hopefully it was something that could be resolved quickly. Now that Rebecca was here with Sophie rather than at the venue, she wanted to get on the phone and make some last-minute checks. She leaned down. "Do you want to go and look at the makeup, Soph? I'll be over in a minute."

Sophie looked uncertain about leaving her, but Samantha gave her the final nudge. "Quick. Go now before she changes her mind about the makeup."

The lure of the lipstick proved stronger than her fear of going alone. Sophie let go of Rebecca's hand. "Will you come over soon?"

Rebecca nodded. "I promise."

As soon as Sophie had skipped off, Samantha lowered her voice. "I didn't get around to showing my mum the seating plan until this morning. She's kicking off about it—doesn't think my stepmum should be at the head table. She reckons it should just be her and my dad from my side."

What had she been thinking, waiting until the day of the wedding to break this news? Not that she could argue with the bride right now either. "Okay. But you obviously do want your stepmum there?"

Samantha pulled a face. "Of course I want her there. She's been with my dad since I was ten. I love her and I want her to be part of it all."

Rebecca took her eyes off of Sophie for a minute and gave Samantha her attention. "Then you need to have her there. It's your wedding."

"I know. But I want everyone to be happy today." Samantha put her hands together in prayer. "Can you talk to her, please?"

This was why she hated doing weddings. There was always some kind of personal mess that needed sorting out. Izzy was so much better at this than she was. Keeping Sophie in her sights, where she was in rapture at the vast selection of cosmetics on display, Rebecca crossed the landing to the bedroom opposite, where Samantha's mother Cheryl was sitting at a dressing table, glass of champagne in one hand and the phone she was swiping in the other. It was easy to see where Samantha got her looks; her mother was stunning. And angry.

Rebecca rubbed her palms together and plastered on her professional smile. "Hi. Cheryl? I'm Rebecca. The coordinator. We met at Samantha's house a couple of weeks ago."

Cheryl looked up. "Of course. I remember. And now you've been sent over to placate me about the head table?"

Rebecca smiled. "Samantha is worried that you're upset. I'm sorry that you weren't shown the seating plan before today."

Cheryl narrowed her eyes. "You don't need to apologize. My daughter gets her sneakiness from her father. She knew I wouldn't like it so she left it until today. Thought I wouldn't make a fuss when it was a done deal, I assume."

"Ah, I see." Rebecca paused. Often, she found that if she left space for people to talk, they told her more than they were planning to. If she was really lucky, they talked themselves into, or out of, their original issue.

It took only twenty seconds of silence for Cheryl to crack. "What you don't understand is that I've had to share her for the last fifteen years with her father and his wife. I'm not unpleasant to the woman and I don't dislike her. Quite frankly, I feel sorry for her, being married to my ex-husband, who is an inconsiderate idiot. And Samantha is right, she has been very good to her over the years and I'm glad of that." Her voice trembled a little and she took a sip of her champagne before continuing. "But this is Sam's wedding. And I'm her mother. I've been thinking about this day since she was about two years old. I just don't want to have to share her today."

Beneath the perfect makeup and false eyelashes, Cheryl's eyes were glassy. She expertly held a tissue underneath her lower lid to prevent any tears from smudging her eyeliner. Rebecca couldn't help but think of Cara, her face a couple of days ago when Rebecca had been braiding Sophie's hair.

Cheryl sighed. "Oh, I know I'm being silly. And selfish. Of course, she can have whoever she wants at the head table. I'm more emotional than I thought I'd be. It's just"—she waved the tissue in Samantha's direction—"she's so beautiful and I'm so proud, but she's not my baby anymore. It just hit me, watching her."

Her bottom lip wobbled and Rebecca reached out for her hand. "She's still your baby."

Cheryl shook her head. "No. That's what people say to make you feel better. But it's not true. And it happens so quickly."

Rebecca looked over to check how Sophie was doing. She was concentrating so hard on not moving while her lipstick was applied; it was impossible not to smile at how cute she looked.

Cheryl followed her gaze. "Your little girl is only small, but I promise you, you'll blink and you'll be right where I am. Making a fool out of yourself by being dramatic and silly. Tell Samantha I'll stop making a fuss. Actually, I'll get myself under control and then I'll go and tell her myself."

Rebecca started to say that Sophie wasn't her daughter and then she closed her mouth again. Maybe it would be her in the stepmother's position at Sophie's wedding one day. "How about if I ask the photographer to take some photos of you and Samantha together now? Before we leave for the church?"

Cheryl squeezed her hand. "Yes. That's a great idea. Thank you."

But before she spoke to the photographer, Rebecca wanted to take a couple of pictures of her own. As she walked toward her, Sophie jumped down from her stool and beamed at Rebecca, who reached out and brushed a hair from her eyes. "You look beautiful, Sophie. Shall we take a couple of pictures of you and send them to Mummy?"

She'd spent the last few days trying to get her head around how hard it was going to be for her to become a mother to Sophie. She hadn't really considered how difficult it was for Cara to watch Rebecca taking her place. It put the braiding awkwardness in a different light. It wasn't that Cara didn't want Rebecca getting close to Sophie; it was just very difficult for her. Before she pressed send on the picture, she wrote a quick message to Cara:

Your daughter looks beautiful.

After a brief hesitation, she sent the same picture and message to Jack. Maybe he'd been right. She had been rushing things. Cara had her appointment with Dr. Green in two days' time. Once that was over, they could all sit down together and make a plan for their future. For Sophie's future.

CHAPTER TWENTY-NINE

Cara

On Monday, Cara took up Jack's offer of using his Uber account to get to and from the hospital. On the way, the driver tried to engage her in conversation about the change in the weather and which radio station she preferred before taking her one-word answers as an indication that she'd rather be left to her own thoughts. Now she leaned with the edge of her forehead against the cool window, watching the raindrops running down the outside. Occasionally, two or three drops would run into each other, forming a larger rivulet, like tributaries joining a river. Every ounce of her was focused on this appointment. Good news wasn't likely, but there had to be a chance. Would there be *any* hope? *Please. Please. Please.*

Dr. Green's office wasn't large—this was the NHS after all—but the seats were more comfortable than those in the waiting area. As always, Dr. Green held out a hand to indicate the seat that Cara should take opposite her own. This was a familiar dance. As soon as Cara was seated, Dr. Green spoke. "It's good to see you, Cara. I'm not going to sugarcoat this because I know you prefer that I give it to you straight. The chemotherapy has not had the effect we'd hoped to reduce the new tumors."

Even though she'd expected it, cold reality trickled down Cara's spine like ice water. Despite feeling almost paralyzed by fear, she had to ask the next question. "What does that mean? Do we try something else?"

Dr. Green's face was the picture of sympathy. "There is nothing else."

It was as if the blood in her veins were turning colder. Though she tried, it was impossible not to let it freeze the tone of her voice. She heard herself speak as if from the end of a long tunnel. "So, what? We just give up?"

The doctor looked her in the eye. "I understand your anger. But we have thrown everything we can at this. There is still so much we—the medical profession—don't know about ovarian cancer."

She was angry, but these were not the hot outbursts she had been prone to. This was more frosty, intense. It came from somewhere deep inside. "What about trials? Aren't you always looking for people to test out new drugs? I'll try anything. Do anything. There must be something you can try?"

Dr. Green leaned forward over her desk. A genuine sadness in her eyes made Cara even more afraid. "Cara, your body has been through so much. It's so weak. I don't think it can even withstand more chemo."

This was ludicrous. In the face of the alternative, her body would stand anything it needed to. "I don't care. I'll try, I'll fight, I'll…"

The doctor reached out and put a hand over hers. "Cara. You wouldn't be accepted into any trials."

So that was it. They didn't want her. The story of her life. She pressed her lips together. She wasn't going to cry in here. She wasn't.

The doctor waited a few moments and then spoke. "I know this is a lot to take in, but we need to talk about palliative care and…and we don't have the luxury of a great deal of time."

Cara felt sick. She closed her eyes as she took that in. Then opened them to ask the most terrifying question of her life. "How long have I got?"

The doctor paused again. It was as if everything moved in slow motion. "I can't give you an exact time. It could be a few months. If we're lucky."

Cara bit down on her lip. *We?* She wanted to scream. *We?* There was no "we" in this room.

The doctor continued. "And obviously you need to prepare your daughter. Make some plans. Have you contacted the cancer support group on the number I gave you?" When Cara shook her head, the doctor didn't look surprised. "You should. They can help, Cara. They can talk to you both. Help you to prepare."

Prepare? How was she going to prepare Sophie for this? How could she tell her four-year-old daughter that she was going to lose her mother forever? But it wasn't fair to vent her anger on Dr. Green; she'd done everything she could. "I know."

Dr. Green patted her hand again and sat back. "Okay. Then let's talk about you and what we can do for you from this point on."

When the Uber dropped her off, she took her time walking up the path to Jack and Rebecca's, putting off the inevitable. This house had become so familiar to her the last few weeks. Would this be the first home that Sophie remembered? Would she forget that they'd ever lived in the one-bedroom apartment with the leaky bathroom faucets and the hot water heater that had to be thumped with the heel of her hand to get it to work?

Once she was inside, it was a relief to shut the door behind her. For a few moments, she just leaned against the door, eyes closed, trying to get enough of herself back into her body before she saw Sophie. All she wanted to do was lie down on the bed and let sleep render her unconscious. But that wouldn't be fair.

Sophie's laughter filtered through the hall. Then the murmur of Rebecca's voice. What were they talking about? Had Sophie missed her at all? God, that was selfish. Wasn't that what she wanted? For Rebecca and Sophie to get close? Wasn't that what this had all been about? There wasn't time for jealousy.

She took a deep breath and pulled herself up. *One foot in front of the other.*

In the kitchen, Sophie was drawing a picture of a party. At least that's what it looked like. Cara kissed her on the top of the head. "Hey, baby, that's a good picture."

Sophie turned on her chair. "Mummy! You're home!" She stood and threw her arms around Cara's neck and squeezed. "I'm drawing the wedding for my perfollio. Rebecca gave me a folder. It's just like hers."

Rebecca had picked Sophie up from preschool on her way home from Izzy's. She smiled at Cara from her open laptop. "We were getting our work done together. How did it all go?"

Cara wasn't about to go into it all now in front of Sophie. She might not have much time, but she couldn't rush that. It needed thinking about. "I'll talk to you about it later. Do you mind if I lie down for a while? Sophie, do you want to come upstairs with me?"

Rebecca's eyes searched her face for a clue but Cara didn't have it in her right now. She would have to sit down with Jack and Rebecca later and go through everything that Dr. Green had said. Right now, though, all she wanted to do was curl up in bed with Sophie in her arms and pretend for just a little while that they were back home in their apartment, just the two of them, and that none of this was real.

CHAPTER THIRTY

Rebecca

Seeing children's playgrounds from afar, Rebecca had always assumed that they were fun, friendly, safe places for families. Not that they were so fraught with danger that she had to watch Sophie like a hawk in case of falls or bangs or scrapes.

"Be careful!" That was the third time she'd said that to Jack since they'd got here. Why was he lifting Sophie to the top of a perilously high slide and then just...letting her go? Was he not going to at least hold on to her? She couldn't watch.

Jack turned and grinned at her. "Stop panicking. She loves it."

After Cara had told them her news two days ago, he'd taken a couple of days off work. This was the first time she'd seen him smile since then. From that moment, a heavy atmosphere of dread had descended on the house. After her brief explanation of her prognosis, Cara hadn't wanted to discuss it further. Neither had Jack. It was as if they were pretending it wasn't happening.

Cara's face when she'd arrived home from her consultant appointment had made it clear that she hadn't had good news. She had smiled at Sophie as if nothing were wrong, but there was no relief. No positivity. No hope.

Once Jack had returned home, and Sophie was in bed, it had taken her only a couple of minutes to explain the outcome of her appointment. The cancer was untreatable and the tumors were growing. Stage 4. Terminal.

Jack had been the first to speak. "Cara, I'm so sorry. I can't believe this is happening to you."

Already thin, she was even more diminished. Nearly four weeks earlier, she had sat in the same chair looking tough and angry. Now she barely took up a third of the seat. Crossing her legs, she almost disappeared. "Me neither. I don't think I ever faced up to the idea that this shitty disease was going to kill me. I was prepared to get ill, to have to endure more treatment, but not…" Her voice had wavered, so she'd paused, chewed on her bottom lip. "Stupid, eh?"

If it was stupid, they were all guilty of it. Hadn't Rebecca and Jack been banking on the same thing? Rebecca had even shown Jack a new housing development that was going up nearby to see if they had anything suitable for Cara and Sophie.

At that point, Jack still hadn't given up hope. "And they definitely can't? Can we get a second opinion? Go private? There must be something—"

"Nope. Believe me, I've asked." Cara was shaking her head slowly. "I've googled. Dr. Green is one of the top consultants for ovarian cancer. She's done everything she can."

Now Sophie was at the top of a wooden climbing frame shaped like a ship, waving frantically. "Rebecca! Look at me! Look how high I am!"

Jack was below her but was also looking in Rebecca's direction. What if Sophie fell?

"Jack. Keep your eyes on her. Don't look at me."

Sophie giggled and ran across a rope bridge that stretched from the bow to the stern. All Rebecca could see was her leg falling between the gaps and snapping like a twig. Where had this anxiety come from? It was crazy. "Jack, please keep an eye on her."

"She's fine, Bec. Stop stressing." Jack was jogging along beside the rope bridge, keeping pace with Sophie, looking every inch the proud father. To her knowledge, he had never taken a child to the park before. How was he taking this in stride? Why wasn't he worrying, as she was, that Sophie might hurt herself? Looking after her at home was one thing, but out in the big, wide world it was a much bigger job. Much bigger.

Jack reached up and helped Sophie down from the bridge, swinging her around until she was dizzy. Now she was at least closer to the ground, although it looked like her arms might come out of their sockets. Rebecca wasn't sure she could cope with watching another precarious climb. "There's a sandbox over here, Sophie. Would you like to play in it?"

Sophie wriggled from Jack's arms and ran to the large sandbox with a playhouse in the middle of it. Jack and Rebecca sat down on a bench alongside it.

Grimacing, Jack rubbed his hands on the front of his jeans. "There was something sticky on the underside of that rope bridge and I don't want to know what it was."

Rebecca wrinkled her nose. "Maybe you should move a bit farther away from me?" She nudged him. "Running around after Sophie looks good on you, you know. It suits you. Being a dad."

He looked at her as if to check whether she was mocking him. "I'm enjoying it more than I thought I would. She's a fun kid. Daredevil. Like her mother."

Rebecca felt a twist in her stomach. Did Cara look at Sophie and see a miniature version of herself? Did that make her happy?

Jack nodded toward Sophie, who was filling a small yellow bucket with sand using a bright pink plastic shell, the concentration and focus on her face almost comical. "I just keep looking at her. She's so young, not more than a baby, really. Running up those steps and down the slide like she hasn't got a worry in the world. While we know what's coming. She has no idea what's about to happen. It's cruel."

Rebecca had had the same thoughts. Cara was Sophie's whole world. How could she even understand what life would be like without her mother in it? What were they going to say to her? How would they explain it?

She'd tried to broach that subject with Cara yesterday. While Jack was upstairs reading to Sophie, the two of them had been in the kitchen preparing dinner. It had seemed like a good time to bring it up. "Have you had a chance to think about what you're going to say to Sophie? I mean, does the hospital give you any guidance on what to say to your child?"

Cara had stiffened immediately. Pulled the vegetable peeler hard across the carrots. "I haven't asked them."

Maybe she should have taken that as a signal to stop, but there needed to be some kind of plan. Was Cara just avoiding thinking about it? Rebecca could help. "I'm sure they will give you some advice if you ask. Honesty is usually the best—"

Cara had flicked her head back toward Rebecca so fast it had almost made Rebecca step back. "And how exactly am I supposed to be honest? When I don't know when it's going to happen myself?"

Then Rebecca had tried to back off. "Sorry, I just thought that…"

Cara's face had been flushed. "Her whole life, I have been the one constant, the one person who always looks after her, who is there for her. Whatever has happened, I've been there to pick her up. To put a bandage on her scraped knee. To show her how to hold a knife and fork. To explain why sometimes people can be mean. How can I tell her that I am going to leave her?"

Rebecca's heart was breaking for her, it really was. But Sophie needed to know before she guessed something on her own. "I can't imagine how difficult this is. But you need to be the one to tell her. Surely it will be much worse for her to wake up and find you're not there anymore? You have to prepare her."

Cara's eyes had flashed with anger. "You're not a mother. How can you possibly understand? Do you not think I feel guilty enough? I don't need you to make me feel worse."

You're not a mother so you can't understand. That was the go-to of every parent she knew. Because she didn't have her own children, she couldn't possibly empathize with whatever they were going through. It was such an easy cop-out. They didn't have to explain their decisions or their thinking because she "couldn't possibly understand."

She hadn't pushed any further when Cara was upset, but it did worry her. This morning, she had taken some breakfast into Cara's room and apologized. Cara had looked so exhausted that Rebecca had suggested on a whim that they take Sophie out to the park to give her a break. Cara's agreement was a good sign that she might have forgiven her. As Rebecca had got to the door, Cara had called her back.

"Rebecca?"

Had she changed her mind about trusting them to take Sophie out. "Yes?"

"I'm sorry too. For biting your head off like that. I'm not used to anyone telling me what to do with Sophie. It's always just been me."

"I'm just worried about her."

Cara smiled, her face softer. "I know. And I'm glad. I will tell her soon. Just give me a couple more days."

CHAPTER THIRTY-ONE

Cara

Cara had cried for a solid hour after they'd left for the park.

In all the years since she'd had Sophie, she'd never felt a loneliness like this. Even when Sophie was a tiny baby and she'd lie on the sofa in the apartment in the early hours of the morning, watching TV with the volume down low so as not to wake Danielle's kids next door, Sophie in her arms and a cold cup of coffee on the table. They had been complete, just the two of them.

Danielle had nagged her many times to start dating, declaring that it wasn't healthy for Cara to spend her life shuttling between work and home with no time for herself, for fun. As usual, she hadn't held back. "What happens when Sophie grows up and leaves? It'll just be you. And by then you'll be too old and saggy to meet anyone."

Cara had laughed and thrown a cheese puff at her, refused to even look at the Tinder profiles Danielle waved under her nose. She didn't want, or need, anyone else in her life.

But once Rebecca closed the front door this morning and she could no longer hear Sophie's excited chatter about whether they were going to the park with the twirly blue slide or the one with the pirate ship climbing frame, the silence of the house settled on her like a shroud. And she felt more alone than she ever had before.

She must have cried herself back to sleep because she woke with a jolt as her mobile pinged. Rebecca had sent her a picture of

Sophie next to a lopsided sandcastle, a smile spread like raspberry jam across her face. Cara's breath caught in her throat. When did she get so grown up? The contours of her face had lost that baby softness. How much more might she change? And how much more would Cara get to see her grow?

All the moments she had taken for granted. Watching *Frozen* together for the hundredth time, listening to Sophie explain in excruciating detail why she hated carrots, watching her draw pictures of the two of them that Cara would have to keep forever because Sophie never let her forget the one time she'd found one in the recycling bin. A million tiny, insignificant, irreplaceable moments.

Sometime in the night, Sophie must have crept into Cara's bed and she'd woken up to find her sharp little knees tucked into the small of her back, her fingers entwined in her own hair. Before she'd lost it to the damn chemo, it had been Cara's hair she played with. Disentangling her fingers and sweeping her bangs away from her eyes, Cara had lain there, just looking at her daughter's beautiful face on the pillow. Her lips slightly pursed, eyelashes twitching: How had she made something so beautiful? How had *they* made something so beautiful—her and Jack?

Tears threatened to pull her under again. She couldn't just sit here and cry; she needed to *do* something. Being alone in the house, at least she could go down to the kitchen in her pajamas without running the risk of bumping into anyone. When she tried to get up, though, even swinging her legs out of bed was an effort. Apart from a trip to the toilet, she had no need to leave the bedroom anyway; as well as bringing her coffee and toast this morning, Rebecca had left her a tray of food and some water on the bedside table. Crackers, a sandwich in foil, a small dish of olives, fruit. She still felt bad about snapping at her. She was only trying to help.

That was another thing Danielle had nagged her about for the last six months. *You need to start asking for help.* It didn't come easy, though. She wasn't used to it. Asking for help felt like weakness. Weakness led to vulnerability. Vulnerability led to pain.

Tucked under a corner of the food tray was the leaflet from the cancer support group that Dr. Green had insisted she take. On the front was a photo of a woman smiling into a phone. *It's good to talk.*

The food almost taunted her; no way was her stomach ready for anything solid yet. Maybe she could keep down some fluids. Her hand trembled as she poured a glass of water from the carafe and opened up the leaflet to read it. There was a list of things they suggested she might want to talk about when she called. Understanding her diagnosis. Financial issues. Telling her family.

Cara bit her lip. It was time to face it. The treatment hadn't worked and she was going to have to work out how to tell Sophie that she wouldn't be around to see her grow up. Before she could talk herself back out of it, she dialed the number on the front of the leaflet.

The phone rang seven times before it was picked up. Cara took a deep breath. "Hi, I...er...I'm calling for advice."

The female voice on the other end was calm and warm. "No problem at all. My name is Julia. What can I help you with?"

Cara stared at a silver flower in the wallpaper. If she kept to the facts, she could do this. *Just say it.* "I'm Cara. I have ovarian cancer and it's terminal. I need some advice on how to tell my daughter. Sophie. She's four. Very bright for four, but, you know, she's young."

Thankfully, Julia didn't offer any flippant condolences. "Okay. Well, first of all, how are you feeling?"

How was *she* feeling? She hadn't called up to talk about herself. "I'm fine. Just a bit tired. I've just had my last bout of chemo, so, y'know, not great."

Julia paused each time before she spoke. Was she writing things down? "I can imagine. And how are you feeling about your prognosis? Has your doctor talked you through everything? Do you have any questions about that?"

Dr. Green had been fantastic throughout. Honest about every stage. Cara didn't want to go through the details now. "No questions. Apart from wanting to know precisely how long I've got. Which nobody can tell me for sure."

Another pause. "And how are you feeling about that?"

For God's sake. This was why she hadn't called one of these lines before. She didn't want to sit around and talk about her feelings with a stranger. What was the point in that? The only reason she was calling now was to find out how to tell Sophie what was going on. Heat rose in her chest. "Look, I know you've probably got a whole script to go through, but I don't want to waste your time or mine—can we just talk about my daughter? What do I tell her?"

Cara knew that she sounded rude, but she didn't care. However, this Julia didn't seem ruffled in the slightest. "Before you can tell your daughter anything, you need to get your own head around what's happening. That's why I am asking you about your feelings. Right now, this minute, how do *you* feel?"

Cara gripped the phone tightly. "If you really want to know, I'm angry. I'm really bloody angry. If I had the energy, I would want to punch someone or something right now."

She was fully expecting to have her call terminated but Julia didn't miss a beat. "It's natural to be angry, Cara. You are grieving for yourself. Anger is a part of that process."

It was more than anger, though. It wasn't the feeling she got from someone stealing the parking space she was about to back into or stealing the scooter she'd saved for three months to buy her daughter. This was a deep, burning, passionate fury that made her want to howl with rage.

Maybe it was because she couldn't see this Julia's face, or that she was a stranger, or that Cara was alone in the house. Whatever it was, Julia's persistence to know how Cara felt made it difficult to control her smoldering emotions. "I know you probably hear this all the time, but why me? Why now? It's just so unfair. Sophie is too young to lose her mum. It's just not right."

If she had heard this a hundred times before, Julia didn't say so. "You're right. It is unfair to Sophie. But it's unfair to you, too, Cara. You are allowed to feel sad for yourself, as well."

A thick, hot lava bubbled in Cara's stomach, threatening to overwhelm her. She had focused so hard on Sophie, on doing everything that needed to be done to ensure that she was safe. And now that was settled—what happened next? What happened to her when Rebecca and Jack played the happy family at the park with her daughter? How long did she have? How was it going to be? Like an explosion, it hit her that she had been so focused on the practicalities that she hadn't thought about the reality of saying good-bye to Sophie. How the hell could she say good-bye to her beautiful girl?

Whatever was rising within her collapsed into ash. "Oh God, I can't bear it. I just can't bear it."

The woman on the other end waited patiently as she sobbed. "Just take your time, Cara. I'm not going anywhere, love."

Once the tears were spent, Julia talked to her in a calm and soothing voice about counseling and how that might help her to process some of these feelings of anger and despair. Once Cara had promised that she would call the number Julia had given her, they returned to talking about Sophie.

"Okay. So, what do you think she knows already?"

Cara took a deep breath and stared at the silver flower again. "I told her that I wasn't well. She knows I had to go into the hospital to have an operation. But I haven't used the word 'cancer' because I don't think she will understand what it means."

"There are some really good picture books for young children that explain cancer in a language that makes sense to them. I'll get your email address at the end of our call and send you some links. I can also arrange for someone to come out and visit you."

It was on the tip of Cara's tongue to say that it wouldn't be necessary for someone to come out, then Danielle's voice rang in her head. *You need to start asking for help.* "Thank you. That would be great." She paused and took a deep breath. There was one question she really wanted to know how to answer. "What if she asks me if I'm dying? Do I tell her the truth?"

"You need to slow down a bit, Cara. Take a breath. First, it's okay to say that you don't know the answers to all her questions. She needs to know that you are being honest with her."

It was all right for her to say slow down, but what if she was running out of time? "I need to know what I should tell her. Do I say that I'm going to die? And how do I say that?"

Julia wasn't going to be redirected that easily. "I'm going to send Jamie out to speak to you. She has had a lot of experience with young children. The most important thing is that your little girl knows that there will always be someone to look after her. There are lots of other things Jamie will suggest—some of them will be in the resources I'll email you—but I think you need to take your time and get everything straight in your own mind first."

Frustrating as it was, maybe Julia was right. She had to get her own head around it first. Plus, she had to remind Jack about getting his name on Sophie's birth certificate as soon as possible. After that, she would make sure that Sophie knew she was safe, that there was someone to look after her if Cara couldn't. And, however much it hurt, Cara would spend as much time as possible helping Rebecca to replace her as Sophie's mother.

CHAPTER THIRTY-TWO

Rebecca

"Hi, I really need to ask a favor." Cara poked her head into the kitchen; her green-tinged skin and eyes ringed with dark circles made her look as if she'd been out on the town all night.

Rebecca lowered the lid on her laptop. "Of course. What do you need?"

"It's not me; it's Sophie. She has a temperature. It might just be a reaction to all the excitement at the preschool Halloween party yesterday, but I'll have to keep her home and I can't...I can't be around her because of my low immunity. I can't risk catching anything."

It was clearly costing her a lot to ask for Rebecca's help. Which of course she would give. But she almost felt sick herself at the thought. The trip to the park on Wednesday had made her realize how much she had to learn about looking after Sophie. "Okay, but you'll have to tell me what to do. I have no idea how to look after a sick child."

Cara held up a small purple box and something that looked scarily like a syringe. "She'll be fine. I've given her ibuprofen to bring her temperature down. She just needs to drink lots of water and have another dose in about four hours. I'm sorry but I really can't risk being around her more now. I'll stay in my room."

"Of course. You go back to bed. I've got this. Just tell me everything I need to do and I'll write it down so that I don't need to keep bothering you."

Sophie plodded down the stairs, dragging her polka-dot duvet. She didn't look terribly sick, although it was tricky to tell from her naturally pale skin. That was something else she must have got from Cara. Jack needed to spend only a half hour in the sun to go nut-brown. Once Cara had settled her onto the sofa, she tore a sheet of paper from Sophie's drawing pad and wrote down the times Sophie could have another dose of ibuprofen. "She probably won't want to eat very much, but it would be good if you can get her to have something to drink." She laid a bony hand on Sophie's forehead. "She still feels warm. Maybe this quilt isn't a good idea."

Sophie gripped onto the blanket like a life raft. "I want to keep it."

Cara stroked the top of her head. "Okay, but if Rebecca tells you to take it off, you must do what you're told. And drink some of this water." She picked up the glass on the table and sighed when Sophie shook her head.

Rebecca was more worried about getting Cara out of the room so that she didn't catch anything. "We'll be fine. You go. Honestly." This prolonged good-bye was making Rebecca anxious. How long did it take for germs to jump from one body to another?

Cara stood but didn't move away from the sofa. "Okay. I wouldn't normally leave her when she's not feeling well, but I really need to…"

"Go." Rebecca pointed to the door and Cara obeyed. When it clicked shut, Rebecca sighed with relief then smiled at Sophie. "Okay, then. What do you want to do? Shall I put some cartoons on the TV for you?"

Sophie shook her head. "Will you read to me?"

Rebecca had about fifty phone calls to make this morning. Still, a picture book wouldn't take long. Then she'd turn on the TV. "What would you like me to read? Do you have a book?"

Sophie reached under her polka-dot duvet, where she had hidden a copy of *The Gruffalo*. "This is my favorite."

Rebecca perched on the edge of the sofa, opened the book, and started to read. She had got to only the third page when Sophie sighed. "You're not doing it right."

"What do you mean?"

"The words don't sound right."

Rebecca hadn't read a children's book since she was a child herself. Her sister's boys had never been interested in books as far as she had been able to tell when she saw them. But it was just words on a page, and she was pretty sure she knew how to read those. Maybe she needed to emphasize the rhyme at the end of every line. She tried again.

Sophie shook her head. "No. It's not right. The voices. When Mummy reads it, she does all the voices."

Rebecca pressed her fingertips together hard. She attempted a voice for the fox and then... No. This was ridiculous. She couldn't do it. "Maybe you should wait for your mum to feel better. How about the TV?"

Sophie shook her head again. "Read me one of those. Your magazines. The one with the lady in the dress."

She was pointing at the brochures Rebecca had put down on the table so that she could read to her. "This? It's just about a wedding venue. You don't want me to read that."

"Yes, I do."

Well, at least it would kill two birds with one stone. Rebecca flipped through a few pages before she got to the part she needed to read: the restaurant. "Henley Grange can cater for up to 250 seated dinner guests or 400 buffet guests. We offer a range of menu options but our fabulous chef is happy to create a menu to your specifications."

She looked at Sophie—how could this be interesting to a four-year-old? But Sophie was leaned in, looking at the glossy photographs with artistic shots of glassware and seating plans. So, Rebecca continued. Sophie got so close that her head was resting on Rebecca's arm. She did feel warm. Remembering Cara's last instructions, she picked up the glass. "Why don't you have a quick drink?"

Sophie wrinkled her face in distaste. "I hate water."

Rebecca had an idea. "What if I get you some fizzy orange?"

Sophie's eyes lit up. Cara didn't let her have fizzy drinks unless it was a special occasion. "Really? Can I?"

"I'll be back in one minute." Rebecca had no intention of going against Cara's wishes. The fizzy orange she made for Sophie was actually mineral water and fresh orange juice. To make it even more authentic, she added a paper straw.

Unfortunately, Sophie wasn't fooled. She took the tiniest of suspicious sips and then stuck out her tongue as if she'd been poisoned. "That's disgusting. It's not fizzy orange! You said I could have fizzy orange."

Being ill brought out a side of Sophie that Rebecca had not seen before. This wasn't the polite little girl who'd been in her house for the last few weeks. She put the glass on the coffee table. "It's fizzy and it's orange. And it'll be there if you want it."

"Mummy makes me a milk shake when I'm not well."

Rebecca seriously doubted that this was true and she was also desperate to get some work done. "I don't have anything to make a milk shake, but I will bring you a glass of milk if you sit quietly and watch some cartoons."

Sophie crossed her arms and nodded decisively. "Deal."

Rebecca had an uneasy feeling that she was being played by a four-year-old. Nevertheless, she brought in a glass of milk, pulling the coffee table closer so that Sophie could reach it.

Cartoons on, she sneaked off to the kitchen to make her calls. She was on hold for Geraldine Stannish—a colleague of Izzy's husband, Tim, who wanted help to organize a charity ball for her daughter's riding club—when she heard a clatter and a yelp followed by Sophie's voice. "Rebecca! Quick! I spilled it!"

The carnage in front of her when she ran into the room looked to be the work of four glasses of milk rather than one. Possibly this was because the orange juice had spilled too. "How did they both tip over?"

She hadn't realized her voice was abrupt but Sophie started to cry. "Where's Mummy? I want my mummy."

Damn. She was going to wake Cara up. "It's okay, Sophie. Just…just give me a minute. Don't cry. It's okay."

She dashed back into the kitchen to get some paper towels, then tried to mop it up with her mobile still pinched between her shoulder and her chin. The damn milk was everywhere, covering the coffee table and dripping into the carpet. It was going to stink if she didn't get some soap on it soon.

Now Sophie was sobbing. "You sh-sh-shouted at me."

For goodness' sake, she had *not* shouted. Just as she was about to explain that, a clipped, well-spoken voice barked in her ear. "Geri Stannish. Are you the fix-it woman Tim promised me?"

Smiley business face on. "Hi. Yes. Rebecca Faulkner. Tim has told me about your ball, which sounds fantastic. Shall we make an appointment for you to let me know your budget and to discuss themes and ideas?"

In the background, Sophie was repeating, "I want Mummy," over and over like a mantra. Rebecca tried pleading with her eyes and putting her finger to her lips.

There was a silence at the other end of the line. "Is everything okay on your end? Your child sounds in pain."

Rebecca tried to keep her voice light. "Oh, that's not my child, and it's just some spilled milk. Just give me a minute and…"

She held the phone to her chest to mute the microphone and reached out to rub Sophie's arm. Sophie shrugged her off, getting louder as she worked herself up, the pitch of her voice enough to make her teeth ache.

There was no calming her. What might work? "Please stop crying. I'll get you a cracker."

As if the sun had come out, Sophie stopped crying and nodded, her face tearstained. "Yes, please."

Rebecca sprinted to the kitchen, putting her phone back to her ear. "Sorry, I'm just getting her a cracker and then we can—"

Geri Stannish interrupted her. "I'm pretty busy today, actually. Why don't you call me back later when you've got your...domestic situation under control."

"No, it's fine, honestly, I'll—" Rebecca stopped speaking. Geri Stannish had hung up. "Damn. Damn. Damn."

With three graham crackers—and a fresh glass of milk—Sophie was finally content to watch some cartoons on the TV. Rebecca gulped at a mug of coffee as she filled a plastic bowl with soapy water so she could scrub the milk and orange juice out of the carpet. She'd actually prefer a glass of wine but it was only 9:15 a.m. She'd been in sole charge of Sophie for less than half an hour and already wanted to drown her sorrows.

And where was Jack? At the office, uninterrupted—that was where. Sophie was his daughter, yet she was the one jeopardizing her work to placate his daughter's every whim. Up until now, Sophie had been so quiet and well-behaved it was as if Rebecca had been lulled into a false sense of security about looking after her.

It wasn't Sophie's fault—she wasn't well. But none of this was Rebecca's fault either. So, why was she the one cleaning up the mess?

CHAPTER THIRTY-THREE

Cara

As promised, Julia at the cancer charity had arranged a visit from a young, spiky-haired support worker called Jamie on Friday evening once Sophie was in bed. Convinced that their meeting was going to be painfully awkward, Cara had been surprised and relieved that Jamie didn't speak to her in a soft voice or suffocate her with sympathy. Instead, she was upbeat and honest and, most importantly, practical. After draping her black leather biker jacket over one of the dining room chairs, she'd accepted a cup of mint tea, recommended some children's books about bereavement for Sophie, and suggested a project for Cara. Which was what Cara wanted to talk to Rebecca about on Saturday morning.

Rebecca had got into the habit of bringing Cara a cup of tea and two ginger crackers each morning. Though it made Cara feel like a maiden aunt, it was strangely comforting, and the ginger really helped with her nausea. This morning she was awake when Rebecca knocked at the door, and as soon as the tea was on its coaster on the bedside table, she launched straight in. "I was wondering if you could get some photos printed for me from my phone. For Sophie, actually."

Rebecca picked up her mug from yesterday that Cara had forgotten to return. "That's a good idea. Of course."

Cara pushed herself up in bed. "And I wanted to get your opinion on something. Jamie, from the cancer charity, recommended I get a box of things together for Sophie. For when I'm not here anymore."

Rebecca swallowed. "Like a memory box?"

"Yes. Exactly. I thought I'd start with photographs." The only way she could do this was to focus on the goal of getting the right objects together. If she stopped too long to think about the purpose of the task, it would be way too difficult. She thumbed through the pictures on her phone to find the one she wanted, then held the screen up toward Rebecca. "Look. Here's one of Sophie when she was first born."

Rebecca wasn't a baby person, she knew that. But who could fail to be moved by this picture of Sophie? She was so tiny, barely six pounds. Her face a tightly scrunched ball, body curled as if she were still safely in the womb.

Rebecca was clearly feigning interest. "Yes, she's very cute."

Cara turned the phone back to herself. "Okay. Maybe only a mother would love them at that stage but look at this one." She thumbed to a picture of Sophie in yellow corduroy overalls. Her second birthday.

This time Rebecca leaned in closer. "She looks like Jack there."

Cara turned it back and looked. "Yeah, it's the pained expression."

Rebecca laughed. "Why don't you download a photo app and get them printed? They'll be here in a couple of days."

"Good idea. I don't know why I didn't think of that." It was difficult to ask the next question. It sounded so pathetic. "Actually, I was wondering if you could help me to put them into an album? Label them with where and when they were taken?"

Rebecca looked confused. "Of course, but why do you need my help to do that?"

She had a fair point. Although Cara was still in bed for half the day, she'd been feeling a lot stronger as the chemo aftereffects started to wear off. "You're more creative than me. And you're good with photos and..." A lump rose in her throat that made it difficult to speak. It wasn't just the lump; a lifetime of looking after herself meant that asking for help didn't come easily.

Rebecca prompted her gently. "And?"

She swallowed down the emotion that was threatening to strangle her. *Stay focused on practicalities.* "It's not just the photos. It's the other stuff. All the items that I'm putting in the box. I want to tell you about them. So that you can tell Sophie."

Rebecca's eyes filled and she stared down at the used coffee cup on her tray. "Oh. I see."

Did she see? Did she understand how important this was? "She's only four, after all. When she looks at these things, she's going to forget. She won't know why they are important. I want someone to tell her. I *need* someone to tell her. And I can't see Jack doing it properly. I need you to do it."

Rebecca swallowed. Looked up and nodded. "Of course. Whenever you want."

Cara leaned down toward a cardboard box on the floor. She would buy something nicer than this battered box that held Sophie's baby things she'd brought with them from the apartment. Rebecca reached down and pulled it up onto the bed for her.

The first thing Cara pulled out was a medical bracelet that looked as if it had been made for a doll. "Like this. She wore this in the hospital. I mean, I know that's obvious, but I want you to tell her how tiny her little wrists were. How they had to make it so small that you could barely read it. The nurse said it was a good thing she didn't have a double-barreled surname." Cara's eyes blurred. She had sat staring at Sophie in the hospital. All the time she was pregnant she had thought about how she was going to cope, where they were going to live, how she was going to work. But she hadn't pictured Sophie as an actual baby. A real little person. For hours, she'd just marveled at how perfect she was.

She coughed and reached inside again. A pink fluffy blob with different-sized ears came out next. "This is Cubby. He was her absolute favorite. She had to have him all the time; otherwise, all hell would break loose."

She passed Cubby to Rebecca, who held it at arm's length and shut one eye. "What even is it? A rabbit? A mouse?"

Cara shrugged. "God knows. She just called him Cubby." Even now, she could picture Sophie's chubby little toddler hands wrapped around its leg. "He was rancid with snot and saliva most of the time. I had to wait until she was asleep and then sneak him away to wash."

Rebecca reduced her hold to just a thumb and forefinger as she dropped Cubby onto the bed. Cara laughed and reached inside for something else.

"This is her baby book. I've written on every single page up until her fourth birthday. The other mums at the clinic used to joke that they started writing in it and then got sidetracked or forgot. But I wrote in every box; every detail about her. I wanted her to have her own history, you know?" Maybe it was because she had nothing from her own childhood, but it had become almost an obsession for her that Sophie would know everything about the first weeks and months and years of her life. Maybe she had been unknowingly planning for tragedy all this time. She passed the book over to Rebecca, who turned the pages slowly as she read.

"This is amazing. So much detail."

"Yep. It starts before she was born and it finishes when she turns five." Her voice wavered and she waited to get it under control. "So, you're going to need to finish it for me."

Rebecca looked her in the eye. For a few moments, neither of them spoke. "You don't know that, Cara. You might be here to finish it yourself."

Cara couldn't handle this right now. She grabbed something else from the box. "And these boots. They were secondhand but she loved them so much. They were all she would wear. It didn't matter what the weather was—rain or sun—it made no difference. Didn't even matter if she was wearing a pretty dress or a pair of jeans. She was so headstrong. Still is at times."

Rebecca was still looking at her face. "It's good to be a woman who knows her own mind."

She couldn't—wouldn't—make eye contact. She just had to keep going. "There are a few of her drawings too. The first one she drew of me." Cara held up a shaky, crayoned semicircle with four—or was that five?—lines coming out of it. There was a circle shape floating above it with marks that might have been eyes and a mouth. She held it next to her face. "Can you see the likeness?"

Rebecca smiled. "It's uncanny."

Cara held the picture in her hand and traced the lines with her finger. "She's always loved to draw. People, animals, houses—it doesn't matter what it is as long as she has a crayon in her hand. I sometimes wonder if she'll be an artist one day." She paused and looked up at Rebecca. "You'll encourage her to be an artist if she wants to be?"

This time Rebecca didn't protest. "She can be anything she wants to be."

Before she lost it altogether, she started to pull other items out at random. "And I'll put in some other things. Like these postcards. They were stuck up on the wall in our apartment. Places I wanted to visit someday. I want her to visit them. I want her to travel and see the world and do all the things I never did. Can you tell her that?"

"I will. I'll tell her."

Cara scrunched the edge of the quilt into her fist. "And tell her that I loved her. Please will you tell her that? That I loved her from the very minute she was born. She was my absolute world and I tried so hard not to leave her."

Rebecca reached out for her hand. "I will, Cara. I will tell her that."

Cara pulled her hand away and wiped at her eyes. How could she put into words what she wanted to say? What she wanted Rebecca to tell Sophie? Even love didn't come close. Every mother loved her child. But Sophie had been her absolute everything. Morning and night, summer and winter, year after year. Without Sophie, she had nothing. Their world had been small, but it had been safe and warm and full of love. And now she had to trust her world, her heart, to Jack and Rebecca.

Rebecca's phone pinged with a message. "It's Jack. Oh, damn."

"What?"

After taking a couple of days off, Jack had barely been home the last few days. Something to do with a big account at work. Maybe it was a problem with that.

Rebecca sighed and put her phone back on the bedside table. "It's nothing important. A party tonight that we'd both forgotten about. I'll let them know we can't come. Shoot. I should have told them days ago."

Surely she wasn't suggesting they stay home because of Cara. "Why can't you go? I'm well enough to look after Sophie now and her cold has almost gone. I'll be fine."

Rebecca shook her head. "No, it's okay. Honestly. I'll send a bottle of wine by way of apology."

This was ridiculous. "Rebecca. Go to your party. If I need you, I can call."

She still didn't look happy about it, but she gave in. "Okay. If you're sure you'll be okay. But I won't drink, then we can come home right away if you need us."

CHAPTER THIRTY-FOUR

Rebecca

Jack's friends Steve and Alison lived in a barn conversion with an acre of land. Their living room was very white, and the furniture had been rearranged to give as much space as possible for standing guests. After a quick hello to their hosts, Rebecca and Jack were on the way to the kitchen to deposit their wine when they bumped into Mark and Christine.

Mark and Jack had been friends since they were at school. Although Jack laughed at phrases like "best friend," Mark was the first of his friends or family that he'd wanted Rebecca to meet. He and Christine, his fellow lawyer wife, were good fun, so for a while the four of them had seen quite a lot of each other. Until Christine had fallen pregnant with their first child and they'd started socializing more with people who had kids.

After clapping each other on the back, and greeting one another's wives, the two men disappeared to the kitchen to get a round of drinks. Rebecca followed Christine to an unoccupied corner where they wouldn't be in the line of traffic.

"So, Jack has a daughter?" Christine looked as if she'd been bursting to ask about it. "That must have been quite a shock." Christine did look sympathetic. She was a genuinely nice person. It was only human nature to be interested in such an unusual turn of events. Christine and Mark were also fully aware that she and Jack had not planned to have children, so they would know better than anyone how much this was rocking their world.

"Yes, it was rather."

Christine reached over and rubbed her arm. Rebecca felt like a fraud; if anyone deserved sympathy right now, it was Cara. "Have you got everything planned out? When she'll come to you, I mean? When my brother split with his wife, they said they would just see how it went with regard to custody and the whole thing was a complete, acrimonious mess. Plus, it's not fair to the kids, is it? They need to know where they stand. Which days they are with which parent. Better all around."

Christine had always been pretty forthright. It was one of the things Rebecca actually liked about her; she always knew where she stood. But this was pretty full-on even for her. "Actually, things have changed a little. Cara isn't very well. We might have to have Sophie with us a bit more than that."

Christine raised an eyebrow; she was swaying. Mark had joked that they'd been here since the party had started and this clearly wasn't her first drink. "Oh my gosh. So you really will be a stepmother."

That word still rankled. "We have a room for her now. Do you remember the guest room next to the upstairs bathroom? We've just made it a bit more child-friendly. I painted the walls myself. Bought new furniture and a few toys."

Christine smiled. "Sounds like you've enjoyed yourself. Have you changed your mind about being a mum? Maybe you can start having some of your own once you've got the hang of it."

Sophie wasn't some kind of a trial run. Like one of those dolls you took home to look after for a weekend in order to understand the realities of motherhood. She wasn't going to spend six weeks with her and then give her back before suddenly making a decision to go for a child that shared her DNA. "I'm not sure that getting the hang of it is the right phrase."

Christine waved a hand in front of her face; to be fair to her, she was pretty drunk. "You know what I mean. Now that you've got one kid at home, it's not a big leap to having another one. One child is the big life change. The second isn't anywhere near as much of an adjustment."

Did she really think she was selling motherhood with this speech? No, it wouldn't be nice. Why couldn't people understand? She wasn't secretly harboring a desire to clean up someone else's literal crap and spend the next eighteen years—at least—supporting them through the metaphorical kind. Rebecca didn't assume that mothers regretted having children, so why did they assume that she might be regretting her decision not to have them?

Having Sophie in the house was going to be hard. She would have to consider the food they would eat, make plans for where Sophie would go if Rebecca had to work. And she hadn't even begun to think about helping her with schoolwork, having her friends to the house to play, what were acceptable levels of time spent watching television. Her head swam at the prospect of all the elements of parenting that she hadn't even considered yet. Suddenly she was tired—too tired for this conversation. It was easier just to agree with Christine. "Yeah, maybe."

Mark and Jack reappeared with drinks. Mark passed her a glass of white wine. "Jack just told me you haven't done a DNA test yet."

Rebecca glanced at Jack, surprised he had been talking at that level of detail with Mark. "No, not yet. There's been a lot going on."

Mark pulled at his ear. His glassy eyes suggested he had been drinking as much as his wife. Was this what happened when you were a parent? First chance of a night out and you got on the beer like a student in freshman week? "Yeah, he told me. About the cancer. It's sad. She was all right, really; definitely didn't deserve that."

Christine's eyes widened. "Cancer? Oh, Rebecca, I didn't realize that's what you meant. I mean, I know she was a little bit reckless when she was with Jack. But no one should have to go through that. Especially with a child to worry about."

It was uncomfortable hearing them talk about Cara in the past tense. She and Cara weren't friends but she felt an unexpected prick of loyalty. "Well, we're hoping that she can keep fighting. There are new treatments being discovered all the time, aren't there?"

Mark laughed. "Yeah, I bet. Getting saddled with a four-year-old is no one's idea of a good time."

That wasn't what she had meant. Jack looked uncomfortable, too, but stayed uncharacteristically quiet. Did he have something on his mind? "I don't think that—"

Jack interrupted her. "Mark filled me in on a few things I wasn't aware of."

"Really?" She looked at Mark, who was fiddling with his ear again.

Christine nudged her husband. "Go on, tell her."

This was uncomfortable. "Yes, tell me. What's going on?"

Mark sighed. "Okay, I don't want you to think I'm being judgmental or sexist or anything. Everyone is entitled to do whatever they want—male or female. Makes no difference as far as I'm concerned. It's not the nineteenth century."

"Get on with it, Mark." Jack took a swig from his bottle of beer, his face pale.

Mark shrugged. "Okay, but remember I am only telling you this in case it's relevant. After Jack finished with Cara, she, well... she put herself about a bit."

Rebecca felt sick and it wasn't the wine. She thought of Cara at home with Sophie, of everything she'd been through in the last few months. They should not have been discussing her behind her back like this. It wasn't right. And it was certainly none of their business whom she chose to sleep with. "I see."

Mark didn't pick up on her reluctance to hear more. "Yeah, a couple of guys I know slept with her. Apparently, she was sofa-surfing for a while and, well, she wasn't sleeping on the sofa, if you know what I'm saying."

Jack put his thumb and forefinger to his eyebrows and rubbed. When he looked up at Rebecca, he was red with shame. "She told me she had somewhere to go. I didn't just kick her out."

She believed him. Despite the shock of the last few weeks, she knew he was a good man. "Did you sleep with her?" she asked Mark.

She felt Christine stiffen beside her. Mark looked shocked. "No. Of course not. I'd only just got married to Christine."

Christine shuffled closer to him. "We were doing up our house. Mark wasn't going out much at that time. He's heard all this secondhand."

Clearly the two of them had been talking about this before tonight.

"Look, I know it's none of my business, but I really think you should get a DNA test done. Soon. I assumed you had proof; otherwise, I would have mentioned all this before. I mean, I don't feel good talking about her like this when she's so ill, but I thought"—he looked at his wife—"*we* thought you knew for certain that the little girl was Jack's. But if you haven't had the test and got the results back, then, well, she might not be."

Jack held up his phone. "I've just ordered a test online. Next-day courier delivery. We'll have it in the morning."

CHAPTER THIRTY-FIVE

Cara

It was extraordinary how many DNA-testing companies there were out there. And how quick it would be to get a result. Rebecca had left them to it, and it felt strangely embarrassing to be doing this alone with Jack. It was crazy. All they had to do was take a swab from the inside of their cheeks. It wasn't as if there were other bodily fluids involved.

The instructions were pretty easy to follow and Cara had already read them aloud for Jack. They had both washed their hands as instructed and were sitting at the kitchen island, each with a swab in hand.

Jack held his aloft. "So, I just rub this against the inside of my cheek?"

Cara checked the instructions again. "Yep. It has to be firm but not uncomfortable."

"Might as well get on with it." Jack stuck the swab—basically a cotton bud—inside his mouth and started to move it around.

Cara turned to Sophie. "Open wide, Soph. This is the magic test I told you about. I just need to rub this on your cheek."

She tried to make light of it but this felt wrong somehow. She pulled funny faces at Sophie to make her giggle as she did it.

Sixty seconds was too long for Jack to stay silent. "Hor how wong?"

Cara glanced at his serious face. "Sorry, I don't speak dentist."

Jack's face creased as he laughed. Was he as nervous as she was? He moved the swab to the side and spoke more slowly. "For how long?"

Cara checked the instructions again even though she knew the answer. "Rub it in a circular motion eight to ten times." She held up the leaflet to prove it. "But we need to do four of them."

She dropped the first swab into a glass and Jack did the same in the glass she'd given him. "We must make sure that they don't make contact with each other."

Jack pretended to wiggle his fingers toward Sophie and then pulled his arm back. "No contact, Sophie." It was sweet of him to try to make light of this. It was only a formality but it felt so clinical. And she could tell he was embarrassed about it too. "Okay. Next one."

"I want to do it." Sophie held out her hand for the swab. "I can do it."

"Okay, but make sure you're pressing hard enough." Sophie's cheek protruded outward with the force of her push. Cara pressed it gently with her finger. "Not that hard, crazy child; you'll come through the other side."

Once the fourth one was done, Sophie ran off to the sitting room, where she'd been drawing. Cara checked the instructions again. "We need to let them dry for at least an hour before putting them in the envelopes."

Jack stood up and stretched. "Shall we just set them aside for now? One of us can come back in an hour and finish up."

Cara imagined that for Jack, "one of us" meant that Rebecca would actually be doing it. For a modern couple, he seemed very happy to let her organize everything at home. He needed to take responsibility for this part at the very least. Plus, she wanted to make sure that everything was aboveboard. It wasn't as if there was anything to hide, but Jack's stumbling attempt to sugarcoat Mark's comments had still stung. Everything needed to be clear and accurate. "I'd feel more comfortable if we both waited here until it's all sealed up."

Jack looked surprised. Then awkward. "Of course. Look, I don't want you to think I don't trust you; it's just—"

"Honestly, it's the right thing to do." Cara didn't want him to finish what was going to be another excruciating sentence. "We should have done it day one. Why don't we start filling out the forms?"

Jack nodded and picked up a pen. "So, once we send all this off, how long does it take?"

Cara read the last box on the instructions. "We can mail it tomorrow and, as long as they get it by ten Tuesday morning, they will email us the results the same day."

Jack frowned as he skimmed through the questions. "I have to check *alleged* father. That makes it sound like I've committed a crime."

"Tell me about it." The words were out before she could stop them.

Jack coughed and rubbed the end of his nose with the pen. "I'm a tactless idiot for telling you what Mark said. I'm sorry. It was all just a bit of a shock. And I guess I felt bad. That night when we bumped into each other again, you said you were staying with a friend. I just assumed you were telling the truth. That you were okay."

"I was telling the truth. When I left your place, I went to my friend Sarah, the one I was with the night we met. She let me stay over, but she had a boyfriend who was practically living there by then and it was a bit 'three's a crowd.' You know what I mean?"

She lifted an eyebrow at Jack and he knew right away what she meant. "Yeah, I think I can imagine what that might be like."

Even in the first couple of days, Rebecca hadn't made her feel as unwelcome as Sarah's boyfriend had, though. Whatever Sarah had said about her being welcome to stay as long as she wanted, his dirty looks and cozy dinners for two had told a different story. "It wasn't comfortable being there so, in the end, I found a cheap room in a shared house. Which was pretty grim." Cold, damp, and dirty, the house itself would have been bad enough, but her new housemates had made it even worse. Jay and Ed would be camped out in the dingy living room from the moment they got home from work, smoking weed and adding to their stack of used ramen noodle containers. The other one, and she'd seen him so infrequently that she couldn't remember his name, would get in from a club in the early hours of the morning and bring random hookups to his bedroom, where they would talk—and other things—loudly into the night.

Jack was nodding as if he could possibly understand. "I can imagine. I remember what student digs were like. Piles of dirty plates in the sink, right?"

She almost smiled at the difference between his life and hers. "Something like that. Anyway, I spent as little time there as I had to. Which meant I was out a lot. There were quite a few nights I didn't bother coming home at all." The men she'd met had made her feel better in the moment. Held, admired, wanted. But the following morning, she'd always felt like total crap. Still, it hadn't stopped her from doing the same thing all over again a few nights later. Jack had left such a cavity in her life, and those men had been like temporary fillings. They'd filled a gap, but they weren't made to last.

Jack reached out and took her hand. Instinct made her want to pull it back. When she didn't, it was more for his sake than hers. "I am so sorry, Cara. If I'd known that you hadn't gone back to stay with Sarah…"

What? she wanted to say to him. *What exactly would you have done?* This time she did pull her hand away. "I wouldn't have wanted you to stay with me out of pity, Jack."

Jack winced. "I know that. It's just hard to think of you being so alone."

"Well, I wasn't alone for much longer. Pretty soon, I realized that I was pregnant." She had never been the kind of woman who knew exactly when her period was due. And that time of her life was so ad hoc and random it had taken her over two months before she'd realized that she'd missed a period. Even when she'd taken the pregnancy test, she hadn't been expecting to see the second blue line.

"That must have been a shock."

To say that it was a shock was an understatement. No way had she been in any position to have a baby. But she hadn't gone to see anyone about ending it either. Once she'd sat down and worked out when she'd had her last period, she'd known that the baby must be Jack's. Plus, she hadn't been stupid enough to not use contraception with anyone else. "It took me a while to get my head around it, but then I did."

She still wasn't sure when she'd made her mind up to keep her baby. Maybe it was because she was Jack's. Had she held on to hope that they would reconcile? Not that any of it mattered now.

Jack looked as if he wanted to ask her something, then thought better of it. If it was to ask how she knew the baby was his, the DNA results would answer that question anyway. Instead, he asked about Sophie. "I wish you'd told me. About Sophie. I wish I could have helped you—whatever happened between us."

For the first time, her memories made her smile. "Once Sophie was born, my life got a whole lot better. The welfare office gave me the apartment next to Danielle, and she was intent on making us best friends from the moment I moved in. Then when Sophie came…" How could she explain it? How could she tell him that looking into Sophie's eyes in those first days had felt like coming home? She swallowed. "She saved me, Jack. Sophie saved me."

"Oh, Cara. I am so sorry that I wasn't there for you. If I could turn back time, I would. Maybe if it had ended better, you might have come to me."

She'd thought about this, too—of course she had. It was just that she'd had longer to think about it than he had. There was no point in making him feel bad for something that was over and done with a long time ago. "And then what? You would have moved me in and we would have played the happy family? For how long? I didn't want you to want me for Sophie's sake. And if and when it didn't work out between us, I didn't want to have to send her to be with you every other weekend. It's me who was wrong. I was selfish."

The last few days, her own guilt had grown. Not so much toward Jack, but toward Sophie. All the things Sophie might have had if Jack had been in her life from the beginning. Somehow, Cara had managed to persuade herself that Jack wouldn't want Sophie. That she was actually protecting her from rejection. But now that she had seen how Jack was with her, she realized that was just an excuse she had used to lie to herself. She checked the final box on her form and folded it in two. Looked up at Jack. "I'm sorry."

Jack reached over and touched her gently on the arm. "Please don't apologize. We just have to get it right from this point on. I know what the doctor said, but she doesn't know you like I do. You're the most stubborn woman I've ever met. You're going to beat this somehow. I know you are. And then everything will be okay. I let you down in the past, but I'm going to make it up to you."

Cara didn't want to stick a pin in his optimism, but he needed to face facts. She slipped both their completed personal information forms into the envelope and laid it in front of the samples they'd collected. "It's not the past I need your help with, Jack. It's the future: Sophie's future. Sophie saved me. I need you to save her."

CHAPTER THIRTY-SIX

Rebecca

Jack had sent off the DNA test on his way to work yesterday, so Rebecca was expecting the results to be emailed sometime today. *How long does it take to mix chemicals and get a result that could make or break our lives?*

This morning she'd been out to visit a new Greek restaurant and had coffee with the owner. It was a big place, over two hundred covers, and she could already think of a few clients who might be interested in using it for an event. The owner had been very welcoming—she'd met half his family while she was there, including his first grandchild, a very cute two-year-old with dark, shiny curls and a thumb-sucking habit. Being around a large extended family hadn't really helped her nerves today, though. She'd been glad to get away and come home.

It was stupid that they hadn't done the test immediately. If this had happened in a TV drama, she would have been the first person screaming at the characters to check first. But Sophie looked so much like Jack and the dates lined up exactly. And everything seemed to have happened so quickly. Was it really only four weeks since Cara had first rung their doorbell?

She counted the days on her fingers. To be precise, it was slightly more than that: four weeks, four days. A month in which the life she and Jack had planned had been turned on its head. Or had it? Today they would know for sure.

She checked her watch again. It was 2:00 p.m. She'd messaged Jack at midday but he still hadn't heard anything from the DNA company. Another half an hour and she'd need to head out to get Sophie.

Cara had an appointment with the palliative care team today. Rebecca had offered to take her but had been relieved when Cara said that the appointment was likely to run into preschool pickup time, so she'd rather Rebecca got Sophie instead. Of course, she was happy to do it, but it rankled that—again—it was her rather than Jack doing the running around. Admittedly, her job was more flexible timewise than his and she was her own boss. However, just because it was easier didn't mean it was fair. She had looked after Sophie a lot more than he had. When Sophie came to stay with them in the future, they would have to come up with something more workable for both of them. *If* she came to stay with them. This uncertainty was killing her.

She sat back from her PC and rubbed at her eyes. It was impossible to focus on the work in front of her—putting together a list of venue options for an insurance company's summer party next year—so she decided she might as well FaceTime Izzy to discuss the photo choices for their next newsletter. Every three months, they sent out a newsletter to clients of all the events that they'd run in an effort to keep their company in the forefront of their minds for future events. Samantha had kindly emailed them from her luxury waterfront honeymoon villa in the Maldives with some of her wedding photos that they could use. Any of them would look amazing, so they just needed to pick one.

Izzy picked up almost immediately. "Hey, how's things?"

She hadn't told Izzy about the DNA test. It seemed too early to be discussing it. And she didn't want someone else realizing how stupid they'd been until she knew how it was going to play out. "All good. Just wondered if you'd had a chance to look at Samantha's wedding pictures. I was going to start putting this quarter's newsletter together."

"Yes, I've been drooling over them this morning. What a fabulous wedding. There's a sweet photo of Sophie. It was nice of Samantha to include her, but wasn't it difficult trying to work and keep an eye on her at the same time?"

She'd given Izzy the debrief from Samantha's wedding last week. Izzy had been greedy for details after being stuck indoors with her little boy recovering from his tonsillectomy. Rebecca had told her about Sophie being drafted in as an emergency flower girl.

Actually, it hadn't been difficult at all. Samantha's pull-out-all-the-stops wedding had included an MC for the wedding breakfast and enough waiting staff for a state banquet. Despite all the last-minute planning, Rebecca had had to do very little on the day apart from watch the delight of a wedding through the eyes of a four-year-old. "Sophie was very sweet, actually. I'm sure she thought she was living the life of a princess. And she was very well behaved."

"Really?" Izzy made a tutting sound. "Careful, you almost sound like a proud parent there."

Izzy was joking, but she had hit a nerve. Rebecca *had* enjoyed spending time with Sophie at the wedding. But that was before they knew the full story about Cara's diagnosis. "It didn't go so well when I was looking after her this week. She spilled milk all over the carpet and I made her cry. Clearly the parent gene is still lacking over here."

Izzy laughed. "There is no such thing as a parent gene. Heavens, if I told you some of the things that I've yelled at my two in the heat of the moment, you'd be coming over here to rescue them both. Parents are humans, too, you know."

It was nice of Izzy to try to make her feel better. There was no getting away from it, though. "I know what you're saying, but I'm just not sure. I don't think I'm up to it."

"I love you, Rebecca, but you have a terrible habit of over-thinking things. No one is expecting you to suddenly become Mother of the Year. As long as she's warm and fed and safe, your job is done. After that, you just need to love them. And that takes time. Even when you give birth to them it doesn't necessarily happen immediately. Don't believe the baby ads. Being a parent can be tough. But you can do it, Rebecca. I know you can. And anyway"—Izzy's tone lightened up—"you only have to have her every other weekend or something. The rest of the time you and Jack can go back to being love's young dream."

Cara's terminal prognosis and the DNA test would have to wait until she saw Izzy face-to-face. "Very funny. Let's press pause on the parenting pep talk. I need to get this newsletter together, so just tell me which picture you like and I'll add it to the other events I'm including."

The rest of the conversation involved checking schedules and planning their next meeting, but they still managed to talk for another twenty minutes. By the time the call ended, Rebecca had just enough time to run a brush through her hair and grab her coat before she had to leave to pick up Sophie. Still no word from Jack.

When she got to the preschool, she had to wait outside with the other parents waiting to pick up. Everyone stood either looking at their phones or at something interesting on the ground. Thankfully, the door opened in a few minutes.

Before she followed the other parents, Rebecca spoke to the teacher at the door and explained that Cara had called ahead to say that she would be picking up Sophie. The teacher directed her to the office at the front of the building and said Sophie would be waiting for her there; she would need to give a password to the preschool manager, who would be with her.

The office door was ajar, so Rebecca could see Sophie as she approached. She was sitting on a tiny chair and already wearing her coat and backpack. In her hands was a lunch bag decorated with a huge unicorn. Something about her looked lost, like an evacuee from another era, and Rebecca wanted to scoop her up and tell her everything was going to be okay. Except she couldn't promise her that, could she?

As soon as Sophie caught sight of Rebecca, her face lit up and she waved. Rebecca couldn't help but return her smile: it was infectious. The preschool manager stood and came to the door. "Hi. Are you here for Sophie? Do you have the password?"

Rebecca nodded. "Yes. I believe it's 'yellow'?"

The manager nodded. "That's right. Sophie here has been telling me that it's her mum's favorite color." She turned to Sophie and smiled at her. "Off you go then, Sophie. See you tomorrow."

Sophie grabbed ahold of Rebecca's hand and, from nowhere, Rebecca felt a rush of pleasure.

All the way back to the car, and on the drive home, Sophie chattered about her day at preschool, oblivious that her mum had been at the hospital today. Although the update from her consultant had been pretty clear, Cara still wasn't ready to talk to Sophie about her prognosis until she had a definite answer as to exactly how long she had. Would anyone be able to give her that information? Maybe she was hoping that her consultant had given her the worst-case scenario when she'd said it might be only months. After all, didn't they have to cover themselves these days so they didn't get sued? When Rebecca had looked online, there had been plenty of cases of people who'd lived with a terminal diagnosis for years. Surely, the longer Cara held on, the greater the chance that a cure might be found? With new drug trials and gene therapy, it seemed as if there were all manner of breakthroughs every day. Since the effects of the chemo had started to recede, Cara was looking okay again. Was it too naive to hope that the palliative care team might give her a more positive viewpoint?

It was almost 3:30 p.m. by the time they arrived home. On autopilot, she poured Sophie a glass of milk and found the channel with the cartoons she liked. Then she sent Jack another message:

Have you checked your email? Did the results come yet?

Surely they would have to arrive soon. A business day ended at 5:00 p.m. Or maybe 5:30 p.m. The results were going to be emailed to both Jack and Cara. Cara wouldn't be able to check hers while she was at the hospital, but Jack had no excuse not to be refreshing his email every few minutes. He must have been as desperate to know as she was.

Sophie was transfixed by her cartoons, giggling to herself at the antics on-screen. Little did she know how much her life might be about to change. She didn't deserve any of this; if only they could protect her from all of it.

Rebecca checked her phone again. And again five minutes later. Finally, she got a short reply from Jack.

I'm on my way home now.

She barely had time to wonder why he was coming home so early when she heard the creak of the front door opening.

CHAPTER THIRTY-SEVEN

Cara

Even meeting with the palliative care team felt like a concession, a defeat. As if she were saying it was okay to stop trying to save her life, holding up her hands in surrender. *I give in. Take me away.*

Since the worst effects of the chemo had worn off, Cara had found it increasingly hard to believe that her cancer was terminal. If she had the strength to keep battling, why wouldn't they help her?

According to the conversation she'd had on the phone, the palliative care team included a number of health specialists: pain management, dieticians, mental health specialists, and others that she couldn't remember. She'd never had so much attention. For this first meeting, she would just see a doctor and a nurse to talk about her medication.

The receptionist took her name with a smile. "We won't keep you long. Please take a seat."

After her conversation with Jack last night, she'd lain in bed asking herself why she had taken so long to get in contact with him. There had been times over the last four years when she'd considered it. Usually when she'd had a couple of glasses of cheap wine with Danielle and become nostalgic. What she'd told Jack about her fear that he might take Sophie away from her had been true, but there had been something else. In the cold light of day, the realist in her couldn't risk the possibility that he simply might not even want to know.

She'd had enough rejection in her life. From memory, her own father had only ever touched her with the back of his hand. When she'd packed her bag at sixteen, he'd watched her leave with his arms folded across his chest, the kitchen door closed so that her sobbing mother couldn't ask her again to stay. Six months later, she'd seen him across the garden of a bar full of underage drinkers. When he'd spotted her, he'd just turned his back. Why put herself through that again? Why put Sophie through the possibility of any kind of rejection?

A young nurse collected her from reception and took her to a room that was a step up from the chemo lounge. Three chocolate-brown leather sofas arranged in a U shape around a rectangular coffee table. Brightly colored cushions and a rug. The NHS pulled out all the stops for the dying.

A doctor stood smiling at her. "Take a seat. Would you like a coffee or tea? Or water?"

Cara took the sofa nearest to the door. "No, I'm fine, thanks."

The doctor and nurse took a sofa each, and the nurse took the lead. "Thanks for coming in today, Cara. Hopefully your consultant gave you some idea about us and what the palliative care team is. Our aim is to give you any support that you might need. Whether that is physical, social, psychological, or spiritual."

They can keep the spiritual, thought Cara in that moment. Wherever her guardian angel was, she wasn't doing a very good job. "She did, yes."

"Although your treatment has stopped, there are medications we can prescribe to help you—"

Cara couldn't just sit here and listen. "The thing is, I haven't given up yet. I have a little girl. I need to keep fighting for her sake."

The doctor leaned forward so that her forearms rested on her knees. Her voice was gentle, as if she were speaking to a frightened pony. "I understand. Sometimes it helps to think about your body separately from yourself. You would never voluntarily leave your daughter—of course you wouldn't. Unfortunately, your body may not give you a choice. Some of this has so little to do with how hard we want to fight, and so much to do with the limits of biology."

Cara could hear their words, but it wasn't really going in. "So, I'm supposed to just give up?"

Like a professional tag team, the nurse took up the conversation. "No, Cara. It's not giving up. Even with a terminal diagnosis, you are still living. We want to improve your quality of life. Whether that's pain management or art therapy or family counseling for you and your daughter."

Cara didn't have time to paint a picture about how she was feeling. She needed to know the facts. "How long have I got? I couldn't get Dr. Green to give me a time frame, but you must have some idea."

The doctor pressed the tips of her fingers together. "It's very difficult to predict, but, looking at your most recent scans, I would say three to six months. Maybe a little longer if you stay clear of any infections or other complications."

The breath was knocked out of Cara's lungs. Six months? Sophie wouldn't have even started school. She bit down on her lip to stop it from trembling. "I'd hoped for longer than that."

"As I said, it's not possible to be precise and we don't want to take away your hopes, but we do want to make sure those hopes are realistic."

For the rest of the meeting, she took in only about a third of everything they talked about. At one point, the nurse had offered ways to reduce stress and anxiety. She'd suggested meditation. Cara just wanted to scream. She didn't want to talk about herself. She wanted to talk about Sophie. How was she going to tell her that her mum was going to die?

When she couldn't take any more, she stood up. "I'm sorry, I just…I'm not ready to talk about all of this yet. I need to…"

They both stood; the doctor was holding a sheet of information. "Of course. We understand that it's a lot to take in. Most of what we were going to talk about today is on this sheet. Take it home, read it through, and let us know when you want to talk again. We're here. You can call us anytime."

Outside, the gray drizzle felt heavy against Cara's face. The bus stop was empty and she sat on the thin plastic ledge, her feet in a puddle. *Probably looking at three to six months. Maybe a little longer.*

She remembered Sophie at six months, so proud to be sitting up, her toys spread around her. At nine months, toddling toward her, Cubby squashed into her sticky hands. At a year, on her first birthday, Danielle had helped Cara to make a cake, grumbling all the while about it being much easier to buy one from the store. That first year had gone so quickly. Would her last one be just as fast?

A sob escaped her throat and she bent double. Hugging her knees, she tried to take a breath but it came in gasps. This was real. This was happening and she had so much still to do. Everyone—Jamie from the cancer charity, Dr. Green, the palliative care people—was telling her to take her time, but that was the one thing she didn't have. She needed to get home to Sophie. She needed to speak to Jack and Rebecca.

When she got back, she let herself in with the spare key that Jack had given her. She stood at the doorway to the sitting room, watching the animated joy in Sophie's face as she followed the characters in her cartoons. How would she be able to look into that beautiful, trusting face and tell her that she was going to leave her?

Sophie threw herself back as she laughed at something on the screen, and she caught sight of Cara. "Mummy!"

Cara held out her arms to scoop her up. "Hey, baby. How was preschool?"

"It was good. Rebecca came to get me. I got to go and sit in the office with Sue."

Cara kissed the top of Sophie's head, smiling at her daughter's self-importance. "Well, that's great."

Rebecca came through from the kitchen and waited until Sophie had flopped down in front of the TV again. She beckoned Cara toward the kitchen. "Have you checked your email?"

Cara followed her, taking off her jacket as she walked. After her appointment, the DNA test had actually slipped her mind completely. "No. Has Jack received his?"

Rebecca shook her head. "Not that I've heard, but he's on his way home." On the kitchen island, her laptop was open. She turned it around so that the screen faced Cara. "You can check your email on here if you'd like?"

She could understand Rebecca's sense of urgency. It wasn't as if she had Cara's certainty about the conception. The web browser was already open, so she only had to type her username into Yahoo! to get into her email.

Rebecca was purposefully *not* looking at Cara as she typed in her password, and Cara wasn't in the mood for small talk. For the next few moments, the only noise in the room was the click of the laptop keys.

The results were there. She double-tapped to open the link in the email and read it through to the end. Then again. Then a third time. Heat rose in her body, her face, her brain. Her finger trembled on the touch pad and her vision blurred. Surely this was a mistake.

Rebecca took her arm. "You look like you need to sit down. What is it? What's the problem?"

Cara pointed to the email. Rebecca scanned it quickly; her mouth fell open.

Just then, Sophie padded into the kitchen. "Can I have a drink?"

When Rebecca spoke, her voice was higher than usual. "Of course, sweetie. I'll get you a glass of water. Go back to your cartoon and I'll bring it out to you."

As soon as she'd gone, Rebecca turned back to Cara. "I don't understand. This says that Jack isn't Sophie's dad. What the hell is going on? Did you *know*?"

CHAPTER THIRTY-EIGHT

Rebecca

It had been only a month since Jack and Rebecca had sat together on the couch eating cheese and crackers after the Friday-night dinner with Jack's boss. It felt like a lifetime ago. After Jack poured them both a glass of wine, they sat there for the next five minutes, clutching their glasses and staring ahead. Neither of them had taken so much as a sip.

He looked at Rebecca. "I feel like I've been hit by a train, to be honest."

That was one way to describe the hard, compressed feeling in her chest. "Me too."

Jack had arrived home about ten minutes after Cara had opened her copy of the email. Having already seen his at work, he had wanted to tell Rebecca in person. Even if he had made it home before Cara, the look of shock on his face when he'd walked through the front door would have told Rebecca what to expect. Cara's reaction wasn't much different. Either she was the best actress on the planet or she was just as shocked as they were: there was no question that she had really believed that Jack was Sophie's dad. After Jack's arrival, she'd taken Sophie upstairs to the bathroom with the promise of a bubble bath.

Rebecca turned her wineglass around in her fingertips. "Do you want to know something crazy? When Cara first arrived, I thought she was after you. Wanting you back, I mean."

Jack coughed a dry laugh. "Because I'm such a catch?"

Rebecca smiled weakly at his attempt at humor. "Seriously. She clearly wanted me out of the way so that she could talk to you and, well, if I'm being honest, it seemed like you were attracted to her."

Jack stared into his glass. "No. It wasn't that. I mean, she is a good-looking woman and I enjoyed talking to her about old times. But it wasn't attraction to her—it was more that it reminded me of being young again, I suppose."

While Rebecca could understand the sentiment, it wasn't one she shared. The thought of revisiting her twenties was not an appealing one. She was much happier now that she had Jack and life was organized and they knew what they wanted. At least, they had.

Everything felt so surreal right now; it was as good a time as any to be open about how she had felt the last few weeks, watching him with Cara and Sophie. "And—if we really are laying our cards on the table—I also thought that you were quick to want to take on Sophie." She took a sip of wine, tried to make her voice sound as nonchalant as possible. "I wondered whether you'd been honest with me about not wanting children."

Jack started in surprise, then shook his head. "That's not quite how it was. Not to start with at least. In the beginning, you were the one telling me that I needed to step up. Pushing me to put a plan in place with Cara for when we would look after Sophie." He held up a hand before she interrupted. "I'm not complaining about that. You were right. I did need to. If she was my child. But now…"

Just as quickly as everything had changed, it had all been turned back again. Like whiplash. She knew how upended she felt by all this, but what about Jack? "But now she's not. Not your daughter."

Jack turned his glass slowly. He looked as if he might cry. "Exactly. Now she's not and we're just us again."

It was like the air was being sucked from between them. Just us. *Just.* "Is that not enough for you anymore?"

"What do you mean?" When Jack looked up at her, there was something in his eyes she couldn't read. He was holding back. She knew him well enough to recognize that.

She had to be sure. They had to be totally honest. "Being a dad these last few weeks... it's really suited you. You've been a natural at it. Has it made you change your mind about wanting children?"

She held her breath. Whatever he said next might change her life.

Jack sighed. He took her hand in his. Oh God, was this where it all fell apart? "No." He shook his head. "No, it hasn't made me want to have children. But Sophie... I have really enjoyed being around her. She's a great little kid. And I'm... I'm worried about her. I'm really worried about what happens to her when Cara can't look after her anymore."

Rebecca's head was a maelstrom. She was worried about Sophie too. Not like a mother would worry necessarily, just as a human being. A human being who could see a little girl about to lose her mother. A little girl with no family that they knew of. It wasn't a maternal feeling. It wasn't. It just wasn't.

"But what can we do?"

Jack looked up at her. "I think we both know what we *could* do. It comes down to whether or not we want to."

Rebecca put her glass down on the table and turned to face Jack properly. This was serious; she needed to know if he was just talking about options or if he really meant for them to keep Sophie. "Adoption? Would they even let us adopt her? I mean, surely there are tests you need to do for that? Isn't there a waiting list or something?"

Jack leaned toward her as if he was trying to read her reaction. "I have no idea. But—if we were interested in doing that—we could ask?"

Rebecca's face felt hot. She fiddled with her wedding ring—the beautiful ring they had chosen together. When they'd known what they wanted. When everything had been clear. And now? "Do you think Cara would want us to adopt her? I mean, you're not her dad. And I don't think she's hugely keen on me. She knows we don't want children of our own."

"Again. We would need to ask." He reached out and took her hand in his again. "But I know we need to talk about it first. We need to be sure that's what we want. We both have busy careers and you're still building up your company. We need to really think about this. Both of us."

One look at Jack's face made it clear where his vote would go. There was an eagerness there that he was failing to hide. If she said she didn't want this, would this be the beginning of the end for them? Something he would hold against her forever? And if she said yes, and they did adopt Sophie, what would happen to their relationship then? To their lives? Most people had time to make decisions like this. Time to decide what they wanted. But they didn't.

It was unspoken, but she'd already seen how adopting a child would impact her life so much more than it would Jack's. She worked from home. She was her own boss. That meant she would be the one doing school drop-offs and looking after Sophie when she was sick.

And this wasn't going to be easy. If they were in a position to adopt Sophie, that would mean that Cara was gone. Sophie would have lost her mother. She would need so much support. So much love. *How do you even start to support a child through that?*

Rebecca's heart thumped in her chest. Right now, she couldn't think straight. Jack was right: they needed time to think. Tomorrow she was booked to go to a wedding fair with Izzy. Maybe a day away from home would help her to get some perspective either way.

CHAPTER THIRTY-NINE

Cara

"Did you know?"

Some women might have been offended by Danielle's question with its connotations of *Are you a scheming, manipulative liar?* But Cara had known her friend too long for unnecessary parsing. That's why she had come here the very next day. The need to be with someone who knew her well and loved her anyway. As well as wanting to escape being in the house she had no right to be living in.

She picked up her mug from where Danielle had balanced it on a couple of copies of *Hello!* on top of her coffee table. "I swear I was as shocked as they were. I mean, I obviously remember sleeping with other men after Jack. It's not something I'm proud of. But I was all over the place once he ended things. Physically as well as mentally."

Danielle nodded and bit into a bourbon cookie. They'd shared their not-so-romantic pasts many times over a bottle of wine: no judgment either way. She pointed the cookie at Cara. "But I don't understand. If you'd slept with other men around the same time, how were you still so sure?"

It seemed naive now, stupid even. But she really had been sure. "I always used condoms. I was angry, not suicidal. Except that time with Jack."

She should have used protection with Jack too. It wasn't as if they had been planning on having a family together. But in an actual relationship, it was easy to let boundaries slide. Yesterday, after the test result, Rebecca's suspicious face had practically accused her of having known all along that Sophie wasn't Jack's child. But she really hadn't.

She could almost see Danielle's brain ticking over as she finished her cookie. "So, all this time you have assumed you knew who Sophie's father is, and now he's not."

"In a nutshell. Yes." Cara rubbed at her cheek with her free hand. This was such a mess.

Danielle held out the cookie packet and Cara shook her head. Danielle took another and held it halfway into her tea. "So, are you going to try and contact the other men? Get them to do DNA tests too?"

If the situation weren't so dire, that would almost be funny. How the hell was she going to do that? Put an ad in the local paper? Have you slept with this woman? "I haven't got a clue who or where they are. I was drunk and needy and barely knew their first names. Although...I do have a vague memory that there was a guy who looked a bit like Jack." She winced at the thought. "It was five years ago. I've got no chance of tracking anyone down."

Danielle nodded. Thank God Cara could speak openly without fear Danielle would be shocked or disapproving. It was only now—when she didn't have her living next door—that she realized how much she valued their friendship. When Cara had first started treatment and couldn't work, she'd been absolutely broke waiting for her first benefit payment. Danielle had bought her groceries and checked in on her and even had Sophie stay over when Cara needed to rest.

That's why she knew that Danielle meant every word when she said, "So, that leaves you back at square one with Sophie. Look, you know I'll take her."

Cara shook her head. "I can't expect you to do that. You already have four of your own to look after. And it's not as if I can give you anything to support her."

"Well, she is *not* going into foster care." Danielle flushed as she spoke. They were both the keepers of a lot of each other's childhood secrets too. Cara knew enough about Danielle's experiences with the foster care system to understand why she was adamant that Sophie wouldn't be looked after by strangers.

She wasn't about to let that happen either. "I know."

Danielle was a really good woman. Cara knew it was a genuine offer to take Sophie in. But she didn't want that either. The short time she'd spent with Jack and Rebecca had given her a window into the world her daughter could have. It wasn't about money or holidays or fancy things. It was about the possibility of a life in which Sophie had choices. Where she could do and be whatever she wanted to be. That wouldn't be so easy sharing a room with Danielle's daughters and going to the local school where nine-year-olds were smoking outside.

Although Danielle didn't look as if she'd given in, she left the subject of Sophie's care for now. "So, what did Jack and his missus have to say about it all? Did they tell you to get packed up and out of there?"

Cara wasn't sure how to answer that. Rebecca must have been so relieved that Sophie was out of their lives. She had made a good show of taking Sophie on, but now she could return to her perfect life with no complications. And who could blame her?

And Jack? He must have been relieved too. The two of them would probably look back on the last few weeks as a nightmare episode from their past. They might even laugh about it from the deck of a cruise ship with margaritas in their hands.

No. That wasn't fair. They *had* made a huge effort with Sophie. They had welcomed her into their lives. She shook her aching head. "No. They were very kind about it, to be honest."

Danielle squinted her eyes. "How kind? 'Adopt the daughter of a dying woman' type of kind?"

Was that a possibility? Was there any way at all they had got close enough to Sophie to want her to stay? "I don't know."

"Seems to me those are your only two options. They adopt Sophie or you leave her with me. Unless you've been hiding a fairy godmother you've not told me about?"

Danielle knew all about Cara's background, the family she'd walked away from. She was right; there were no other options. "If they are willing to adopt her, can you just do that? Can you just give your child to someone like that? Would they need to get checked out?"

Danielle opened her mouth to answer, but Sophie appeared at the door with Poppy following behind her. "Mummy, can Poppy come home with us? Can she come and play at our house?"

Poppy looked very hopeful about that. Sophie had probably painted a virtual picture of her new bedroom and toys. And she already thought of Jack and Rebecca's place as home. How quickly children could adapt to a new reality. Would she adapt to another change so soon? "Not today, baby. Why don't you go and play for a bit? We've got to go in a minute."

As they ran away to play, Cara heard Sophie making promises about building blocks and dollhouses and other treasures that she'd show Poppy at "my house." She started to cough and Danielle frowned at her. "Are you okay? You don't sound so good."

Cara rooted around in her bag for a packet of tissues. "I think I've got a bit of a cold. Sophie wasn't feeling well last week." She blew her nose. Her head was really starting to throb now.

Danielle looked concerned. "Do you want some aspirin?"

"No, I'll be fine. Just need to get home and sleep, I think." She was doing it now: calling Jack's place home. Which it wasn't. She stood up to put on her jacket. "Do you know if Lee has rented my old place next door yet?"

Danielle held out her hands. "No idea. I can call him and ask him if you'd like? How long have you got before you need to move out of the palace of dreams?"

Cara laughed, but even that hurt. "I don't know. It's all been a bit..."

But she didn't finish. Danielle's face blurred in front of her and she felt herself begin to fall.

CHAPTER FORTY

Rebecca

The exhibition hall was full of stalls and people. Bright white smiles and long tanned legs lured people to see the latest in venues, invitation design, balloon art.

Rebecca had already read the wedding fair itinerary and circled the stalls that they wanted to visit so that she could maximize their time. Although weddings were almost always Izzy's side of the business, they liked to attend events like this together and, as usual, she needed to rein in Izzy from wandering off. The woman needed child reins to keep her under control. Even the thought of that brought Sophie to her mind and she pushed her out again. "Okay. We want stand G47. Glenmore House. They have a new wedding package that I'd like them to explain."

Izzy wasn't even looking at her. She was peering over at a stall that was giving away multicolored drinks with decorative fruit floating on the top. "Okay, but can't we just wander and find the people you think I should speak to as we go?"

Did Izzy even know her? "We only have four hours and I want to make sure we don't get sidetracked."

"You mean *I* don't get sidetracked, right? I don't think you've ever taken a track on the side in your life." Izzy nudged her and smiled, but she wasn't in the mood.

A ridiculously handsome man of around twenty—probably a part-time actor paying the bills—stepped out in front of them with a fistful of pens and Post-it notes. "Good afternoon, ladies, can I interest you in a lovely free writing implement?"

Izzy beamed. "You had me at free."

Before Rebecca knew it, he'd managed to corral them toward his stand, which was for stationery: invitations, seating plans, save-the-date cards, menus—limitless options on premium-quality card stock. This was not what they were here for, but Izzy was already stroking a glossy, linen-finish program. The handsome man-child obviously sensed that Rebecca wasn't as interested. He thrust a Post-it note pad at her. "Do you have kids at home? I can give you a few more of these for them if you'd like."

He was clearly too young to realize that he shouldn't say that to a woman, even if she did look of an age to be popping out children. Rebecca crossed her arms. "No children. And I'm fine, thanks."

Izzy looked up. "Sophie might like one. My two go mad for a sticky note. And you said she likes drawing. Why don't you take a couple for her?"

Something twanged in Rebecca's chest. "Sophie won't be around much longer."

Izzy frowned. "What do you mean?"

The young man was clearly only there as bait because he left them alone to go out onto the concourse and hook more prey. His older and less attractive colleague leaned in. "You clearly have a good eye for class, ladies. That's our new luxury range of wedding stationery. Can I interest you in the other items in the range?"

Ever the professional, Izzy flashed him a smile. "That would be great, but I just need a conversation with my partner."

She took Rebecca's elbow and steered her out past the handsome man until they were anonymous members of the crowd. "What do you mean, Sophie won't be around? What's happened?"

Rebecca took a deep breath. "Jack isn't Sophie's father."

Izzy looked as if she was about to choke. "What? Are you sure?"

Rebecca nodded. "DNA test. We found out yesterday."

Izzy covered her mouth with her hand. Other people walked past them: brides-to-be with their proud mothers in tow, event coordinators picking up brochures, stallholders checking out the competition. *This* was her world: she knew where she was here. Izzy reached out and put an arm on her shoulder. "Let's go get a cup of coffee."

She really didn't want to talk about it. "I'm fine. Let's just go to—"

Izzy had her elbow again. "You might be fine. I'm not. Come on."

The coffee bar was über-trendy with about forty different choices of coffee, milk, and size of cup. Izzy made her scout for a seat while she stood in line for two flat whites.

In usual Izzy fashion, she got served pretty quickly, and Rebecca waved her over from the seats she'd found. Izzy slid the cups onto the table and pulled her chair in close, her voice low. "Look, I don't mean to sound like a Judgy Judy, but I'm surprised you guys didn't ask for a DNA test from the beginning. I mean, this is you, Rebecca. You cross-check everything."

Rebecca tried to sip her drink from its compostable cup but it was scalding and burned the edge of her lip. "I know. I feel like a complete idiot. We meant to do it, but . . . I don't know. Sophie just looks so much like Jack, or at least I thought she did. And he seemed to think it was entirely probable that she was his. And then the, you know, the cancer. It just didn't seem like a priority."

She'd been over and over it in her head. It *was* entirely out of character for her to just have accepted that Sophie was Jack's daughter without proof. If that wasn't vindication for all the other times she'd been accused of squeezing the life out of things with her triple-checking, she didn't know what was. The vindication didn't make her feel any better, though.

Izzy was slowly shaking her head. "Sheesh. I don't know what to say; this is . . . I honestly don't know what to say. What was Jack's reaction?"

Jack had been in shock. In some ways, it was worse than when Cara had knocked on their door that first night. Was it really only a month ago? "He's as lost as I am."

Rebecca and Jack had been circling around each other this morning. Afraid to say the wrong thing. Giving Sophie her breakfast had felt... well, it had felt as if she were seeing her for the first time. Suddenly, all the ways she had looked like Jack just kind of fell away. It was crazy.

"And what about Cara? Has she got any idea what she's going to do now that Jack isn't Sophie's dad?"

She hadn't seen Cara before she'd left this morning. Jack had known she'd wanted to go over to Izzy's before the exhibition and he'd offered to wait with Sophie until her mother got up. She was so tired first thing in the morning that they hadn't wanted to disturb her. Maybe she hadn't been asleep. Maybe she had been lying there trying to figure out what the hell she was going to do next. "I think it's early days. I mean, it's not like we're going to kick her out. They don't have anywhere to go."

The coffee shop was filling up and there were people eyeing their table, waiting for them to go. Rebecca just wanted to go to the stands they'd planned to visit and then get back. "Come on, let's get this done."

If Izzy had any more questions, she kept them to herself. "Okay, but you know you can talk to me about this whenever you want. Nothing you can say will shock me. Honestly. And in the meantime"—she held out her hands—"take me where you want me to go."

The stall Rebecca wanted to see was on the other side of the exhibition space. They had to run the gauntlet of overeager stall-holders thrusting brochures or flyers into their reluctant hands. It was avoiding a toothy orange person with a bag full of spray tan vouchers that made Rebecca mistakenly enter the Bouncing Balloons stall, almost getting knocked to the ground by a life-sized inflatable bride and groom. "Sorry."

Izzy giggled behind her. "I don't think they mind."

Hot and uncomfortable, Rebecca turned to find her way out of there. Balloons were not her thing. There was something decidedly tacky about an inflatable archway in the shape of a heart. Terrible for the environment too. But there was a pearly yellow balloon bobbing alone that she could just imagine Sophie holding in her pudgy little hand. She mustn't think about that. "Get me out of here."

She was striding back along the main concourse when Izzy caught up with her. "Hey. Wait for me. Where's the fire?"

When Rebecca turned to look at Izzy, her vision blurred. "I'm sorry, I…"

Izzy's face fell and she put her hand on Rebecca's shoulder. "Oh, Rebecca, don't cry. Oh, honey, what is it?"

"I can't do it." It was only as she said the words that Rebecca realized the truth of them. "I can't let her go."

Then her phone rang.

Once Cara had finished, she passed the cup back to the nurse. "Do you know how long before they're going to let me go…home?" She faltered on the last word. Where even was home right now?

The tear of Velcro sounded loud in that small space as the nurse tore apart the blood pressure cuff and wrapped it around Cara's arm. Watching her capable fingers making it secure, Cara was suddenly surprised at how thin her arms had become. She felt the tightening as the machine did its work and the nurse read the dial. She nodded her approval. "Your blood pressure is okay. You've got a chest infection, so we need to make sure the antibiotics are doing their job."

There was no way she wanted to stay in here overnight. She needed to get back to Sophie as soon as possible. What if she was frightened? Had she seen the ambulance taking Cara away? "So, how long will that be? Another hour? Two?"

The nurse tilted her head to look at her. "Normally we would keep you in overnight to monitor you. But, under the circumstances, the doctor might discharge you and let you recover at home. As long as you come straight back in if you feel at all unwell. Have you got someone to come and get you?"

Cara chewed at her lip. Danielle would come and get her if she needed her to, but that would depend on her eldest daughter being at home to watch the younger ones. She didn't want to ask Jack or Rebecca. "I'm fine to get a taxi."

The nurse frowned. "There's no way we can discharge you if there's no one at home to look after you."

She needed to think quickly; she wasn't about to stay here and pick up some bug at the hospital. There was too much to do. Too much to organize. Rebecca and Jack were good people, but how long would they let them stay now? "There is someone at home. They just might not be able to come out to get me." It wasn't a complete lie; Sophie would be with her wherever they ended up. Sophie was her home.

The nurse would have seen Cara's file, so she knew why Cara didn't want to be in the hospital for any of the time she might have left. Her tone was sympathetic. "Well, we'll see. Hopefully we've caught the infection this time. But you're going to be susceptible to every bug that's going around. You need to think about isolating yourself as much as you can."

If only she had the luxury of a partner or family that would enable that to happen. "It's a bit tricky. I've got a little girl. And I'm on my own." She bit at her lip again to stop it from trembling. She had been on her own with Sophie forever. She hadn't felt sorry for herself and she hadn't asked for help from anyone. But this was different.

The nurse was very kind. "I understand. It's difficult, but kids are miniature germ factories. Is there anyone who can help you out with her?"

It wasn't just Sophie who had got used to being at Jack and Rebecca's. On some level, Cara had felt as if she had a safety net for the first time in her life. Her appointment with Dr. Green had been devastating and terrifying, but at least with Jack and Rebecca there, she knew that Sophie would be okay if the worst happened. And now?

The nurse was still there, waiting for a response. "Maybe. I'll call someone."

When the nurse left, appeased for now, Cara ran through the options in her head. The more she thought about it, the more she kept coming back to the same answer: Jack and Rebecca were her only hope. Jack might not be Sophie's biological father, but he had enjoyed spending time with her, hadn't he? And Sophie loved spending time with him. And Rebecca.

This chest infection might get better, or it might not. Either way, she didn't have time to be polite or hopeful. She needed to make this happen. Somehow, she had to find a way to persuade Jack and Rebecca to look after Sophie. She would beg them if necessary.

Her handbag was in the locker by the side of the bed. It took her a while to reach it with her left hand and then pull it onto her lap. Her mobile phone was in the side pocket at the front. She found the number she was looking for. It rang twice before being picked up.

"Rebecca? Hi, it's Cara. I need your help."

CHAPTER FORTY-TWO

Rebecca

It was taking some time to extricate Sophie from Danielle's house because she wanted Rebecca to verify to her eager-faced friend Poppy that she did indeed have her own bedroom and her own desk and, yes, Sophie had made cupcakes and helped to plan someone's wedding.

Somehow, Danielle had managed to allay Sophie's fears about the ambulance in the few hours since Cara had been taken in, further helped by a phone call from Cara to tell Sophie that everything was fine and that the doctors had given her some medicine to make her chest better.

Now Danielle was eyeing Rebecca suspiciously, her arms folded across her cleavage. "I can keep her here, you know. I'm more than capable."

Her defensive tone made Rebecca feel like someone from social services. "I'm sure you are. But Cara asked me to pick her up and take her home. Hopefully they're going to let Cara out in the morning anyway."

The two little girls had disappeared back inside to find Sophie's shoes, and Danielle pulled the front door almost closed behind her, lowering her voice. "She really didn't know, you know."

"Sorry?" Rebecca had to lean forward to hear her. For a moment, she thought Danielle was talking about the cancer.

The fingers of Danielle's right hand were hooked around the open edge of the door to stop it from shutting. Her left arm was wrapped across her stomach, hand on her right hip as if she was hugging herself. "That Jack isn't Sophie's dad. The DNA test. She was completely shocked. And she definitely would have told me if she wasn't. She had thought Jack was Sophie's dad the whole time."

Rebecca knew this. It was obvious from Cara's reaction that she had been blindsided by that result. They all shared the blame for not doing a DNA test immediately. Even now, she couldn't explain why they hadn't. Was it Jack's reaction? Her own misguided belief that Sophie looked like Jack? Who knew? But they hadn't. And this was the result. She lowered her own voice to the same level. "I don't blame her."

Danielle pushed the door open to check for Sophie then stepped out into the communal hallway, still holding the door handle so that no one could pull it open from behind. "What are you going to do?"

Rebecca needed time to get her own thoughts straight before dealing with someone interrogating her about the next step. "Sorry?"

"About Sophie. And Cara. Are you kicking them out?"

Why was she being made out to be the bad person here? "I don't think that's any of your business."

Danielle lifted her chin. "Cara is my best friend and she is too ill to be figuring this all out. She needs somewhere to stay for a while . . . somewhere nice to . . ." Furiously, Danielle wiped away the tears rolling down her cheeks.

Rebecca softened. If Cara was this woman's best friend, it was no wonder that she was looking out for her. "Look. We're not about to *kick them out*. But we do need to talk about it all. Now that we know Jack isn't Sophie's father, it's even more complicated than it was at the beginning."

There was a little knock on the other side of the door. Sophie lifted the letterbox flap. "Can I come out, please?"

"Of course, sweetheart." Danielle opened the door and crouched down to Sophie's height, zipped up her pink padded coat. "You be a good girl for Rebecca. And give your mum a kiss from me when she gets home, okay?"

"Okay." Sophie wrapped her arms around Danielle's neck and gave her a hug, then reached out for Rebecca's hand. How quickly this felt normal.

Danielle came back up to Rebecca's eye level. "Cara has my number. Let me know. If they need anything. Let me know."

Rebecca nodded. "I will."

The new ISOFIX car seat she'd ordered for Sophie had turned up the previous day and—in light of the DNA test—she had planned to send it straight back. Now she was glad she hadn't.

Maybe it was being in the back and not having to look Rebecca in the face that gave Sophie the courage to ask the questions she wanted to ask. "How sick is Mummy? The ambulance took her away. Is she going to die?"

Clearly, she hadn't been as reassured by Cara's call as Danielle had assumed. Rebecca wanted to stop Sophie from worrying, but it wasn't her place to answer any questions about Cara's long-term health. Probably best to keep it vague for now. "She's got a really bad cold and the doctors need to give her some medicine in the hospital so that she can get rid of it."

Sophie had obviously been considering this. "But I didn't go to the hospital when I had a cold. We just had French toast."

Rebecca kept a smile on her face as she glanced at her in the rear-view mirror. "I know, but Mummy was already sick, wasn't she?"

Sophie didn't meet her eye when she asked her next question. "With the cancer?"

What had Cara said to Sophie about her condition? She'd never heard them speak about it but Cara seemed to think that Sophie knew what she needed to know. Did Sophie know how serious it was, though? Rebecca didn't want to make things any worse. Didn't want to make Sophie scared. But she couldn't lie. "Yes. The cancer."

Sophie was quiet for another few streets, drawing a face in the steam on the car window. Then she spoke again. "I had a bad dream last night."

"Did you? What was it about?"

"Nothing."

How absolutely confusing and frightening this situation must have been for Sophie. No child should have to deal with her mother's terminal illness. It was too big for such a little girl. However much she wanted to soothe her fears, Rebecca wasn't the right person to be helping her. What if she said the wrong thing? But she couldn't say nothing. Couldn't just dismiss it as unimportant. "Do you have bad dreams a lot?"

Another glance in her rearview mirror confirmed that Sophie was nodding. "Sometimes I have them a lot and sometimes they go away and then they come back again."

Rebecca took a deep breath. "Are they about your mum?"

Sophie was looking out of the window again now. "Sometimes."

How could Rebecca explain it to her? She needed to say something that would make her feel listened to without making her more anxious. "Well, it's normal to have bad dreams when you're worried about somebody. And when your mum is not feeling well, it's natural to be worried about her."

Sophie seemed to consider this for a few moments. And then she repeated the question that she really wanted answered. "Is my mummy going to die?"

Rebecca could barely open her mouth to speak. It was so unfair that this little girl was going to lose her mother. She was too young; it wasn't right. But Cara had sounded so weak on the phone. Rebecca knew that something like this could be the end for her.

She wanted to tell Sophie that everything was going to be okay. That, whatever happened, she and Jack would look after her and keep her safe.

But how could she promise her that when she had no idea if that was even going to be possible? "How about we get home and then you can call Mummy and speak to her again?"

CHAPTER FORTY-THREE

Cara

After a frustrating overnight stay, Cara finally persuaded the hospital to let her out late on Thursday afternoon. Dr. Green had checked in on her and explained what they both already knew: her immune system was dangerously weak and a virus or infection like this could be the final straw for her body. If the antibiotics couldn't get ahold of it, she was looking at weeks, if not days.

She could have stayed in the hospital, but she'd read enough articles about MRSA and the like to know that she wouldn't be totally safe there either. No, if she only had a little bit of time left, she was going to spend it with Sophie. And that's what she needed to talk to Jack and Rebecca about.

Jack had come to pick her up from the hospital. He'd taken the day off work because Sophie had stayed home from preschool with Rebecca and she couldn't bring her into the hospital. Cara had asked Rebecca to send her makeup bag with him. Sophie was already going to be scared; she didn't need her mother coming in looking like the walking dead.

Sitting next to him in the car was strange—like old times. Like that day, back when they were together, when they'd taken it into their heads to drive to Brighton for the day. Lying beside him in bed, she'd happened to mention that she'd never been, and he had jumped up and grabbed his car keys, and they'd been on the A23 in no time. She smiled at the memory.

Jack must have noticed the smile. "Are you feeling better?"

"I'm not sure 'better' is the right word, but I'm upright at least."

Jack winced. "Sorry."

She was being mean, and this wasn't the time to be difficult. "No, I'm sorry. I do feel a bit better than I did, but I need to start facing facts."

Should she talk to him about it now? Sound him out while he was on his own? Two weeks ago, she might have, but it was obvious that she needed to speak to both of them. If Rebecca thought she'd gone behind her back, it wouldn't help her cause one bit.

The first priority when she got home was seeing Sophie to reassure her that her mum was okay. But when she arrived, Sophie was tentative, as if she was frightened to touch her. "Hey, baby, where's my welcome-home hug?"

Sophie hovered for a second and then ran at her, buried her face in Cara's hip and shook with tears. Cara stroked the back of her silky head. "Come on, shall we go upstairs for a story and a cuddle?"

Rebecca and Jack kept themselves scarce while Cara lay with Sophie and told her that she had to take antibiotics and they were going to fight her bug and get her better again.

While she was explaining, Sophie could barely meet her eye. "Is it my fault?"

"What do you mean?"

"Is it my fault you have the bug? Was it my germs that made you sick?"

It may well have been the bug that Sophie had had the other day but there was no way Cara was telling her that. "Of course not. It's Mummy's treatment. It makes me more likely to get a bug. The doctors are used to it."

That seemed to appease her a little. At least she was looking at Cara now. "And does it hurt? If I hug you, does it hurt?"

"Not at all." She squeezed Sophie close to her, pressed her nose to the top of her head, and breathed her in. If she could just hold this moment forever, she would never want for anything else. "Having you here is the best medicine I could ever have."

Eventually, Sophie was persuaded that her mum wasn't going anywhere and disappeared downstairs to have a snack. This gave Cara the window she needed. She called Jack's phone and he answered almost immediately.

"Hi. Are you okay? Do you need something?"

Already, she was feeling tired again. She needed to speak to them now. "Could you and Rebecca come upstairs for a minute? Make sure Sophie is occupied in front of her cartoons or something?"

Jack paused. He must have realized something was up. "Of course. We'll be up in five."

True to his word, Jack knocked gently on her bedroom door five minutes later. "Okay to come in?"

She pulled the covers up higher. "Of course."

Rebecca came in first and Jack followed; his obvious embarrassment was ironic considering they'd explored every inch of each other's bodies in the past.

Rebecca spoke first. "How are you feeling?"

"Exhausted, to be honest. And achy. Really achy."

Judging by the look of concern on Rebecca's face, she must have looked really bad. "Can we do anything to make you more comfortable? Do you want anything to eat?"

Even a small shake of her head hurt. It was too soon for more painkillers, though. "I just need to speak to you both about Sophie and then I'll sleep."

Rebecca glanced at Jack. They shuffled farther into the room. Jack smiled at her. "We wanted to talk to you about Sophie too."

"Let me talk first. I need to get it out. I know what I'm about to ask you isn't right. I know that I've brought so much upheaval to you these last few weeks and I am sorry for that. I really did think she was your daughter, Jack."

She held her breath for a moment. This was harder than she'd thought it was going to be. Jack looked as if he was about to speak so she carried on. "Sophie is my daughter and I will do anything to make sure she is safe. Anything. You are a good man, Jack. You've always been a good man. Even when I hated you for leaving me, I had to admit that you had been honest and kind and fair. You just didn't love me, or at least not enough to stay with me forever."

Jack lowered his gaze to the floor. She didn't want to make him feel bad. She just wanted him to understand. To really understand. "Sophie needs someone like you in her life. She needs dependable and good. She needs to be loved." She turned to Rebecca, who had tears in her eyes. "I know you don't want children, Rebecca. I know that wasn't your plan. But you will be a good mother to her—I know you will. You are clever and ambitious and...way, way more tidy than is probably healthy. But you have a big heart. I know I am asking a lot. I am asking you to change your whole life to look after a little girl who you didn't even know a month ago. But she's a wonderful kid and you won't regret it. I know you won't."

Rebecca reached out to take her hand and then stopped herself. "Cara, I—"

"No, don't speak yet. I need to say everything." She had to get it all out. "I was thinking about this while I was in the hospital last night and I'm actually pleased you don't want any more children. If you and Jack had kids, you might love them more than you love Sophie. But this way, she gets to be the center of your world like she has been the center of mine. With you as parents, there is nothing she won't be able to have or see or do. You can give her everything I want for her. An education. Travel. Dreams."

Tears were flowing freely down Rebecca's cheeks now. Cara reached for the hand she had almost offered moments before, grasping it as tightly as she could manage. "Do you think you could love her?"

Rebecca looked as if she was struggling to speak. She nodded and whispered, "I think I already do."

Jack cleared his throat. Were his eyes shining too? "This is what we wanted to talk to you about. We've been discussing the same thing."

As Cara let her breath out, it vibrated over her throat. Had she said enough to persuade them? "And?"

"And . . ." He glanced at Rebecca and she gave a small nod. "We want to adopt Sophie."

Cara's heart lifted; that was half the battle. Now for the rest. "I am so pleased. And grateful—I really am. But I don't think we have the time for that. My doctor was pretty clear. I don't know how long I have, and adoption might take too long. We might not have enough time."

The effort of speaking made her cough, and Rebecca poured her a glass of water.

Jack waited for her to finish coughing. "I don't understand. I thought this was what you wanted?"

Rebecca put her hand on Jack's arm to stop him from asking any more questions. "What is it you want us to do?"

Cara's heart began to beat faster. "I want to be sure that Sophie will be with you. I want Jack to legally be her father. That way I know she will be safe." She looked at Jack, pleading with everything she had. "I want you to put your name on Sophie's birth certificate."

CHAPTER FORTY-FOUR

Rebecca

Jack ran his hands through his hair. "What do we do?"

Sophie had finished watching her favorite cartoon and was back upstairs with Cara. She'd asked Rebecca if she could take her art box up with her so that she could draw her mum some pictures, so Rebecca had helped her to carry them and had given her one of the huge hardback books that she kept under their glass coffee table for her to use as a surface. Jack had joked that at least someone was getting some use out of them.

Jack had closed the kitchen door and was leaning against it, eyes closed. "It's illegal, isn't it? What she's asking us to do?"

"I would imagine so. I've not googled it."

Jack opened his eyes and looked at her. "Me neither. I'm almost frightened to look it up in case anyone checks my search history."

She didn't want to look it up because she didn't want to know for sure. Didn't want to know what the going rate for prison sentences was if you lied on a birth certificate. Maybe it was better not to know. Go in blind. "I read something once—a newspaper article—that said there are a surprising number of men who are named on birth certificates and don't know that they are not the father of the child in question."

Jack nodded. "Yeah, I mean, people are always having affairs, right?"

"All the time." Rebecca laughed. Then put a hand to her mouth. It must have been the shock. "Sorry."

Jack waved her apology away. "You've got nothing to be sorry about." He was quiet for a moment. "Do you think the DNA people keep a record of the results they send out?"

"Probably." She should have been thinking about this more seriously, but her mind was upstairs, with Cara and Sophie. No one should have to go through what they were about to. If there was anything she could do to make it easier for them, she would. Anything.

Jack began pacing the floor of the kitchen: a sure sign he was processing, reasoning, planning. "So, they—the DNA people— would know that I'm not her father. Her biological father, I mean."

Already he was making the distinction. Did he think of himself as Sophie's father? "Yes. They must know."

"And do you think they are linked in any way to the people who issue the birth certificates? Like, they have to share information with them?"

Rebecca had no idea and he knew that. These questions were rhetorical; Jack was trying to sort this out in his own mind. Weigh the potential risks. "I don't suppose they are linked but I don't know. I'm not sure it'd be legal for them to share private medical information."

Jack slumped down on the kitchen stool next to her, stared into the coffee that he hadn't touched. They sat in silence, lost in their own thoughts.

A strange calm had settled over Rebecca. Anyone who knew her would imagine her imploding at the very idea of Jack signing his name on a legal document when he knew that he was lying. It went against everything she believed in. But right now, all she could think about was Cara's face. Her absolute fear when she spoke about Sophie going into the foster care system. And the thought of that beautiful little girl losing her mum and then being taken away from the life she knew. And what if they couldn't find a family for her? Or the family they found weren't nice people? What if…? She tightened her grip around her mug. *No.* That wasn't going to happen. *No. No. No.*

Jack broke the silence. "There's no one else, is there?"   .

There was Danielle, Cara's friend. But if that was an option, surely Cara would have been speaking to her now rather than them. Rebecca had seen her tiny apartment with four kids living there already. "No. No one else."

"I can't bear to think of her being…out there. Being with someone other than us." Jack stood up and recommenced his pacing. "Surely they would let us look after her? Social services or whoever it is who decides these things. I mean, it's what Cara wants, isn't it? It's what Sophie wants. And we have a nice home, good jobs; we're good people. Why would they say we couldn't look after Sophie when Cara…when she's gone?"

He couldn't bring himself to say that Cara would die. He had loved her once. In the middle of all that was going on, she'd not thought that he might be grieving for Cara too. "I'm sure there's a good chance they would. Like you say, we are perfectly capable of looking after a child, and Cara wants us to have her. But if they didn't…"

Jack stopped pacing and turned to look at her. "It's a risk."

She nodded. "And we don't have very long. The way she looked when you brought her home from the hospital…We just don't know how long we have." It was strange how calm she felt. How matter-of-fact. When this was probably the craziest, most out-of-character thing she had ever done.

Jack swallowed. "And Cara might be…gone before everything is sorted out. She wouldn't know for sure."

Rebecca nodded. "She wouldn't have that peace."

"Oh my God." Jack's voice cracked and he reached out and squeezed her hand. "It's all so bloody unfair."

It was getting harder not to cry. It *was* unfair. "She is clearly such a good mum. Sophie is a lovely kid."

Jack's eyes were bright with unshed tears. "She really is, isn't she? Clever and funny and beautiful." He frowned and stared at the back of Rebecca's hand, following the shape of her knuckles with his thumb. "Cara used to be like that, too. Well, most of the time. Other times she was... I can't explain it; it was like she'd been broken. Everything would be fine and then she would do something nuts. Like she was trying to wreck everything. Trying to get me to leave her. It was like I was constantly being tested."

Had Cara been like Sophie as a child? What had happened in her life to give her that brittle, fragile shell? "And she doesn't want that for Sophie."

"No. She doesn't." He looked up. "And I can stop that from happening."

Was he serious? As if this wasn't a massive commitment for both of them. "You? Not us?"

"Sorry, you know what I mean. Of course it will be both of us. And we need to be really sure. Once I've put my name on that birth certificate, there will be no going back. It's a legal document. I will be legally responsible for Sophie until she's eighteen."

Eighteen. They weren't just talking about looking after a little girl. She was going to grow into a teenager, a young woman. They would be negotiating schoolwork and friendship issues and boyfriends. This was forever.

Jack still held her hand. Butterflies started up in her stomach. They were going to do this. They were. It was illegal but it was the right thing to do, wasn't it? It was the right thing for Cara and the right thing for Sophie. They just had to hope that she would see it like that too. "We can't lie to Sophie. How is that going to work? We will have to tell her what we've done."

Jack wiped his eyes with his free hand. "I know."

"And how will we do that? We can't wait until she's eighteen and tell her. If we tell her now, she might let it slip to someone. How is this going to work?"

"I don't know. I really don't know."

There were so many loose ends. So many unknowns. So much risk. And responsibility. Just the thought of it all made Rebecca's head swim.

Jack came closer toward her. "I'm sorry, Rebecca. I feel like this is all my fault. And I don't want to pressure you into this and I don't want to lose you, but I can't..." His voice broke. "I can't..."

Rebecca put her other hand on top of his. "I can't either. I guess we have to wing it, right?"

Jack reached out to her and placed his hand on her cheek, wiped away tears she hadn't even noticed. "I guess we do."

He held her close and she breathed in his warmth and strength. They could do this. Together they could do this. But they needed to do it soon.

Gently, she pushed him away. "I'm going to call the courthouse now and get an appointment as soon as we can. You can work out how we get Cara there before she is too ill to go."

CHAPTER FORTY-FIVE

Cara

"Okay, Cara. Jack has managed to get a wheelchair so we just need to get you dressed and then we can be on our way."

The last couple of days, Rebecca had started saying "we" when she actually meant Cara. It was irritating but understandable when Cara had to be helped to do absolutely everything. It wasn't that she couldn't get dressed or get herself a glass of water or even walk to the toilet unaided. It was just that everything was a huge effort and she didn't seem to have any energy at all.

The wave of grateful relief she'd felt when Jack had agreed to be added to Sophie's birth certificate had given way to a gnawing anxiety that something was going to go wrong. What if the rules had changed? What if she said something or he said something that gave the game away? The sooner they had that certificate, the happier she'd be. She needed to be sure.

Rebecca knelt on the floor in front of her so that she could step into the trousers she was holding out. Cara wrestled with telling her that she didn't need her help when obviously she did. It took Rebecca five minutes to get her dressed. Left alone, it was more like twenty-five.

According to the clock in the hallway, it was 10:00 a.m. "What time is our appointment again? I thought you said it was at twelve."

Rebecca nodded. "It is. Normally it's closed between twelve and one but my friend Izzy knows someone at the courthouse so they've managed to squeeze us into a special appointment."

"So, why are we leaving so soon? Are you worried Jack won't be able to push me very fast? I know I must be pretty heavy."

She was trying to make a joke. She knew as well as they did what a bag of bones she was these days. Rebecca smiled weakly in acknowledgment of her poor attempt at humor. "I was hoping you might be well enough for a cup of coffee first. It was Sophie's idea. She mentioned a café in the town center that you take her to for a treat. Something about an Oreo milk shake?"

Candles Café. It had been their place. The owner always gave Sophie a free cookie with her milk shake. "I think I could manage that. Although I'm not sure I can imagine Jack there. It's not quite him."

"We weren't planning on joining you. I thought it might be nice for you to go with Sophie on your own. We can take you there and go and get some shopping done and then come back. Sophie said you always go just the two of you, so I thought you might like to go?"

She didn't need to add "for the last time" in order for Cara to hear it. Who would have thought that a little café would make her want to drop her head and cry? "I'm not sure if we'll get in. It's a small place."

Rebecca pulled her coat from the rack in the hall. "It's fine. I've called ahead."

If Cara kept breathing slowly, she might be able to do this without tears. "Thank you. It's a really lovely idea."

The café was just as it always was. Rattling cups on saucers, the hiss of the coffee machine, and the loud, grainy whirr of the blender making milk shakes from a list of different sweets and cookies.

Jack wheeled her inside and into the corner, where the owner had reserved them a table. The first time they'd come here, Sophie had been in a stroller. Now she was the one who needed help.

Sophie scooted across the bench opposite and picked up the menu, pretending to read it. "I will have an Oreo milk shake, please, and Mummy will have a big coffee. I am paying with my money." She pulled out a purse that Cara hadn't seen before. Rebecca must have given it to her. And the money.

Jack smiled at Cara. "I'll leave you in your daughter's capable hands. We'll come back in thirty minutes."

The door jangled as he left and a young girl came to take their drinks order. After laying out the money from her purse, Sophie worked out that they could afford cake too. Although Cara didn't have the appetite for cake, she wouldn't spoil Sophie's fun ordering it; she could always wrap it and take it home.

Sophie looked so grown-up all of a sudden. Ordering their drinks, counting out the money, slipping the change back into her tiny purse. What would she look like in another five years? Or ten? What kind of woman would she become?

When the waitress had come to take their order, she'd brought Sophie some crayons and a coloring sheet. This—as well as the Oreo milk shake—was why it was their favorite place to come. Eagerly, Sophie tipped the crayons out onto the table and selected the blue one: her latest favorite color.

"Do you remember when yellow was your favorite color?"

Sophie wrinkled her nose in disgust. "No. My favorite color is blue. Dark blue first. Light blue second."

Cara laughed. "I know it is now, but it used to be yellow. Like mine." So much more had changed than her favorite color. So much more would change in the years to come. And she wasn't going to see any of it.

The waitress returned, slid a tray onto the table, and unloaded a large milk shake and what seemed to be a bucket of coffee: there was no way she could drink all that. The cake, too, was large enough for a giant; she felt sick even looking at it. "The manager said the cake is on the house. And he's sorry you're not well."

Cara looked over at the rotund man behind the counter. He lifted a hand to acknowledge her nodded thanks.

Sophie put her lips to the striped pink paper straw and sucked hard. She sat back with her cheeks as full as a hamster and took a minute to swallow. "Delicious."

"Don't drink it too fast or you'll get—"

"Brain freeze!" Sophie giggled as she joined in.

This was a good idea. However nice Rebecca had made the spare bedroom, it was good to be out of it. And good to spend time with Sophie, just the two of them. She could almost pretend that everything was normal.

"Mummy, are you going to get better soon?"

This wasn't the ideal place for this conversation, but Cara had promised herself when she'd lain in that hospital bed that she would be honest with Sophie from now on. "Mummy is very sick, baby."

Sophie took another mouthful of milk shake, swallowed it, and went back to her drawing. "I know. Rebecca has to help you."

Cara's stomach tightened. It was difficult enough accepting the help, much less talking about it. "She does. Rebecca is a big help. Do you like her?"

Sophie looked up. "Of course. She is married to my daddy."

It was incredible how quickly Sophie had got used to the idea that Jack was her father. Maybe it was true that children were a lot more resilient than adults gave them credit for. Cara was really hoping so. "Good. I'm glad you like her. I like her too."

Sophie picked up the red crayon. "So, are you going to get better?"

Maybe there was no right time. Maybe it was now. "No, baby. Mummy's medicine didn't work. I'm not going to get better."

Sophie pushed so hard on the crayon that it snapped in two. Her head down, a large tear splashed onto the picture.

Cara leaned forward. "Come here, baby. Mummy needs one of your special cuddles."

Sophie climbed up onto Cara's lap and pushed her face into her mother's chest. Cara held her tightly, just as she had done when Sophie was a tiny baby and she'd had to balance her with one hand while holding a fork in the other. She pressed her nose into Sophie's hair. "It's going to be okay, baby, I promise. Everything is going to be okay."

She stroked Sophie's back. It was going to be okay. Because she was going to make it okay. They were going to put Jack on the birth certificate today; and then, tonight, she needed to speak to Rebecca. To tell her everything about Sophie. She needed to know her favorite milk shake, favorite color, what kind of vest she liked to wear. Cara wouldn't be able to be Sophie's mother for much longer, but she could make sure that her new mother would have everything she needed to make Sophie happy.

CHAPTER FORTY-SIX

Rebecca

"Do you need anything else?"

Rebecca had made the room as comfortable as she possibly could. Apart from the new soft bedding and plump pillows, she had a jug of iced water with lemon, fresh flowers and a selection of books and magazines, and they'd hung a flat-screen TV on the wall.

"I can't even *think* of anything else. You've been very kind."

Cara had deteriorated so quickly in the last few days. Her cheeks had hollowed even more and she'd barely had the strength to hold a glass of water. The gentle visiting nurse had quietly suggested a hospice, but neither Jack nor Rebecca could think about separating her and Sophie. The nurse had tried to explain that the hospice wasn't like a hospital, that Sophie would be able to spend as much time with her mum as she wanted, but how could it be as nice as this? Here, Sophie could wander in and out of her mum's bedroom whenever she wanted. This morning, Rebecca had found her curled up at the foot of Cara's bed like a kitten. They couldn't deprive Sophie or Cara of a single moment together.

Rebecca opened the drawer under the bed to slide in fresh sheets. "Sophie is downstairs with a pencil in one hand and a cheese sandwich in the other. I've told her to make sure she doesn't get the two confused, which started her giggling and pretending to draw with her sandwich. Do you want me to leave you to rest, or would you like some company?"

The visiting nurse had also told them to keep a regular check on Cara's condition. They were to call her if she took a turn for the worse. In the meantime, she'd said, all they could do was keep her comfortable. The morphine was taking care of the pain, but her poor lips were so dry and sore, and no amount of Vaseline seemed to make much difference. She licked them before she spoke in a gravelly voice. "I wanted to talk to you, actually. I need you to know how grateful I am. To you and Jack. I know that I have thrown a grenade into your life."

They'd been over this already. Rebecca didn't want Cara to keep thanking her. "She's a very cute grenade, though."

Cara laughed, her throat wheezy. This damn chest infection was ravaging her poor, weak body. "She is very cute. I'm not biased, am I?"

Rebecca shook her head. "Definitely not. She is a beautiful little girl. And clever too. She's going to do something amazing someday." If anyone had told Rebecca two months ago that she would feel so attached to a child so quickly, she would have laughed and called them mad. It wasn't just that Sophie was a good kid; the fact that she was about to lose her mother made her so vulnerable that Rebecca just wanted to cover her in love and keep her safe.

"That's what I think too. She's going to be this incredible person. That's the reason I had to do this. I've been lying here thinking that I should have told you both about the cancer from the start. You've been so good about it that I feel really bad about deceiving you. I just wanted you to get to know her a little. I wouldn't have asked for help for me, but for her I'd do anything."

"I can see that. She knows that too."

"I know she knows that *now*. I mean, I tell her enough. My parents weren't big on that, you know. Affection. Love. I wanted her to always know how much she meant to me. She's been my life."

This wasn't the first time that Cara had alluded to her troubled home life. It made Rebecca respect her even more. From the little she'd said, there had been no motherly role model, but she'd done such a great job with Sophie. Rebecca's stomach flipped over; she was going to be a hard act to follow.

Cara broke into her thoughts with a seemingly random question. "Do you remember anything from when you were four?"

Rebecca stopped tying the corners of the bag in the wastebasket she was emptying and stared into the middle distance, trying to conjure up her early childhood. "Yes, I think so. I remember the toys I played with. I remember a vacation at Cornwall when a wave soaked me fully clothed and my parents had to buy me replacement clothes from a secondhand shop nearby. And the Christmas when my grandad fell asleep and we covered him in discarded wrapping paper."

She smiled at the memory of the paper rising and falling with her grandfather's snores and saw that Cara was scrutinizing her. "Sounds like you had a pretty good family. But do you actually *remember* those things? Or is it because you've seen photographs and people have told you about them?"

It was certainly true that those things had become part of their family folklore. "That's impossible to answer, isn't it? I am pretty sure I remember them, but you're right—maybe I've re-created them from things I've been told."

Cara sighed. "Yeah. That's what I've been thinking about. I don't think I have any memories from when I was Sophie's age. It doesn't bother me because I doubt they'd be good. But I want Sophie to remember. I want her to remember me."

Her voice cracked and it tore at Rebecca's heart. "Of course she'll remember you. She adores you. You don't forget a love like that. Even if you're four."

Cara chewed at her poor lips. They were trembling. "I hope you're right. I really do. But you had people to tell you about when you were small. Who is going to tell Sophie about all our memories? Who is going to help her to join the dots from the fragments in her mind? Who is going to tell her how much I adored her?"

How excruciating this must be for her. "Tell me. Keep telling me all the things you want her to know. I'll write them down. I'll record your voice. I'll video you if you're up to it? Let me help you."

Cara lay back with her eyes closed. Until she spoke, Rebecca thought she had fallen asleep. "It's weird, isn't it? In real life, we would never be friends."

Did being terminally ill remove all need for politeness? "Ouch. Tell it like it is."

One eye opened slightly. "Sorry. That wasn't meant to be rude. I just mean we're very different. It's a wonder Jack was attracted to both of us. Maybe I was good for fun, but you are good for marriage."

"Ouch again. I *can* be fun when you get to know me. You know, when you're not asking me to raise a child I've only just met." Rebecca winked at Cara so that she knew she was teasing.

Cara had closed her eyes again but she was smiling. "I'm saying this all wrong. What I mean is, I never would have expected when I met you that we would be here so soon. I hadn't even factored you into the whole thing. But I'm glad. I'm glad that Sophie will have you. I think you're just the kind of mum she needs."

Rebecca perched on the edge of the bed. It was getting difficult to breathe. "I hope you're right. But you can't leave me to it yet, you know. I haven't learned how to do all the things I'm going to need to do. I don't know how to be a mum."

Cara shook her head slightly, her eyes still closed. "None of us do. Giving birth doesn't give you new powers, you know. Quite the opposite. I spent the first year of Sophie's life feeling like a complete and utter failure. And she's four now, and soon she'll be going to school. I know as much about that as you do. You just kind of find out as you go along."

That's what Rebecca was afraid she'd say. "Play it by ear, right?"

Cara smiled. "Yep. Play it by ear."

Rebecca thought of Izzy's remonstrances about her inflexibility at work. Jack complaining that he was never allowed to hatch a surprise. Her intergalactic stress levels at Samantha's wedding. "Not really my strong point."

Cara patted her arm. "Oh, I don't know—I think you've been doing a pretty good job of it lately." She took a deep breath; her chest rattled in complaint. "Not many people I know could take a curveball like their husband's ex-girlfriend turning up at their door with a child and everything else that's happened since. You've been incredible, Rebecca. I'm not sure I know how to thank you. But I want to. I don't think...I mean, I don't know..."

She started to cough and Rebecca reached out and took her hand. "Shh. Don't speak if it's difficult. You don't need to say anything. And you don't need to thank me. I just wish I could do more. I wish I could help you stay with Sophie."

Cara gave a small but definite shake of her head. "You have done more for me than anyone has ever done in my whole life."

Rebecca's heart ached for her. For Sophie. For the life they should have had together. "And you have trusted me with the most precious thing you have. I think that makes us even."

Cara tightened her grip on Rebecca's hand. "Take care of my baby, Rebecca. Tell her she was loved from the minute she was born."

Tears welled in Rebecca's eyes. "I will tell her every day. I promise."

CHAPTER FORTY-SEVEN

Rebecca

"Are you ready, Soph?"

Jack, dressed in a black suit with a yellow tie that Sophie had insisted on, held out his hand for hers. In the last few days, they'd discussed at length whether Sophie was old enough to attend her mother's funeral, but she had been so sure she wanted to come that they had relented. It was going to be just them, Danielle, and a few of Cara's old work colleagues, anyway. The crematorium had been very accommodating about putting together a service that would help Sophie as much as possible.

In the end, Cara had slipped away quietly, two weeks after they'd visited the courthouse to put Jack on the birth certificate. It had seemed that she was recovering from the infection she'd picked up, but then it had come back with a vengeance, too strong for her weakened immune system to fight off. Once they'd realized that she might not make Christmas, they'd brought it forward. Squeezing a tree and presents into her bedroom and eating Christmas pudding perched on the end of her bed. Sophie deserved one more Christmas with her mum.

Now Sophie stood up from the sofa, where she had been sitting really still so that she didn't mess up the new dress Rebecca had taken her to buy. She'd wanted to know what people wore for a funeral and Rebecca had told her she should pick whatever she wanted. That was why she'd picked the yellow dress, because her mummy had said that yellow was her first favorite color and she thought it might be her mummy's favorite color too. "I'm ready, Daddy."

She had started calling Jack "Daddy" in the last couple of days, tentatively at first and then with more confidence. She still called Rebecca by her name, so they assumed that was the way it was going to be.

When they got out of the car at the crematorium, Sophie noticed the memorial plaques among some of the flower beds and she asked Rebecca what they were. "They are the names of the people who have had their funerals here. People write their names and then a little message about them so that they can remember them."

Sophie frowned. "What kind of message?"

"Well, this one"—Rebecca pointed at the plaque nearest to them—"says, 'Ted Brown, much-loved husband, father, and grandfather.'"

They walked on toward the crematorium, but Sophie was obviously turning this new information over in her mind. Just before they joined Danielle outside, she stopped and pulled at the hem of Rebecca's coat, and Rebecca crouched down to listen to her. "Will my mummy have one of those messages?"

"If you would like her to have one, we'll make sure of it. Do you know what you would like to write on it?"

Sophie nodded. "I want it to say, 'Best mummy in the world.'"

Rebecca swallowed. She didn't want to make this harder for Sophie by getting upset. "That sounds perfect. She was the best mummy in the world, wasn't she?"

Sophie nodded and started to cry. Rebecca folded her into her arms, closing her own eyes tightly and barely daring to breathe. Her heart was aching for this little girl who had lost her mother and for Cara, who wouldn't be here to see her grow. With every ounce of her being, she hoped she was up to the task of helping Sophie through this and beyond.

Sophie pulled away and looked at Rebecca. "And you can be the best number two mummy in the world."

Now she couldn't keep from crying. "I will do everything I can to be the best number two mummy, Sophie. I really will." She took a tissue from her bag and wiped Sophie's face and helped her to blow her nose.

Then she took Sophie's left hand, and Jack took the right, and they walked in together to say their final good-bye.

EPILOGUE

"Mum, how many times are you going to take this picture?"

The blazer Sophie was wearing came down to her knuckles, and her crisp white shirt was just a little too big. Still, she was every inch the middle school student now.

Rebecca held up her phone, trying to get the angle that Sophie assured her was the way to get the best shot. "Just one more. I want to send it to your dad."

Jack had offered to take the morning off work so that they could both take Sophie on her first day but she'd been mortified, rolling her eyes at the very idea. "I'm eleven, you know, not five."

How could she be eleven already? The last seven years had flown by. Some had been easier than others. If Izzy's eldest was anything to go by, they had plenty of teenage storms ahead too.

At the bottom of the stairs, Sophie picked up her backpack, which was empty apart from the pencil case and paper they had bought at the beginning of the summer. Still, with it on her back, she looked like a turtle. A very beautiful turtle.

Last night, Rebecca had stood at the entrance to Sophie's bedroom, where a picture of Cara watched over her from her bedside table as she slept. When her eyes were closed, there was still a whisper of the little girl she'd been when they'd first met. Back then, Rebecca had had no idea how much she would come to love this face. Looking at her standing there now, it hit her again. It was overwhelming.

Sophie turned with a thoughtful look. "Do you think she would have been proud of me? My mum?"

They had been honest from the beginning, explaining to Sophie that they were going to adopt her and be her parents from that point on. She had asked who her dad was if it wasn't Jack, but up until now she'd been content with the answer that they honestly didn't know.

There had been tricky times when she'd said to her teacher at school that Jack wasn't her real dad, but they had managed to explain that away by saying she'd been mixed up with her mother dying and everything else. Once she was old enough to understand, they had told her that Jack was on her birth certificate because it was what her mother had wanted and because it meant that no one could ever take her away from them.

How could anyone not be proud of her? Her clear, bright eyes that wanted to see everything the world had to offer, her huge heart with which she loved everyone and everything. "Yes, my darling. She would have been bursting with pride. Just like I am. Just like your dad is."

Sophie grinned. "I forgot to tell you, when Dad came to pick me up from the promotion day, one of the teachers joked how alike we look. How funny is that?"

Rebecca wasn't surprised. Hadn't she thought that four-year-old Sophie looked like Jack? That was why they hadn't pursued the DNA test at the beginning. "I can see why. You have the same mannerisms."

Sophie rolled her eyes. "Urgh. Don't say that."

Rebecca laughed. Sophie made her laugh a lot these days. It was weird when your child grew up to become someone you wanted to hang out with, spend time with.

Her child. They were two words she thought she'd never say. It wasn't something she had wanted or needed in her life. But Sophie had come along and—somehow—they had made their way through.

Of course, she had had to endure the smug "We knew you'd come around" comments from some quarters and it was pointless trying to explain that she and Jack would have led a perfectly happy and fulfilled life together without kids. In fact, when Sophie was about seven, she had asked about brothers and sisters. Rebecca and Jack discussed it, but nothing had changed. They both loved Sophie. She was their daughter. But they didn't want another child. They had taken care to sit down with her and explain that in some detail, but she had merely shrugged and said, "Can I have a kitten instead?"

Now that little girl was two feet taller and standing at the front door with her hand on the doorknob. "Can we go now? I don't want to be late."

They were going to be about twenty minutes early, but Rebecca didn't want to dampen her enthusiasm. "Have you got everything?"

The increasingly familiar eye roll made an appearance. "Yes. I made a list and checked it all off as I packed it."

Some character traits were handed down without biology. "Okay, let's get in the car."

Once they were in the car and on their way to Sophie's new school, she seemed more pensive. "Do you think I'll be in a class with my friends, or will I be on my own?"

"I don't know, but you'll be able to see your friends at recess."

She was quiet again for a bit. "And do you think the work will be like St. Catherine's, or do you think it'll be really difficult?"

"I don't think they'll make it difficult right away."

She looked out the window. "What if I hate it there? What if I don't make any friends? What if...?"

Rebecca reached out and laid her hand on Sophie's. "Someone very clever once told me that you have to take life as it comes and deal with it as it happens. I think she called it 'playing it by ear.'"

Sophie smiled. "Okay, Mum. Let's do it."

They parked on a road two streets away from the school, where Sophie had negotiated that Rebecca would drop her off. Sophie got out of the car but didn't close the door. Instead, she hesitated. Looked toward the school and then back at Rebecca, biting her bottom lip in the way she always did when she was nervous about something.

Rebecca leaned across the passenger seat toward her. "Don't overthink it. See how the day pans out. Sometimes it's the stuff you don't plan for that brings you the most happiness."

And as she watched her daughter walk away to join a throng of other students, the truth of her words settled in her heart and she whispered into the air, "There she goes, Cara. I hope you're proud."

ACKNOWLEDGMENTS

Grateful thanks to my brilliant editor Isobel Akenhead, who never fails to make my books better than they ever would have been. Also, thanks to DeAndra Lupu for her insightful copyediting, Laura Gerrard and Deborah Wiseman for proofreading, and to Kim Nash for brilliant PR and for hosting a really fun "Bookchat" on the Bookouture Facebook page, which I enjoyed immensely. Thanks to all the Bookouture authors for their support and high jinks. Particularly to Susie Lynes for letting me sit in her kitchen and rattle on about vague plot ideas and asking the right questions to help me get them on paper.

When you write about real-life experiences, there is a responsibility to get the details right. My heartfelt thanks to Debbie Wiley for generously sharing her experiences with me and not getting fed up with my random questions for weeks afterward. Your honesty and openness helped immeasurably in describing Cara's experience. Any mistakes are mine. I'd also like to shout out to Kerry Woodbury, whose fabulous blog *My Left Boob* helped many people and who is much missed. Go find it on Facebook.

As well as writing, I teach English at the Coopers' Company and Coborn School and I want to give a big shout-out to all my students who have encouraged and celebrated with me since my first book came out in 2018. This year, I have had to say a very hurried good-bye to my class because of lockdown so I want to take the opportunity to say: 13.1—you were an absolute pleasure to know and I will miss you all incredibly. Don't forget to celebrate Biscuit Thursdays!

My friends and family deserve to be thanked after every book as I couldn't do it without their faith and encouragement. Special thanks to my mum for looking after the kids and dog when I am on deadline and to Dan for realizing when NOT to make the joke about "putting more man-eating sharks in it."

And finally, to everyone who has bought, read, and reviewed one of my books, I am truly grateful. I hope you enjoyed this one too.

ABOUT THE AUTHOR

Emma Robinson is the author of several bestselling women's fiction novels. She also blogs about the funny side of parenting and has contributed to podcasts such as *Funny Women*. While her early novels are humorous, her recent work focuses on emotional themes and these novels are both heartbreaking and life-affirming. Emma enjoys writing stories that explore the power of family and friendship in the most challenging circumstances. Emma currently lives in Essex, England, with a husband, two children, and a small black dog.

Find out more at:

EmmaRobinsonWrites.com

Facebook.com/MotherhoodForSlackers

Twitter: @EmmaRobinsonUK

Instagram: @EmmaRobinsonUK